Also by Alice Taylor

Memoirs
To School Through the Fields
Quench the Lamp
The Village
Country Days
The Night Before Christmas

Poetry
The Way We Are
Close to the Earth
Going to the Well

Fiction
The Woman of the House
Across the River

Essays
A Country Miscellany

Diary
An Irish Country Diary

Children's
The Secrets of the Oak

ALICE TAYLOR

HOUSE OF MEMORIES

BRANDON

A Brandon Original Paperback

First published in 2005 by Brandon
an imprint of Mount Eagle Publications
Dingle, Co. Kerry, Ireland, and
Unit 3, Olympia Trading Estate, Coburg Road, London N22 6TZ, England

ISBN 0 86322 339 7

2 4 6 8 10 9 7 5 3 1

Cover design: id communications, Tralee
Typesetting by Red Barn Publishing, Skeagh, Skibbereen
Printed in the UK

To Diarmuid, in memory of a day in West Cork

CHAPTER ONE

DANNY HAD NEVER been in a bank. He stood outside the Bank of Ireland in Ross with a knot of fear in his gut. Behind that impressive façade and heavy doors was a world about which he knew absolutely nothing. Although the thought of going in there and asking a complete stranger for a loan crippled him with anxiety, he forced himself up the limestone steps. Looking in through the heavy glass door, he tried to figure out where exactly he should go when he got in there. He was tempted to turn back. A thin woman in a fur coat marched out and gave him a disapproving look. His throat tightened with nervousness, and he felt the sweat in his armpits. Finally he grasped the brass handle and pushed, but even the heavy door seemed reluctant to let him in.

High arched ceilings and glossy mahogany counters gleaming with brass rails caused him to blink in awe. The sound of drawers opening and closing, the clinking of coins and the voices of people who belonged in this world swam around him.

He was a child in school again with a spiteful voice whispering in his ear "yella belly". His heart was pounding and he swallowed hard. Which way now? He was so nervous that his eyes could not focus properly. To steady himself he looked down at the floor, and words engraved in the limestone flag danced up at him: "Bank of Ireland . . . Founded in 1812". An oak floor shining in front of him like a dark brown sea looked as if nobody had ever walked on it. He glanced down uncertainly at his heavy boots, but as he dithered with indecision the door was pushed in behind him by a burly, impatient man, and he had no choice but to move forward. Feeling that his legs could be taken from under him, he stepped on to the glossy floor and heard his tipped boots clatter noisily. He felt eyes turn in his direction. In here the men were all dressed in Sunday suits and the women in good shoes. Nana Molly had always said that her shoes told a lot about a woman. If his grandmother was right, there were a lot of rich women in here. In his working pants and darned jumper, he felt shabby and wondered if he smelt of the farmyard. He should have changed his clothes before coming, but he had made the snap decision this morning as he let the cows out after milking. He had not thought about clothes or appearances, and if he had he would have thought that they did not matter. Now he was not so sure.

But what the hell! He was here and there was nothing wrong with his darned jumper. He looked around with determination. In front of the openings in the frosted glass panels, people waited to be served. At one opening was a little woman in a long black coat who did not look as intimidating as some of the others. He might feel more comfortable behind her. She looked like a country woman. He lined up behind her and was amazed to see, over her shoulder, that she was pulling rolls of red twenty pound notes out from inside her long coat and was pushing them in to the girl behind the counter. *God,* he thought, *it's hard to know who has money in here.* He wondered if he was in the right place to ask to see the manager. He looked around to know if there was anybody who might tell him, but everybody seemed preoccupied with their own business. A man with a peaked cap looked at him curiously, but he felt too intimidated to ask him, and when the little woman moved, a slim girl with long blonde hair looked out at him with mild curiosity.

"Can I see the manager?" he gasped nervously.

"Have you got an appointment?" she asked briskly.

"No," he gulped.

"Will I set one up for you?" she inquired pleasantly.

"No, I want to see him now," he insisted.

"That may not be possible," she told him.

"I can wait," he persisted.

Danny was determined that he was not going to leave this bank without seeing the manager or whoever needed to be consulted about getting the loan, because if he went home now he might never work up the courage to come back again. He had agonised long and hard about coming to the bank in the first place, and now that he was here, he was resolved to see it through. All his instincts had warned him against asking for a loan, because it was an old bank loan that had caused all the problems in the family. As a result of it, his father fought all his life with the Phelans and would have nothing to do with the bank. But his father had let everything run down so that the whole place was on the brink of ruin when he died. Now Danny was determined to turn everything around and had a long-term plan. Today was the first step. His mother would be flabbergasted if she knew what he was doing, but then his mother had no spirit left after years of living with his father. It was up to him to get the whole mess sorted out and get things moving.

"Would you like to sit over there?" the blonde girl asked him, pointing to a bench in the far corner. "I'll see what I can do."

"Do your best," he implored her, and she looked momentarily startled by his desperation.

"Your name?" she inquired

"Danny Conway."

As he sat on the glossy wooden bench, he took a few deep breaths to try to stop his heart from thumping. He felt that he might skid on to the floor if he moved suddenly on this smooth bench. He remembered how Fr Brady always told them to breathe deeply if they were nervous before a match. If only that was all he had to worry about now! At least before a game all the lads were nervous together. In here he was on his own and he was the odd man out. Everyone else seemed to know what they were about. Customers came in and made a beeline for different sections, exchanged pleasantries with the staff, did their transactions quickly and were gone. Drawers opened and closed, and a soft hum of conversation wove in and out behind the counters.

There was nobody waiting in his corner. Was this where they put you if you were asking for a loan? Was he the only one looking for money? Did everybody know that if you were sitting here that's what you wanted? Hopefully no one from Kilmeen would come in and see him waiting like a beggar. He looked up at the ceiling. Apart from the church, it had the highest ceiling that he had ever seen. Normally he would have been very impressed with a place like this, but today it unnerved him. He looked over at the granite slab inside the front door. The inscription on that slab read 1812 and it was now 1962, so this bank was one hundred and fifty years old. It had to be in through this very door that his grandfather Rory Conway had come with his friend Edward Phelan and got the loan that was later to cause such bitterness between them. It made him feel that he was stepping back into the shadow of his grandfather, and the very thought chilled him. Maybe the two of them had sat waiting on this very bench. It looked solid and shiny enough to have seated hundreds of people waiting over the years. Had they chatted as they waited? They probably had because they were friends, but they had no idea then what trouble their visit to this bank was going to cause. On that day they had set in motion a chain of events that had poisoned their own lives and ignited a feud that had smouldered between their two families for years. The shadow of that old loan had moved like a threatening monster in and out through his own childhood. He swallowed hard as a wave of foreboding swept over him. Maybe it would be better to get out now. Shades of all that had gone before him were gathering back to unnerve him.

"Mr Harvey will see you now." The blonde girl broke into his thoughts and led him towards the far end of the counter where she lifted a flap and led him across an open area of yet more glossy floor. As he followed the slim, suited figure, he could feel a cold lump of apprehension in the pit of his stomach. He had to get this right, but he had no idea how to go about it. Desperation had driven him in here. Over the last year he had worked day and night to improve things on the farm, but now he could go no further without money. He had gone to the shops and priced everything that he needed and had added up the total costs in a little notebook. The shop people had been helpful, but his father had never done business with any of them, and the Conway name did not inspire respect or confidence. He also knew that they felt he was too young and inexperienced to be trusted with much credit. He just had to convince this man that he could pay off the money when he had got things going well.

"Well, Mr Conway, what can we do for you?" The large, dome-faced man behind the wide, green-leather-topped desk gazed at him speculatively.

"I want to get a loan of a thousand pounds," Danny blurted out.

"It's not quite as simple as that," the pale man who filled the swivel chair told him as his fingers played piano notes on the desk. His hands were soft and white.

"I have all the details here," Danny told him, eagerly pushing his little notebook across the counter. It was dog-eared from being carried around in his pocket. Mr Harvey picked it up and gazed curiously at the rows of figures.

"These are all outgoing," he said. "The bank is more interested in returns and security for our loan."

"I have no security," Danny told him bluntly.

"Then we are both wasting our time," Mr Harvey said evenly.

"But I need the money to get the farm going," Danny pleaded desperately.

"Where is this farm?" Mr Harvey asked.

"Over in Kilmeen," Danny told him.

"Oh," he said thoughtfully, and Danny sensed that he was recalling something that he had heard about the name Conway and Kilmeen.

"My father is dead and I'm running the farm now." Danny knew that he was gabbling, but he felt that if he kept talking he might say something to help his case before this smug man would dismiss him.

"Do you own this farm?"

"Well, I kinda do, in a way."

"You either do or you don't," the man behind the desk told him briskly.

"Well, it belongs to my mother and the rest of us."

"That's not a great position to be in."

"But it will be mine when we get it all sorted out," Danny assured him.

"Does your mother and the rest of them know that you are looking for a loan?" he asked. "And when you say the rest of us, who exactly are you talking about?"

"Two sisters and three brothers," Danny told him.

"And where are they?"

'My two sisters are in Dublin."

"What are they doing?"

"Well, Mary, the eldest, is teaching, and Kitty is still in school."

"In school in Dublin?" the bank man said in surprise.

"It's a long story," Danny said abruptly, wishing to God he would stop asking awkward questions.

"And your brothers?"

"One working in England and two in America."

13

"So they would all have a claim on the farm, as well as your mother, of course."

"They would but . . ."

"So you are in no position to give the deeds of the farm as security for the loan," the bank man cut in.

"No," Danny admitted.

"Then how did you expect to get a loan?" Mr Harvey asked in a puzzled voice.

"I was never in a bank before," Danny admitted, feeling his face go red.

"Oh," the bank man said thoughtfully, "and how old are you?"

"Twenty-one," Danny told him.

"A bit young to be running a farm on your own."

"Well, I'm the only one left at home since my father died last year. My mother is with me, but she spends some of her time in Dublin with my sisters. I have improved things a lot on the farm, but now I cannot go any further without money to repair the buildings." Danny knew that he was gabbling again. He wanted desperately to convince this bank man that he was down to the wire, but he was beginning to think that he might be grasping at straws.

"I understand your position," the man said not unkindly, "but the bank cannot give out money without security."

"But I'm honest and I work hard and I would pay it back," Danny pleaded.

"I can appreciate all that," the man said quietly, "but my hands are tied."

"So it's no good coming in here looking for money?" Danny said in despair.

"Without security, I'm afraid not."

"So no matter how hard-working or honest I am, it makes no difference to the bank," Danny protested, feeling angry and frustrated at the injustice of it all. The man across the desk nodded in agreement.

So his grandmother was right. Her words winged back over the years: "Danny boyeen, when you are in the arsehole of the world, it is very hard to get out of it."

She had it all figured out, and nothing had changed since her day. He looked at the well-dressed man behind the large desk and felt an unbridgeable gap between them. This man knew nothing about sagging roofs and cows that could go hungry in the winter.

As he walked down the street he felt physically sick with disappointment. Desperation had driven him into the bank. It had been his last hope, but now that hope was shattered. There was no other avenue open to him, and he could not survive another winter without money. Some of the farm buildings were in dire need of repair, and the barn had to be resheeted before the winter or the hay would rot. What the hell was he going to do? He was so immersed in his misery that he was impervious to the street around him.

Normally when he came into Ross he enjoyed wandering around and looking at the shop windows, especially those of the hardware shops. Sometimes when he came to the end of the main street, he would look back at the different shop fronts. He liked fine buildings and was always impressed by the tall, three-storey houses that stood shoulder to shoulder along both sides of the street. Back in Kilmeen there was just one shop that sold a bit of everything, but here there were different shops specialising in clothes, furniture and things that he would never be buying. But he enjoyed looking, and for him the hardware stores were like Aladdin's caves. In there were the tools and everything that he would need to fix up Furze Hill. The last time that he had come to Ross, pricing things that he would need and making a list of all the expenses in his little notebook had given him great satisfaction and brought the realisation of his dream a little closer. That day, at the back of his mind, the plan to visit the bank for a loan came into being. The loan was going to be the gateway into his plan of bringing the farm right. The thought of it had filled him with a warm glow of anticipation.

He remembered his grandmother talking about the way things were when she was a child in Furze Hill. It had been a thriving place then. He had loved the way she had always called it Furze Hill, with a note of pride in her voice. No one else but Nana Molly called their farm Furze Hill. She had made it sound like a good place, and as a child he had felt a swell of pride in his chest. But as he grew older there came a sense of unease when he heard the neighbours refer to it as Conways' place with a touch of contempt in their voices. His father had earned that contempt, but as a young fellow growing up it had been hard to swallow the shame.

So much suffering and anguish had taken place in their house that he sometimes wondered if he could ever wipe out the memory of it. But if he could only build up the farm, he might in some way wash away the shame and bring back a sense of pride to the family. He wanted his mother to be able to dress well and walk tall down the street of Kilmeen as if she owned half of it, like Martha Phelan from Mossgrove.

Mossgrove, across the river from Furze Hill, was a well-run farm. It had always been a thorn in his father's side, and in later years it had turned into an obsession which in the end had led to his death. Not that Danny regretted his death, although sometimes he felt guilty to be so relieved that he was gone. He was grateful to Martha Phelan for that, but she would never know that he knew. Would never know that he had watched her that night on the river bank when she had set the old fellow up. What she had done had required nerves of steel, and on that night she had given them all their freedom.

He was so intent on his thoughts that at first he did not hear when a voice called to him from a car parked beside the kerb, but when a horn beeped beside him, he swung around to see Kate Phelan smiling at him through the car window. *Oh God!* He needed a Phelan now like a hole in the head, but she leant across and opened the car door.

"Danny," she smiled, "would you like a lift back to Kilmeen?"

It was the last thing that he wanted, but it would be awkward to refuse Kate Phelan, who had always been decent to him. Despite the trouble between the families, Kate had a strange friendship with his grandmother, which had annoyed his father intensely. But because Kate Phelan was the district nurse, he could not prevent her calling to Nana Molly when she was sick. Kate had been there the night Nana died and had been instrumental in getting Kitty out of the house and up to Dublin to Mary. Kate Phelan probably knew more about his family than he did himself.

"I'll be glad of it," he lied, slipping into the seat of her small Morris Minor where his legs were too long and his head dented the roof.

"How are you, Danny?" she asked as she eased the small car away from the kerb and headed down the main street home towards Kilmeen.

"I'm fine," he told her grimly.

"You didn't look too fine as you came down the street right now," she said quietly.

"I suppose," he agreed.

"Danny, I don't want to pry, but I saw you come out of the bank. Is that why you're so miserable looking?" she asked bluntly.

"Well, I don't want to . . ." he began, but she cut in before he could go any further.

"Danny, I've watched you over the last year and seen what you have done with that farm across the river. You are beginning to work miracles."

Her sympathetic tone was his undoing.

"Well, the miracles are going to stop," he blurted out angrily, "because the bloody bank manager won't give me money to keep going."

"I thought that might be it," she said evenly.

"All that hard work," he raged, "and now I can't go any further without money. It wasn't that I didn't enjoy the work, because I did. For years, when the old fellow was alive, I had dreamed of pulling the place together. My grandmother had told me about the way it used to be as if she had wanted to put it into my head so that one day I would know what to do when the time came. Now the time has come. I have the freedom now that he is gone. It was great to get started, but now I want to go further," he finished, thumping his fists together with frustration. He had not meant to tell Kate Phelan all his troubles, but once started he could not stop.

18

"You know my father ruined all our lives. He couldn't keep his bloody paws off my sisters, and he beat the spirit out of my mother, and he ruined the farm. Now I want to undo some of that harm. But I can't do it without money, money, money," he finished angrily.

"Danny, you can't carry the burden of your father," Kate told him gently. "He's dead, and try to let his sins die with him."

"Die with him?" he cried. "Every day I walk in the awful shadows that he left behind. We had no childhood. We lived with a brute. You know what my mother is like. She's afraid to open her mouth because every time she did she got a belting. I want to give her back something that she lost when she came to Furze Hill. Do you know that she was in the same class in school as Martha Phelan and look at the difference. Martha looks like her daughter."

"None of us look as good as Martha," Kate assured him. "I am a good few years younger than my sister-in-law, but she looks better than I do."

He wished that he had the courage to tell her that he preferred the way she looked, small, dark and friendly, unlike the elegant, aloof Martha who always made him feel uncomfortable.

"I know what you are telling me is true," Kate was continuing, "and . . ."

"Oh and there was much more than anyone will ever know," he cut in, "but now we are free of him! Every day I am grateful for that, and the more improvements I do in Furze Hill, the more I wipe him out of there. That day last year when he fell into Yalla Hole was the best day of our lives."

"Well, it's best to put it all behind you," Kate advised gently.

"That's why I'm working so hard on the farm," he told her desperately. "It's making me feel free of him, apart from the satisfaction of seeing it coming right. That's why I need the money so badly."

"Did you ever think of talking to Jack about it?" Kate asked.

"Jack Tobin?" he said in surprise. "Sure, what would Jack know about being short of money?"

"Mossgrove went through tough times when Ned and I were young and my father drank too much. Jack was there and got us through. My mother and himself slaved to keep Mossgrove going then."

It surprised Danny to hear that they ever had money problems in Mossgrove. To him the Phelans in the farm across the river always seemed to have everything. It was hard to imagine that they had had hard times at any stage.

"So Jack could give you sound advice," Kate told him, "if you don't mind discussing your problems with him."

He wondered what Jack Tobin could tell him that would solve his problem. Advice was not much good when it was money you wanted, but then on the other hand, what had he to lose? After almost sixty years working with the Phelans, Jack must have learned a lot about farming, and if they had been short of money, he knew about this problem too. As well as that, when Kate Phelan was so nice, he would not like to throw her advice back in her face.

"Will I call to Jack some night?" he asked.

"Would you like me to tell him about your situation so that he could have a think about it before you come?" Kate asked.

"That might be a good idea," he agreed.

"Well, that's a step in the right direction anyway," Kate said with relish.

"I don't seem to have that many directions open to me," he told her grimly.

Kate dropped him off at the end of the road up to Furze Hill. When her car had disappeared around the corner, he walked across the road to the little stone bridge, leant over the bridge and watched the water. There was a pool of despair inside in him. Over the years whenever he was coming home from the village on his own he leant over this bridge, and sometimes the water had a soothing effect on him. But on bad days when his father had been on a rampage, with his mother showing evidence of his violence, or if he had heard the door of Kitty's room opening stealthily in the night, he had sometimes looked at the swirling water and thought that to sink down into it would have been a way out of all the terrible things that were happening. But it had always been only a fleeting thought because he knew that to do it would be giving in to his father. He could not let his father win. If he had given in he would not have been there for Nora that night in the wood. His father hated him for that.

Next to his mother he was the prime target for his father's rages. He would crash his fist into his face shouting, "You're no Conway." When he was very young he had taken that as an insult, but as he grew up he felt otherwise. Now he looked down at the calm water swirling out from under the bridge and wondered what it would be like to sink into its swirling current. He would not jump in from this height but climb over the stone wall further down, then walk through the soft high grass and over the bank and into the water. Walk until it was deep enough that he could lie down slowly. It would be such a tranquil ending. Their lives had been so violent that he did not want a violent end. Just oblivion! He knew that his mother had survived her ordeals by the power of her belief in something above and beyond his understanding. But he knew that hers was a different God from his father's. When they were young his father had marched them up all up to a front seat in the church every Sunday, and as he grew older and listened to Fr Tim's sermons on love and kindness, he wondered if his father ever heard them.

As he walked up the hill, he tried not to think about the implications of his visit to the bank. Would Jack be able to advise him in any way? That was the only flicker of light at the end of a dark tunnel. But as well as the money problem, there was the other niggling worry that he had tried not to think about but which the bank man had pulled up front. Ownership of the farm had to be sorted out. His mother and the girls had tried to arrange the signing over after the funeral, but Rory was the one who would not agree. Liam and Matty had not even come home from America for the funeral and were happy to go along with whatever their mother and the girls decided, but Rory wanted to stick in there for everything. Being the eldest he felt that he had prior claim, but he was like the old fellow and was not a farmer or a worker. If Rory muscled in they were all back to square one. After the funeral last year, he had returned to England, but Danny knew that he would be back.

CHAPTER TWO

JACK SAT THINKING by his cottage fire. After supper he loved to sit smoking his pipe in the quiet kitchen and listen to the clock ticking. He seemed to spend a lot of time reflecting these days. *Is it a sign of old age?* he wondered. But he did not feel old, although lately when he went to lift a heavy bag of spuds or oats, he had to have a second go at it before he succeeded, but it annoyed him if Peter rushed to help. It was the last straw altogether if Nora thought that she should come to his assistance. He wished that they would not do it even though he knew that it was kindness on their part. Their mother Martha, on the other hand, never interfered, and he did not know whether it was because she did not care or because she understood. With Martha you were never quite sure of anything. Over the years, just when he had decided that he had her measure, she made another move which turned his entire reckoning upside down. Over twenty years ago she had married Ned and moved into Mossgrove. During that time they had worked together but had not become friends. Maybe he could never quite forgive the anguish that she had caused to Nellie, whom he had loved dearly, and the wedge that she had tried to drive between Ned and his mother. The Phelans were his family, and anything that upset them upset him. He had been with them since he was a lad of fifteen and had worked there with four generations of Phelans. During those years, his roots had grown deep down into the soil of the farm that he always regarded as his homeplace.

He closed his eyes and thought back to the first day that he had gone down to begin work in Mossgrove. That morning he had been as happy as a bird because Billy Phelan and himself had gone to school together and were best friends, so the idea of working together every day was an enjoyable prospect. But the old man, Edward Phelan, was a stern taskmaster, determined to train them well. At first he was so tired at night that he wondered if he would ever be able to keep going, but gradually, almost without realising it, he fell in love with the land. It was a love affair that began for him as a teenager and never wavered but grew deeper with the passing years. For Billy that love affair never began, and from the beginning he battled against the land and his father, and the only good thing that he did for Mossgrove was to marry Nellie, who loved the place like old Edward.

In later years, Ned had grown up and followed in his grandfather's footsteps. They had great days in Mossgrove then before Ned married Martha and she had moved in and tried to wrong-foot them all. But Nellie would not hear a word against her and bent over backwards not to rock the boat. It had made him sad that after all her years of dedication to Mossgrove she had finished up like a shadow in her own house. It had annoyed Kate as well, but, of course, by then Kate had left Mossgrove and gone to England where she had trained as a nurse. When she came back as district nurse to Kilmeen, she bought her own house in the village.

But at least at the end of her days Nellie had the joy of her two grandchildren, Peter and Nora. The irony of the whole thing was that even though Martha had resented Nellie, she had now in Nora a daughter who was a carbon copy of Nellie. Life had a tendency to level things out as it went along. But the one thing that he felt it could never level out was Ned's accident. That had been a crippling blow. He had loved Ned like a son, and his death had been an earthquake in the midst of them all.

But in time things had settled down again, and now Martha and Peter were doing a great job, with occasional fireworks between them. Matt Conway's death last year had made things easier. He did not like to write off a death as a blessing, but in this case he had to be honest with himself and admit that it was hard to view it as anything else. That fellow had been a thorn in the side of Mossgrove for years. As long as it had been the land and animals that he threatened, it was in some way bearable, but when he had attacked Nora last year it was too much. Matt Conway had been worse than his father Rory, for whom old Edward Phelan had guaranteed the bank loan. But, of course, Conway did the devil when he would not pay it back though he had enough money to do so. Instead he had bought extra fields near the village with the money. That had driven Edward Phelan mad. He had felt betrayed. So he had hauled Rory Conway to court and beaten him and got the two river fields off him which were judged to be the equivalent of the two that he had bought. By God, but those two fields had caused trouble down through the years!

All water under the bridge now, he thought as he put a few extra sods on the fire. The February evening was turning chilly. He had spent too much time thinking and let the fire run down. Now as the flames licked up between the sods, he stretched out his stockinged feet beside the warmth. Toby shifted himself to become more comfortable and curled up again beside the soft socks and was soon shivering in his sleep as he chased imaginary rabbits. While he had been sitting lost in thought, dusk had crept into the cottage, and now the fire sent leaping shadows dancing up the walls. The lustre jugs on his mother's dresser glinted gold in the glow of the fire, and the only sound apart from the crackling of the logs was the soothing tick-tock of the clock. The clock was older than himself and had hung above the fire since he was a child. Every Saturday night after the ten o'clock news on Radio Éireann, just as the Hospital Sweepstakes programme began, his mother had wound that clock. She had waited until Bart Bastable began, "Makes no difference where you are, you can wish upon a star," and then she had reached into the clock for the key. For years after her sudden death, he sometimes thought that he could hear the sound of the clock being wound.

He loved his kitchen with its door opening straight out into the garden and narrow window looking down over Nolan's fields. At night the lights of Kilmeen twinkled in the distance. At the northern side by the road, he had planted trees giving complete shelter to the cottage. But behind those trees, he kept his hedges cut low so that he could enjoy the rolling

26

countryside and see the cows in the fields around the cottage. The surrounding view was a wide backdrop to his garden. *My garden*, he thought, *is as far as my eye can see.* It was the joy of his life. Mossgrove was the big picture, but his own acre around the cottage was his private little cameo. The patch at the front facing west was his flower garden which he walked through every time he left the cottage, and when he sat inside the window having his meals he could look out into it. In this way he felt that his flowers gave him double delight. But the long acre at the southern side of the cottage was his harvesting area where he grew his own fruits. When his mother Emily was alive, she had made all kinds of preserves, and when she had died he missed the pot of home-made jam on the table. When he had found her old dog-eared Mrs Beeton and had started to make his own, it doubled once again his satisfaction in fruit growing. When he had all his vegetables and potatoes sown in the early spring, it was a great feeling to stand at the top of his acre and admire the long straight drills full of buried promise. That promise was realised later when he eased the spade under his early potato stalks and their pale perfection burst out of the dark brown earth. It was a resurrection! That evening when he put those early potatoes on to boil, he felt a deep gratitude for the plenitude of his little corner of God's earth.

His bedroom at the back of the cottage faced east. Every morning the early light poured in, and during the summer he could watch the sunrise. After his mother died, he had planned to take down the wall between the two bedrooms so that he would have two east-facing windows, but for years he had put it on the long finger. Then one morning last year Peter had come up from the farm with Davey Shine, and by evening he had one big room with two windows facing east. It was a source of wonder to him to watch the light changing in the morning sky. These windows also looked out over his haggard where his hens and ducks were housed. At first light the rooster was his alarm clock. The windows of his little parlour faced over the vegetable garden. The parlour was for special occasions, and every Christmas he lit the fire in there. In the small sideboard he kept the set of china that old Mrs Phelan had given his mother when she got married, and in the tall linen press by the fire he kept the tablecloths that his mother had embroidered. At night when her darning was done, she had picked up her embroidery. He knew that of all the things she did with her hands her embroidery gave her the greatest pleasure. In the winter she did it by the fire, but when the light was good in the spring and summer she sat in her rocking chair inside the kitchen window. She loved that view and used to say, "It is good to have your evening window facing west to say goodbye to the day and the morning window facing east to welcome in the new day." Now he knew what she was talking about. It was one of the pleasures of growing older that your sense of appreciation broadened and deepened. Now he too was glad that the front of the cottage faced west, because every evening he sat inside the kitchen window and watched the sunset, and every evening it was different. Then the cottage gathered itself around him like a soft shawl.

Long ago old Edward Phelan had told him, "Jack lad, always be guided by nature when you plan your building because we can never improve on her. When we work in harmony with her she will repay us, but if we wrong her we will pay a terrible price." He was right. The old man had so much wisdom and he had passed it all on. He had been good to him in so many ways. Every spring he was given a calf and a lamb; they were reared in Mossgrove and were known as Jack's calf or Jack's lamb, and when they were sold he got the money. As well as that, when the big sow farrowed he got a bonham, and when it was later sold as a fattened pig he got the money too. He had discontinued this practice himself when the going was tough during Billy's time, but Ned, remembering it since he was a child, began it again when he was in charge. It had finished when Martha took over, but by then he no longer needed it. He had a reserve for a rainy day. He was grateful to the old man for that security.

When his mother had died suddenly when he was eighteen, the old man had stepped in and paid for the funeral and later put up a headstone, and no one knew about it but the two of themselves. Jack had missed his mother dreadfully: his father had died when he was a baby and he was an only child, so when she went he was on his own. The months after her death were raw and hard. Often the old man had called at night and stayed for hours. That support in his bereavement had welded a deep bond between them. Sometimes he found a bunch of flowers on his mother's grave, and he knew that it was the old man remembering.

Suddenly he felt a soft cheek against his and was startled into wakefulness, causing him to straighten up, moving his feet and disturbing Toby, who looked up at him in annoyance.

"Kate," he said with delight. "I must have dozed off."

"You must indeed," Kate laughed from behind him as she put her hands on his shoulders and began to massage between his shoulder blades.

"Oh, that eases my old bones," he told her appreciatively.

"How's the old ticker doing? Are you taking things any easier?" she asked.

"Yerra, I'm great for an ould fella," he told her.

"Well then," Kate said as she drew up the rocking chair beside him, "tell me all the news from below."

"What kind of news?" Jack teased.

"You know that anything that moves in Mossgrove is news for me."

"Well, all is quiet in Mossgrove. While Martha was in America, Peter got his hands on the control knobs, and I feel that he might keep them there."

"Is she satisfied with that?"

"I'm not sure. You know with Martha you can never be quite sure of anything. She seems satisfied enough, but that might only mean that she is hatching something that might turn us all upside down when she gets going again," Jack said.

"Life is never dull around Martha," Kate mused, "but nothing came of the great romance that we all thought would blossom in New York."

"Well, we are assuming that it didn't, but I suppose when he didn't come back with them that was that. But it didn't surprise me that it happened that way. Somehow I can never see Martha getting married again. In many ways Martha is a solo operator," Jack concluded.

"I thought that she might have married him for the money," Kate said thoughtfully. "I know that sounds terrible, but Martha likes power, and think what she could have done as Mrs Rodney Jackson."

"Martha would prefer to make her own money," Jack decided.

"You are probably right," Kate agreed. "You know Martha better than any of us."

"Hard to know Martha."

"Well, I didn't come to discuss Martha," Kate told him. "I am here to discuss money problems."

"Oh," Jack said in surprise.

"Not my money problems," Kate assured him.

"Whose then?" Jack looked at her inquiringly.

"Danny Conway's," she told him.

"Aha! I thought that he couldn't keep going much longer without needing hard cash at the rate he was doing improvements," Jack said thoughtfully, "but how did you get involved in it?"

Kate filled him in, and as he listened he nodded his head slowly and smiled with understanding as she told about the grandmother.

"So old Molly Barry has left her mark," he said slowly. "The chances were always there that there was bound to be one throwback. And Danny is the one! I thought that it was looking that way. And he has even resurrected the old name Furze Hill. It was always known as Furze Hill when I was a child, and it was a grand place then. The Barrys were fine people."

"But what happened?" Kate's voice was full of curiosity.

"Molly Barry married so far beneath her that she could never again straighten up," Jack told her.

"Good God, Jack, that's a deadly pronouncement," Kate told him in a shocked voice.

"Just telling it as it was," Jack declared. "Rory was a blackguard of the highest order. There is no other way to describe him. Molly was a strong-willed only child who had seldom heard the word no. She was very spoilt. Conway could be charming, but there was a bad drop in him. They eloped and were married before anyone knew anything about it. I'd say that the day she got married was the last good day that she had. He was no good, and she discovered it in her own time. But I suppose her biggest disappointment was that their son Matt turned out the same as his father. Matt was a bit of an oddball and pushing on in years when he married Brigid, who was far younger; and then he got worse if anything. He treated Brigid like dirt, and then, of course, there was the business with the daughters. So Molly's hardship did not die with Rory."

"But how come old Rory Conway was so friendly with grandfather if he was that bad?" Kate asked in a puzzled voice.

"Could never understand it," Jack told her. "They went to school together, and I think that your grandfather always thought that he could straighten him out. Then he fixed the loan because he did not want to see Furze Hill go to the wall, on account of Molly. The Barrys were the old stock, and your grandfather had great time for them, and he wanted to do everything he could for Molly."

"Well, Jack, this is all news to me," Kate exclaimed. "You live in a place all your life and you think that you know all that there is to know about the people, and then you come on an unopened chapter."

"Life is full of unread chapters, Kate," Jack smiled. They sat quietly together, both occupied with their own thought, and the logs shifted in the fire, sending out a spray of sparks that caused Toby to draw back hurriedly. He looked around, unsure of the safety of the stone floor, and jumped into Jack's lap where he settled down comfortably. Jack rubbed behind his brown ears, thinking that it was time to put on the kettle, but Kate broke into his thoughts.

"And while we are at it now, Jack, what is the story of that old stone house beyond Conway's own house?"

"That was more of Rory Conway's madness. He got the daft notion that it would be cheaper to live in a smaller house. The rates were high on Furze Hill and would be less on a smaller house, so he stripped the slates off that fine old house and moved into that other poke of a place. He was friendly with your grandfather then — that was before the split — and the old man made him sheet it afterwards, so at least that kept it from the weather."

"And they never used it since?" Kate asked.

"No. Rory Conway locked it and boarded up the windows, and over the years it got buried in furze bushes and trees. The place is not called Furze Hill for nothing, you know. By then, of course, Molly and himself were having blue murder, so he was probably doing it to spite her as well. She had loved that old house. It was her childhood home, and I suppose we all love our childhood home."

"Not I'd say if you were one of the present generation of Conways," Kate told him.

"No, I suppose not," Jack agreed evenly.

"I've always felt sorry for the young Conways. Their father gave them a terrible life, and only for old Molly it would have been worse. Even when she was dying she was looking out for them. I had great time for her."

"She was a real Barry," Jack said, "and it was hard to get to the end of the Barrys. She probably sized up Matt's clutch and decided which had the most Barry blood in them and primed

Danny to be ready if the tide ever turned in his direction."

Then Kate took him by surprise: "Jack, did you ever think that there was something strange about the way Matt Conway died?" she asked searchingly.

"I did," he admitted reluctantly.

"Do you think that Martha had something to do with it?" she persisted.

"She could have," he told her slowly, remembering the morning beside Yalla Hole, "and I think that Danny might have seen more than was good for him."

"How do you mean?" Kate demanded.

"There are certain things in life, Kate, that are best put behind us, especially when I'm only putting two and two together and not sure of anything; so we'll let it at that now."

Looking into a fire, Jack thought, *is a great place to think. You can see the future take shape between the sods and the logs.* He knew that Kate was thinking back over all that they had talked about, but he was thinking ahead to the future of Furze Hill. Despite all the bitterness between himself and Rory Conway, old man Phelan had mourned the condition of the house and farm across the river. He had hated to see Molly's life ruined and good land neglected.

"So where do I come in to all this?" he asked Kate.

"Well, Jack, this is your chance to find out if Molly Barry's instincts were right," Kate told him with a smile.

"Doesn't this put me in a strange situation now," Jack mused. "I've spent my entire life struggling against the Conways, and here I am now being asked to get into their boat and start rowing with them. I suppose the strangest thing of all is that I'm being asked by a Phelan."

"What did you think of Molly Barry, or Molly Conway as I always thought of her, but after this conversation I feel that she was more Barry than Conway," Kate said.

"You forget, Kate, that she was a lot older than me, but my mother and herself had been good friends, and I know that your grandfather had great respect for her. Any time that I met her, I'll have to say that I was always impressed by her. Even though she saw hard times and had come down in the world, she never lost her sense of dignity and pride."

"Never forgot that she was one of the Barrys of Furze Hill," Kate smiled.

"Maybe that," Jack agreed, "because despite everything there was always a bit of grandeur about her. Rory tried to drag her into the gutter, but she never quite joined him there."

"You know, Jack, when I was nursing her before she died, I must say that I found her a formidable old lady. But there was something admirable about her, too. One thing that sticks in my mind is that she was always hinting that she knew more about us than she was ever prepared to say."

"She probably did too, because she was around for a long time, longer than any of us, and she had a mighty memory," Jack told her. "Anyone around here who wanted to check back on anything asked Molly Barry, and she was always right. She knew everything about everyone, and there was a rumour that she kept a diary. But she was a bit of a closed book."

"And now all her secrets are gone with her," Kate concluded.

"Secrets have a way of lurking in dark corners," Jack told her.

Later, when Kate had gone home, Jack walked across the kitchen into the small parlour. He stood inside the window and looked across the valley at Furze Hill. In the bright moonlight, the sagging rusty roof of the barn was a foxy patch in the surrounding green. Kate's request had taken him by surprise. The possibility of himself getting involved with Furze Hill was an unexpected turn of events. He smiled to think that Molly Barry was still shaking the dice. She had once said to him, "Remember, Jack Tobin, that you owe the Phelans nothing." At the time he did not know what she was talking about, but years later he understood.

CHAPTER THREE

K ATE PUT THE saucepan of strained potatoes to the back of the cooker. Her kitchen was small, and she had painted it a rich yellow to brighten up the quarry-tiled floor. She took a tea towel from a little press beside the Aga and covered the potatoes. They had burst their creamy jackets, and their floury insides smiled out at her. Jack grew great potatoes. She could hear his voice now: "Fine plury spuds breaking their hearts laughing." Every first Saturday on his way through the village to confession, he brought her a bag of potatoes, vegetables and home-made jams. Over the years he had taken the place of the father who had died when she was young, and in more recent years even filled the gap left by Nellie, and no one else understood her sense of loss after Ned as well as Jack.

She checked the meat in the top oven and put the potatoes and vegetables into the bottom one to keep warm. Her Aga was very kind to dinners that had to be kept warm for long periods, which often happened in her job and with David, who could be kept late at school or delayed after a match. She took the dishes off the dresser and put one of Emily's embroidered cloths on the table. Jack had given her some of his mother's cloths, and she used them constantly because he had advised, "Use them, Kate girlie; no good in keeping them for your wake." He wanted her to enjoy and appreciate the long hours that his mother had put into them and keep alive the memory of the woman whose photograph was hanging over the fireplace in his parlour, the woman whose faded face was smiling but full of sadness. Kate had often looked at the photograph and wondered about her sad eyes. Once as a little girl she had asked Jack about the pretty lady in the photograph and he told her quietly, "That lady talked very little about herself." After that she asked no more. If Jack wanted you to know something he told you; otherwise you did not ask questions.

She respected everything about Jack, especially his sense of decency and integrity and his unlimited kindness. When she had mentioned, after buying this house, that she wished she had a dresser like the one in Mossgrove, Jack had turned up six months later with a smaller replica that fitted perfectly into her kitchen. She had never known until then that he had made the original with her grandfather, old Edward Phelan, and had not forgotten how to carve every minute detail. Later he had made her kitchen table. David and herself spent a lot of time in their kitchen, and she had put a comfortable sofa under the sloping ceiling by the stairs where she sometimes slept if she came back late after a night call and did not want to wake David. Sometimes on a chilly evening if he came home tired from school, he took a short catnap before dinner. Remembering the great use that Ned and herself as children had made out of the old one in Mossgrove, she had bought the sofa thinking that it would be lovely too for her children. But unfortunately that had not happened.

She walked over to the back door and looked out into her back garden where Jack and herself had spent many evenings digging and planting. When she had bought this house after coming back to Kilmeen, the garden was a jungle, but to Jack it was a challenge. He had rubbed his hands in gleeful anticipation when he saw it.

"Kate girleen, we can do great things out here."

They had shared the joy of creating a little haven where she went if she came home tired from work. Sometimes in her job she had to deal with deaths and tragedies in her patients' lives, and when she had comforted them she herself needed a quiet place to recover. She recalled a practical sister on the ward in her training hospital in London telling her, "Nurse Phelan, you can't die with every patient." That sister had thought that she was too soft to be a good nurse and needed to toughen up a bit, but it was sometimes difficult to stand back from the patients' problems, so this garden was her healing place. David was not a gardener, but when he came home from school drained after a day's teaching, she smiled as he headed out into the garden to sit under the old beech tree. They were lucky that someone had planted that tree long before she bought the house. Sometimes when she sat under its sweeping branches, she thought kindly of the person who had planted it and felt that she was sheltering beneath the leaves of their foresight. If she joined David there, he smiled and said, "This place clears my head." He put all his energy and dedication into the school that he had set up, and it gave him immense satisfaction when his students did well. It was the first secondary school in the parish, and it was giving the children a chance of education and a job at home instead of taking the boat, as Jack called it.

She would be for ever grateful to Rodney Jackson, who had given his aunts' old home to house the school, making it possible for David to stay in Kilmeen. The rent that he was paying was nominal, not alone because Rodney was extremely wealthy but because he had a deep interest in Kilmeen, where he had come on holidays to his aunts while growing up in New York. He had also helped Martha's brother Mark, who had been painting since childhood. They had all taken his talent for granted until Rodney Jackson had seen his possibilities and mounted an exhibition of his pictures in New York, where he had sold out. Now commissions were coming in to Mark's home, where his mother Agnes was constantly amazed at the prices that Rodney insisted that Mark should charge. Martha, who had never been impressed by her brother's ability to do anything right, was slightly cynical of his success as an artist. But it had taken them all by surprise the previous summer when Rodney had shown a sudden interest in Martha and invited herself and Nora to attend Mark's opening in New York. Kate had been filled with curiosity as to how things would develop between them, but Martha and Nora had come home and Rodney had remained on in New York, so she assumed that Martha had declined his proposal. But there was no way that she could ask Martha.

As Kate dished up the dinner she heard the front door bang. She knew that it could not be David, who always moved quietly, and she smiled when she heard something clatter on to the tiled floor of the hall and Fr Tim Brady burst into the kitchen with pages dropping from an overfull folder. Beneath an unruly mop of black hair, his thin, boyish face smiled ruefully at her. Sometimes when he was training the team he was mistaken for one of them.

"I thought it might be you," she told him.

"How did you know?" he asked breathlessly.

"You always move as if you are about to catch the last train out of town," she told him. "And sometime your luggage is not quite going to make it," she added pointing to the pages on the floor.

"Never!" he protested. "I always thought that I was the quiet, silent type."

"Rather the direct opposite," she told him, "a volcanic whirlwind of legs, hands and hair flying in all directions."

"You make me sound like a lunatic," he protested.

"But a nice one," she told him. "Sit down there now and have dinner with us to see if I can put a bit of fat on those skinny bones."

"Your choice of words, Kate, leaves a lot to be desired," he laughed, sliding into a chair across the table from her, "and somehow I think it is better that the more tactful David rather than you is in charge of our local corner of education. You might not be the best in dealing with a doting mammy who thinks that she is rearing a potential Einstein. You lack a certain delicacy in your choice of delivery, whereas David would soothe her down and she would go home knowing the truth but not blaming him that her son is not a genius."

"Yes, my darling husband has the master's touch with people, and I'm sure that a lot of the mothers feel sorry for him, married to that dark, stubborn Phelan one."

"Ah, but Kate, when they get a pain they need you. Did you ever consider that we could run this parish between the three of us. You could deliver them, David could educate them, and I could bury them."

"You should tell Fr Burke," she told him.

"We'd let that to David. The PP is very impressed with him, but that could be partly because he is the doctor's son and the PP is a bit of a snob. It goes against the grain with him that his curate was reared in a pub."

"I'm sure that he finds you a great trial, but then he does not love me either since that run-in we had about the trees around the church . . . Oh, that's David now," she finished.

"I didn't hear a thing," Fr Tim decided, having listened.

"No, David is the quiet type," Kate told him.

"Hello, quiet man," he called out.

Kate smiled, and she thought how different these two men were and yet what a strong friendship had developed between them. Fr Tim was a great support to David, giving all his free time to training the school teams. He was good with the young because he had a great zest for life. Kate felt that the older people in the parish did not appreciate him fully because he lacked a certain gravitas. But as she had stood with him by the bedsides of the sick and dying, she had discovered that he had unplumbed depths of spirituality. There he was a different person from the laughing, vivacious tearaway who outran the footballers up and down the playing field. Any family who had him with them for a death and bereavement saw the other side of him, and they never forgot his goodness.

As David came into the room with a stack of copybooks under his arm, Kate felt the usual warm glow enfold her. She was always more complete in his loving presence. Now his dark eyes were full of amusement as he viewed Fr Tim and herself.

"What's all this about the quiet man?"

"Your wife has been busy undermining my self-confidence by telling me what a big-mouthed, long-legged, awkward galoot I am and what a nice, quiet, gentle soul you are," Fr Tim told him.

"Well, isn't it nice to be appreciated," David said, ruffling Kate's hair as he passed behind her chair.

"You must be the most appreciated man in the parish," Fr Tim told him, "all the mothers thinking that you're wonderful and the leaving cert girls hanging off your every word."

"Oh, the first years might be impressed by me, but by the time they come to leaving cert they have gone off me because by then they have discovered that I'm a slave driver," David told him, "but it's you, Tim, that the leaving certs girls think is great."

"Do you think that it has anything to do with my half-starved look?" he joked.

"Not really; just a case of any half-respectable-looking male under forty and teenagers full of awakening hormones," David said ruefully as he joined them at the table. "But enough of that rubbish. Have you the Kilmeen team made out for Sunday or did you forget?"

"Forget! You know that I never forget anything," he protested much to their amusement. "It's right here, boss," he said, bringing a page out of his folder on the floor and waving it in front of David, who took it and studied the list.

"I see that you have Danny Conway in goal again," David said thoughtfully.

"Why, what's wrong with that?"

"He nearly fell asleep there last Sunday. Only for Davey Shine we were wiped out," David said ruefully.

"I suppose he wasn't up to his usual, but then Shiner, as the lads call him, covered well."

"But Shiner should not have to be carrying Danny. You can't win matches with fellows trying to cover for each other," David protested.

"Yes, but Shiner won't play as well in front of any other goalie, because himself and Danny understand each other and can anticipate each other's thinking."

"I think that Danny's lapse could be temporary," Kate cut in. The two men looked at her in surprise. In their world of GAA, she seldom voiced an opinion.

"How do you know?" Fr Tim asked with surprise.

"Well, it's a long story. Have you both the time to listen?" she asked them.

"As long as it takes," Fr Tim told her. "Don't you know that the GAA is the second religion in Kilmeen, so it's my second job. We're all ears."

When she had finished there was silence for a moment as they digested the story. "What will Jack be able to do for him?" Fr Tim wondered.

"Kate thinks that Jack can raise the dead," David smiled.

"Well, he raised Mossgrove from the dead when Dad died," Kate told them. "I know that money is all-important to Danny now, but an experienced head is a great thing in farming and could spare him a lot of money in the long run."

"Somehow I don't think that it's the long run that Danny is worried about right now," Fr Tim said. "Has he anyone to help him at the moment?"

"As far as I know, Davey Shine goes over every evening when he is finished in Mossgrove. Danny didn't tell me that, but I heard Martha complaining about it."

"How did she know, because I doubt that Shiner told her?" Fr Tim asked.

"She probably saw him across the fields. You can see Furze Hill quite clearly from Mossgrove, and much doesn't go on unknown to Martha," Kate told him.

"That's typical of Shiner now to help out; he has a great heart. Of course, himself and Danny always stuck together. I remember him the time of Matt Conway's funeral; he was never far away from Danny," Fr Tim said.

"It's Rory that I'd be worried about," David broke in. "When we had him playing with us he was nothing but trouble. Money could solve the first problem, but there are some problems that nothing can solve, and Rory I think could be one of them."

"We'll have to wait and see how it all turns out," Kate concluded, "but I thought that I'd fill you in so that you'd understand Danny, and maybe you might get a chance to help in some way."

"A rescue team?" Fr Tim smiled.

"More than Danny needs a rescue team," David told him.

"How come?"

"The Kilmeen club is going to grind to a halt without funds, and we can't expect the likes of Danny and others like him who have nothing to put on the wind to buy jerseys and hurleys."

"You're right there," Fr Tim agreed.

"Well, how do we make money?" David asked him.

"You're asking the wrong man," Fr Tim told him. "My

brothers got all the money brains in our family. I was the academic."

"That makes two of us," David said ruefully.

"Any ideas, Kate?" Fr Tim asked.

For a long time it had bothered Kate that there was so little activity for the young in the village, but especially the girls. Nora and Rosie Nolan were for ever complaining about it, maintaining that the boys had hurling and football but that they had nothing, and she agreed with them.

"Why not run a fund-raising event," she suggested.

"Like what?" Fr Tim demanded.

"Well, let the young decide that," she told him. "Why not form a club of the boys and girls and then let them do it together and divide the returns between the Kilmeens and the club. If the Kilmeens go it alone, they won't have all the young with them, but the club would be a parish effort and everybody would be on board."

"That's a great idea," Fr Tim declared enthusiastically.

"Where would they meet and run their events?" David asked.

"The parish hall, I suppose," Kate said. "Sure there is nowhere else."

"Oh, oh, that's the first stumbling block," Fr Tim decided. "I can imagine the face of the PP when I ask him for the hall for a gang of young ones, and we'll have to ask him as it's parish property."

"Yerra, you wouldn't do to ask him at all," Kate told him. "We'll have to send David."

"Great idea," a relieved Fr Tim declared.

"So I'm to take the bull by the horns," David smiled.

"And bull is the operative word," Kate said.

46

They sat for a long time discussing the pros and cons of the new venture, and as they chatted Kate realised that between the three of them they knew most of what went on in the parish. This aspect of Kilmeen irritated Martha, and she often complained that it was like living in a fishbowl, but it never bothered Kate. She had often discovered on her rounds that some of people's problems, when they were aired, were not really as big as they had thought. She was always nervous of the problems that went on behind closed doors, and when she came on a problem like Matt Conway and his daughters, she nearly lost her faith in human nature. But then old Molly Conway, with her determined efforts to protect her grandchildren, restored it.

"Kate, where are you gone off to?" David's amused voice broke in on her thoughts and she heard the doorbell ringing. "That will be Rosie Nolan," David said rising. "She is coming in to go over some maths. Nora is very anxious that she do honours maths and get a good leaving cert to go to college with her."

"Is that what Rosie wants?" Kate asked in surprise. "I thought that Rosie has this big dream of becoming a showband singer."

"She probably has, but Nora is determined that she will do a good exam and have something else behind her as well," David told her.

"Well done, Nora," Fr Tim said. "The singing could be a shaky number, but Rosie could make it because she has a great voice and she is all up for it."

"Well, for the next half an hour she must be all up for Euclid," David declared.

When he had gone, Fr Tim poured himself another cup of tea, and Kate smiled as he filled her cup without asking.

47

"You're a rale tay boy," she told him.

"A family failing," he smiled.

"How are they?" she asked.

"They're all fine. The pub is humming away, but since Brian got married Dad is feeling that he is not as needed as he was. He does not say anything, but I can sense it in him. I suppose after Mom died he had been stretched to the hilt trying to get us all reared and educated, and now it's done. He's coming over to me next week to do my garden and straighten out my garden shed. But I know that he is only doing it to pass away the time. He loves gardening, but mine is very small. Dad was used to a very full life. He was a builder, you know, before he bought the pub. Made his money on the buildings in England and then came home and bought a pub."

"Smart move," Kate told him. "Can't go wrong with a pub in Ireland."

"Suppose so, but Kate, you have no idea of the drivel you have to listen to in a pub."

"Prepared you for the priesthood," Kate smiled.

"Maybe," he agreed, "but I suppose that it was my mother's death when I was a teenager that really started me on that road. Her death opened up all kinds of questions about what life was all about."

"Did you find any answers?" Kate asked.

"No," he told her, "and I'm beginning to think that there are none and that we must all struggle along the best way that we can."

"Any regrets?" she questioned.

"Sometimes when I shut the door behind me at night, I think that it might be nice to have someone to sit down and have a chat with and discuss the day that is gone. When I see David and yourself so happy and contented together, I regret that it can never be mine."

"Nothing is perfect, Tim," she told him lightly.

"You regret very much that you and David don't have children?" he questioned gently.

"My one regret in life," she told him, "and yet I feel that it is not right to complain when we are so happy together, and David never makes any issue out of it. It's I have the problem with it."

"Well, that's only natural, I suppose," he said.

"You know, when I think of the likes of Matt Conway having children and abusing his daughters and David and my not having any, wouldn't you question what God is thinking?" she demanded.

"God isn't very good at answering questions, Kate. But hearing about Danny's efforts to sort out Furze Hill, maybe it is up to all of us to help the Conways to recover from the life he inflicted on them."

"I feel so helpless on that score," she told him.

"Well, who knows but ways to help might open up yet," he smiled.

"That's what I like about you, Fr Tim: you are the eternal optimist."

"Inherited from my father, because he is a firm believer that if you keep plugging on things will eventually work themselves out."

"He's my kind of man," she said, "and. . ."

"Oh my God, I almost forgot to tell you that I had a letter from Rodney Jackson this morning," Fr Tim interrupted, diving into his pocket, "and he is coming after Easter. He says that he has big plans for Kilmeen. I didn't half read the letter as I was rushing down the street when I met Johnny and just opened it and sconced over it and pushed it in here," he finished pulling a crumpled envelope out of his pocket.

"Typical of you," she told him, "but I'd better get the spare room tidied out for him and see . . ." But she was interrupted by a gasp from Fr Tim who was busy reading down through the letter.

"Listen to this bit: 'For a long time I have felt that Kilmeen is in the need of a small hotel as the catering facilities are so limited and there is no place for any tourist to stay in the village."

"Tourists!" she echoed.

"Just listen," he told her continuing: "While the school at the moment is occupying my family home, I feel that the house would lend itself better to being restored and made into a small, intimate, first class hotel. . ."

"Jesus," Kate gasped, but Tim continued reading from the letter, ". . .but this is only part of a larger plan, and I will discuss it all with you when I come. Please tell Kate that I'm looking forward to her hospitality."

Fr Tim put down the letter and looked across at Kate's stricken face.

She felt as if somebody had given her a kick in the stomach.

"What on earth is he talking about? The school is in the old Jackson home since it started. There is no other place for it. He just can't kick us out now," she gasped.

"Where did all this come from?" Fr Tim wondered. "There was no mention of it when he was here last summer. What has happened since?"

With Fr Tim's question something clicked in Kate's brain. Martha had happened since. Last summer they had all been surprised when Rodney Jackson had fallen in love with Martha. *We should have known*, Kate thought, *that it was never going to be straightforward.* Nothing was straightforward with Martha. Even if she had no great feelings for Rodney, he was still a bright prospect for getting what she wanted in life. He was too good a business opportunity to pass up. Rodney would never mean to wrong anybody, but Martha was a manipulative woman, and Kate had seen how she had outmanoeuvred Ned and got her own way in everything. While she was in New York, Peter had taken over in Mossgrove and was not going to relinquish his grip. There was too much of his mother in him to give in to her. Jack had often said that it took your own to level you, and Peter had edged Martha out of the running of Mossgrove. She had surprised them all by accepting it. Now Kate felt a piece of that jigsaw slip into place.

CHAPTER FOUR

NORA CHECKED THE list of subjects in the timetable on the parlour table. Every evening before beginning her homework, she allocated a certain amount of time to each subject, and though it did not always work out, it still brought a bit of order into her study. She had tried to get Rosie to do this but gave up in the end because Rosie Nolan would never adhere to a plan.

The parlour was a good place to do her lessons. It was a restful room with flowing cream drapes that Nana Agnes had made when Mom was getting the house ready last year to impress Rodney Jackson. As it happened, Rodney Jackson had been so impressed with the house and the whole lot of them that it looked as if he wanted to become part of them. She liked Rodney Jackson but not enough to want him as one of them. He had been delighted with the old family pictures in the parlour, and Peter had been highly amused at that, because Mom had evicted them years previously and had only brought them back because Peter was making such a song and dance about it. Nora was glad that they were back, especially Nana Nellie, who had a kind face, and she liked looking at the picture of Dad and Mom on their wedding day. Dad looked a bit uncomfortable, but Mom was beautiful. Secretly she wished that she looked like Mom, with her high cheekbones and wonderful green eyes. But she did not want to be like Mom, whom she knew that the neighbours, even though they might be a little bit in awe of her, did not like very much. The other mothers were all chatty and friendly, but Mom did not go in for small talk. Though her school friends were impressed by Mom's appearance, they were never very comfortable in her presence, and Mom made no effort to put them at their ease. She sometimes wished that Mom was more sociable, but Mom was Mom, and there was no way that she was going to make an effort to impress anyone.

But the picture that dominated the room was the one that Uncle Mark had painted of Great-grandfather Edward Phelan. Aunty Kate had taken the original picture when she got married and had got Mark to paint a portrait for Mossgrove. It hung on the wall at the end of the table where he could keep an eye on everything. He had steely grey hair and eyes that followed you all around the room. Nobody, not even Mom, would dare to shift Great-grandfather. Everyone knew that he was the foundation stone of Mossgrove, but he was also the one who had started the huge row with the Conways. Growing up, even though she did not know all the details, she accepted that there was an unbridgeable gap between them and the family across the river.

She tidied up the books on the table and was pleased that she was finished with the writing exercises. Now all she had to do was the reading and learning off, and she could sit by the fire after the supper and do those. When doing her homework she did the subjects that she liked least first, and then the night got easier as it went on. This was her last year and she was determined to do her best and get the results that she would need to get to college. She had her heart set on doing teaching so that she could join Uncle David and teach in his school. Everything about Uncle David impressed her, and secretly she thought that Aunty Kate did not really appreciate him enough. He was one of the reasons that she was determined to do well. Peter called her a slogger, but he helped her in any way that he could. He was very good at maths, but she preferred English, especially poetry, and dreamed of one day opening up the world of her favourite poets to students. When she had told Rosie about this, she threw back her long mane of blonde hair and rocked with laughter.

"In the name of God, Nora Phelan, there's about as much interest in poetry in Kilmeen as there's in outer space," she declared.

"We are a poetic people," Nora asserted.

"And pigs can fly," Rosie told her.

Now the muted sound of the kitchen clock striking six echoed through the house. Having stacked up her books, Nora left the parlour and went across the front hallway to the kitchen. After putting on the kettle, she went over to the radio and tuned into Radio Luxembourg and was delighted to hear Elvis Presley singing "Wooden Heart". She danced around the kitchen to the soothing sound of Elvis and closed her eyes, imagining what it would be like to dance with Uncle David. Then she began to lay the table. They would soon be in from the cows and the yard jobs. Sometimes she wished that Mom would come in early and get the supper and not always be depending on her to do it. Mom and Shiner did the yard work and Jack and Peter did the cows. Peter and Jack worked in complete harmony, and it had always been like that. She sensed that Jack had filled Dad's shoes and become Peter's support and adviser, and she remembered Aunty Kate saying that the same thing had happened for her when Grandad had died. No wonder they all loved Jack. He was the heart of Mossgrove and of their lives. Sometimes she worried when she saw him trying to lift something that was too heavy and tried to help. But Mom had advised, "Let Jack do things his own way and don't be trying to make him feel like an old man."

"But, Mom," she had protested, "sure at seventy-five he can't be whipping bags of wheat and spuds around."

"If he feels able, don't interfere. Jack would prefer to burn out fast rather than rust out like old mowing machine. Haven't you often heard him say that?"

"But I don't want him to burn out fast," Nora protested. "I would die if anything happened to Jack."

"Norry, my dear, you must toughen up a bit or life will crucify you," Mom said firmly.

"Did life crucify you, Mom?" she asked curiously, because Mom never talked about her emotions.

"No," Mom had declared grimly, "because I learned early in life that if you saw something that you wanted you went right for it."

Nora wondered if that included Rodney Jackson. She did not want Mom to marry him. Peter and herself had discussed it, and Peter had concluded, "She might not marry him, but he is going to come in useful in some other direction."

Davey Shine was the first to come in the back door, and Nora knew by his face that himself and Mom were after a confrontation. He was running his finger through his wiry red hair, causing it to stand upright above his normally happy round face. Davey was broad and short, but what he lacked in height he made up for in muscle. Now he grinned ruefully at Nora.

"Your mother," he told her, shaking his head, "has the happy knack of acting like Queen Muck and thinking that she can control all around her. Wouldn't you think that I'd be used to her at this stage?"

"Davey, you know she doesn't mean it," Nora assured him.

"Not so sure of that now," Davey decided. "I go over every night to help out Danny across the river, and your mother thinks that she has the right to tell me that I'm working here and not at Conways'."

"I think that you are great to be helping Danny," she told him warmly, "but you are probably tired and that's why Mom's annoyed you. Normally she doesn't bother you and it's Peter does all the complaining."

"God, you had better say nothing about me being tired," Davey warned her, "because that's exactly what your mother is complaining about."

"But it's all in a good cause," she told him.

"Nora, my girl," Davey smiled at her as he dried his hands, "sometimes I think that you are in the wrong nest."

"Oh, she's in the right nest all right," Jack assured them, overhearing the remark as he came in the door, "her grandmother down to the ground."

"Oh the blue blood of the Phelans!" Shiner laughed,

throwing the towel across to Jack. "There you are now, wash your dirty paws before you dine with your betters."

"There is none better than Jack around here," Nora asserted. "Jack is the best, and there would be none of us here only for him."

"Jack, you have them all brainwashed," Davey told him. "Peter thinks you're God, and Nora thinks that you made the world, and even herself is a little bit in awe of you."

"Is Mom in awe of Jack?" Nora asked with interest as she laid out the cold meat and boiled eggs on the table.

"Just a bit, but even a bit is a big thing with the boss woman, and now here comes the big boss himself," Davey announced as Peter came in the door. He put his head down and pretended to shadow-box in front of Peter. Peter tried to wrestle him to the floor, but his tall athletic figure was no match for Davey's solid frame.

"The trouble with you, Phelan," Davey said looking down at him, "is that you are all long legs and speed, but when it comes to holding your ground you are no match for me."

"But you've no speed, Shiner. I'd outdistance you without trying," Peter told him as he straightened up and joined Jack and Nora at the table.

"Speed is not much good, my boyo, if you're caught in a corner," Davey told him, slipping on to the long form beside Jack inside the table.

"Do you know what ye remind me of?" Jack asked them.

"Well, we don't," Peter told him, "but I'm sure that you're going to tell us."

"Bran's two pups out in the barn, and they might have more sense than the two of you."

"And you're like Bran, Jack, full of age and wisdom," Nora smiled.

"Where did that come from?" Jack wondered.

"Yeats," Nora told him.

"So we're having Yeats for supper in Mossgrove now. There is no doubt but things are looking up around here," Shiner decided.

"Davey, what do you think of poetry?" Nora wanted to know.

"Well, now let me think," Shiner said slowly, sighing deeply and stroking his chin. "This is heavy stuff after a day piking dung."

"Ah, Davey," Nora protested, "this is serious. I'm researching an idea that I have."

"In other words, Shiner, you're a pilot project," Peter told him.

"That's agricultural language, my boy," Shiner told him in a condescending tone.

"Nora and I are on to higher ground at the moment. Now let me think. I learned poetry in the Glen school, and a lot of it did not mean much to me, but then one day there was a poem about the sky and blackbirds and I liked that. So to me poetry is someone putting pictures that I like into words."

"I knew it! I knew it! I knew it!" Nora waved her hands in the air with excitement. "Davey, you're a genius," and she ran around the table and planted a kiss on top of his wiry head.

"You should have aimed a little lower," he grinned up at her.

"Forget about that," she told him. "You're after saving my belief in the human race."

"You know, Norry, sometimes. . ." Peter began, but then

changed into song, "You speak a language that the strangers do not know."

"Well, between poetry and singing, we're like a Bunratty banquet," Shiner declared.

"What's all the racket about?" Martha demanded, coming in from the back porch having washed her hands and taken off the long apron that she usually wore around the yard. Nora always marvelled at how her mother could come in from the yard, having spent an hour feeding calves and hens, and still look elegant. Aunty Kate had once described Mom as a black swan, and Nora thought that it was a perfect description. There was not a rib astray in her glossy black hair coiled in a knot at the back of her long neck. Now she slid gracefully on to a chair at the head of the table, and with her arrival a more restrained air descended on them. Nora saw Shiner glance at her mother out of the corner of his eye. He was gauging whether she was going to forget or continue the argument that they had started out in the yard, and she did not leave him long in doubt.

"Now, Davey Shine," she began, "I expect you to arrive here on time in the morning and not to arrive with the two eyes hanging out of your head with exhaustion."

Nora knew by the surprised look on Peter's face that he did not know what Mom was talking about, but she felt that it came as no surprise to Jack. How did Jack know everything?

"What are you talking about?" Peter demanded, preparing for an argument because he recognised the tone of voice that was normally reserved for him.

"Our Davey Shine," she informed him icily, "is haring across the river every evening when he finishes here and spending until the small hours of the morning slaving with Danny

59

Conway, trying to bring law and order into that wilderness over there. How can he do a day's work after that?"

"Well, to be honest," a surprised Peter told her, "I saw no difference in Shiner's work."

"That's because half the time the two of you are so busy discussing football that you don't know what's going on around you," Martha declared.

"Hold it right there now, Mother," Peter asserted forcefully, "this place is running like clockwork now, and it's due in no small way to Shiner, and what Shiner does in his own time is Shiner's business. This is 1962, you know, not the middle ages."

"So you have no problem with him helping out the Conways, who spent years trying to bankrupt us out of here by burning our hay and hurting our cattle, not to mention other things?" she demanded.

"Now that's another question altogether," Peter told her.

Nora felt that her mother was backing Peter into a corner and forcing him into confrontation with Shiner, and even though she hated getting involved in arguments between Mom and Peter, she blurted out, "Well, I think that I owe Danny Conway a lot, because only for him the night of his father in the wood might be . . . might. . ." Suddenly the old fear flooded back, and the whole scene in the wood swam in front of her eyes: the terror of Matt Conway forcing her to the ground and tearing her dress and then her amazement when Danny came from behind to hit him with a hurley, yelling for her to run. For months afterwards she had nightmares in which she was still running, but since the trip to New York they had faded. Now the terror was back. She ran sobbing from the kitchen into the parlour.

The door opened gently, and it was Jack who came in quietly and sat into the armchair across from her. "It is good to get that crying out, Norry," he reassured her.

"I don't know where it came from, Jack," she sobbed. "I thought that I was over it."

"Sometimes there are hurts buried in crevices of the mind, girleen, and it eases us to to clear them away. You'll be the better of it," he told her.

"You make it sound as if it was a good thing that happened tonight, Jack," she smiled through her tears.

"It was," he assured her. She looked across at Jack and her heart overflowed with love for him. All her life he had been there when she needed him. He had been there to comfort her on the night that Nana Nellie had died. She had loved Nana Nellie and, with the unerring instinct of a child, sensed that Jack did too. Mom was no comfort then because she knew that Mom had never loved Nana Nellie. And on the terrible day when Dad had been killed and her whole world had been blown apart, it had been Jack who had comforted and sheltered her. Mom could not cope and had gone to bed, and it was Jack who had looked after herself and Peter and had kept the farm running.

"Was there a big argument in the kitchen when I left?" she asked hesitantly.

"Not a bit of it," he assured her with a smile. "You put a stop to the whole carry-on. Shiner is free to do what he wants, and we'll all do as we see fit. So now, girlie, you keep up the learning and get to teach this poetry thing that you have in your head."

The following morning, as she walked up the boreen from Mossgrove to Jack's cottage, she thought back over his advice.

He was right about the studying, or "the learning" as Jack called it. But besides that, her head was full of things that she wanted to do. If she came back teaching with Uncle David, she had a dream of putting on Shakespeare in Kilmeen and bringing him alive on stage. There were so many other things that she dreamed of, such as poetry readings, book clubs and plays. It would be lovely if they had a little theatre in the village. She had not discussed the details with anyone because she was afraid of getting her dream punctured. She was determined to hold on to that dream.

Toby was waiting at the gate of Jack's cottage, and he went wild with delight at the sight of her. He was there every morning and evening without fail. "Toby, I think that you have a watch," she told him as she leaned in over the gate to rub behind his ears. Jack's haggard was full of scratching hens, quacking ducks and the gander holding court with his two geese in the far corner. It was a hive of activity. Jack had the gate into his vegetable plot wired along the bottom, but when everything was harvested in the autumn, the fowl got the run of the entire acre and were delighted with the extra territory. This morning they were engaged in their different pursuits around the small yard.

As she walked down the hill towards Nolan's, she went over in her mind the poetry that she had learned off the night before. One morning the previous week she had been so intent on doing this that she had not realised that she was reciting out loud until an amused Sarah Jones had looked out over the small white gate in front of her well-kept cottage. Now she stopped to call good morning to grey-haired Sarah, who was feeding her hens in a corner of her well-manicured garden. Sarah was a close friend of Jack's and had been of Nana Nellie, and Nora knew that Sarah often called to Jack's cottage to feed his hens and ducks if for any reason he was delayed in Mossgrove. She always wore a floral coat overall that somehow wrapped Sarah up in a small, clean, happy package. Now she looked questioningly at Nora's bag of books.

"That's a heavy load of books for a young one to be dragging along with her," she said sympathetically, leaning over the gate.

"I don't always have so many," Nora told her, "but today all the subjects are on."

"You're a great girl," Sarah assured her, "and I won't delay you now because Rosie will be out at the gate waiting."

"Rosie is never waiting," Nora said. "She is always running after herself at the last minute."

Sarah smiled with understanding as she slipped her hand into the pocket of her apron and produced a bar of chocolate. "You can share this between the two of you on the way in the road," Sarah told her.

"That's great," Nora said, even though privately she thought that she might be getting a bit too old for this kind of thing. Ever since she was a little girl, Jack and Nana Nellie had always pulled small treats out of their pockets. Over the years since Nana Nellie had died, Sarah had slipped into her shoes. Sarah was very friendly with her other grandmother, Nana Agnes. These two women and Jack were the pillars of her life.

As she approached Nolan's gate, she was surprised that Rosie was waiting, and she could see from her face that she was bubbling with excitement.

"You're late," Rosie accused.

"I'm not," Nora protested. "I'm always later than this and you're never out at the gate."

"Well, this morning is different," Rosie announced.

"I know by your face that you have news about something. Your face tells everything that's behind it."

"Isn't it terrible the way that I can't keep anything to myself," Rosie lamented, "because even though I might not want to tell it, my face tells the whole story before I open my mouth."

"But look at it this way," Nora comforted her, "you'd make a great actress because your face would be full of expression, and it will help with your singing too."

"You're a great comfort to me," Rosie laughed, giving Nora a clap on the back.

"My God, Rosie, you're as strong as a horse," Nora told her, wincing under Rosie's exuberance.

"Don't say that," Rosie protested. "You know that I'm trying to lose weight and become tall and willowy like you."

"But, Rosie, you're lovely and curvy, and all the lads think that you're gorgeous."

"I'm not interested in all the lads, only one, and he lives in a house where he has a mother like a model and a sister like a hunter, so he's used to being surrounded by elegant females."

"But why would Peter want a girlfriend like his mother or his sister?" Nora asked her.

"Don't know," Rosie sighed, "but whatever he wants, I must not have it because he treats me like he treats you."

"But, Rosie, your brother Jeremy treats me like he treats you."

"And that's grand for you because you have no interest in Jeremy," Rosie wailed, "but you know I've always had this big crush on Peter. I've had it for as far back as I can remember."

"Don't know what you see in him," Nora said dismissively,

thinking that compared with Uncle David Peter was as dull as ditch water, "but Aunty Kate says that boys are slower to develop than girls, and anyway you want to be a showband singer, so you will need time to concentrate on that."

"Well, that's rich coming from you and you ramming it down my throat every day to forget about singing and concentrate on my exams," Rosie protested.

"Well, I didn't mean to forget it altogether," Nora explained; "just wait until the exams are over. Then you might be the next female Elvis. Did you hear him last night on Radio Luxembourg? He was on just after six."

"No," Rosie wailed. "Dad was in from the cows and wanted to hear the bloody news on Radio Éireann. Being an Elvis fan in our house isn't easy. Mom is more interested in Din Joe than Elvis."

"Same with my crowd," Nora assured her, "but I suppose you were better studying instead of listening to Elvis."

"You are so bloody sensible you make me sick," Rosie told her in disgust.

"You don't think that I'm sensible when I talk about my poetry plans," Nora protested.

"Well, that's your blind spot, and we are all entitled to one," Rosie assured her blithely, "but now to get back to my news."

"What is it?" Nora demanded, even though she knew from experience that Rosie was not going to just tell her straight out.

Rosie stood in the middle of the road, drawing herself up to her full five feet four, and with outstretched hands announced in a dramatic voice: "We are going to have a youth club in Kilmeen."

Her announcement had the desired effect. Nora came to a standstill with a delighted look of amazement on her face. "Wow," she gasped, "that's great! How do you know?"

"Well, that's the embarrassing bit," Rosie told her reluctantly.

"It must be to make you blush," Nora declared.

"Well, this will sound worse than it really was," Rosie assured her.

"Stop hedging and out with it," Nora instructed.

"Why are you so damn honourable?" Rosie protested. "It always makes me feel so bad if I have to confess that I did something dodgy."

"Come on," Nora persisted.

"I listened outside your Aunt Kate's door."

"You what!"

"Well, it actually sounds worse that it really was," Rosie protested. "You know that I had a maths grind with your Uncle David yesterday evening? Well, when I got to the door it was open, so I just pushed it in and before I could call out or ring the bell I heard him, Fr Brady, and Kate talking about the youth club. My ears stuck out, and before I knew what I was doing I was listening. I was glued to the floor with curiosity, and then I was stuck because I couldn't go in as they'd know I was listening. So I had to steal out quietly and ring the bell and pretend that I had just arrived. I felt a bit bad about it, but it was worth it because now we know and can be prepared."

"For what?" Nora demanded.

"To bag the important corners, and run the club our way."

"What do you mean?"

"Nora, sometimes I despair of you," Rosie wailed. "What good is a youth club if we have a collection of old fogies or, worse still, a gang of yobs running it?"

"So we'll be running it?" Nora asked.

"You got it! And the first thing on the agenda is a dance in the hall on Easter Sunday night," Rosie declared.

"But how will we manage that?" Nora demanded.

"You just watch me!" Rosie told her.

CHAPTER FIVE

J ACK OPENED THE rusty gate into the farmyard of Furze Hill. He stood for a long time surveying the scene in front of him. It was Sunday evening and he knew that Danny was playing a match with the Kilmeens, and he had come now because he needed time on his own to walk around and get a feel of the place, to form a plan. When the lad would eventually come to him, he wanted to have some ideas in his head. Since Kate had spoken about helping Danny, he had thought of nothing else. When he was a young fellow himself, he had always been grateful to old Edward Phelan for his encouragement. The old man had always talked over his suggestions and sometimes improved on them, and they had implemented their plan together. In this way they had improved Mossgrove. But it would be a big undertaking to turn Furze Hill around, especially when the cash flow was non-existent, although he had brought Mossgrove back on track himself after Billy had died, and money was scarce then too.

Now, as he looked around the yard, he realised that Mossgrove had never sunk this low. There was not one decent farm building in the yard. But the entire yard was well brushed and clean, and all the overgrowth and briars that he remembered since the day of Matt Conway's funeral were cleared away, and the stone wall of the piggery just left of the gate was almost entirely rebuilt. It was obvious that Danny was making a huge effort to bring the place around. To have done this much in so short a time told of dogged hard work.

He inspected the piggery that was being restored and decided that Danny was getting that right, but when the walls were finished he would have to put in a new door instead of the broken iron bedhead that was serving as a makeshift door now. That door must make feeding the pigs a tough undertaking. Now the pigs, hearing the footsteps outside, were presuming that it was feeding time and were screeching and poking their snouts out through the bars of the bedhead. He could only imagine what a job it must be trying to get in through that contraption with the pigs screaming for food and jumping on you.

Next was the hen house, which was a bit of a shambles, but then hens had the ability to function in any kind of a thrown-together situation. They were scratching around happily, but laying boxes and perches seemed to be in short supply. Jack knew from watching Martha in action in Mossgrove that a well-set-up and organised laying unit repaid well, and he remembered that Nellie's egg money had sometimes kept Mossgrove floating when times were tough. So something would need to be done to improve things here. This hen house needed to be enlarged and reroofed. As he went slowly along, he was doing mental arithmetic as to the absolute minimal cost of turning things around.

Next on his pathway was the dwelling house. At right angles to the hen house, which made it the building that faced you as you came in the gate, was the long low house which, in the Barrys' time, had been an old cow house. Conway had not even bothered to roof it properly. With its rusty galvanised iron, it must be bitterly cold in winter, and there had to be leaks. Windows that had been broken over the years were patched with bits of wood, and even the front door had been chewed at the bottom by his dogs and must cause freezing draughts on windy nights. Molly Barry had called it "the poke". Looking at it now, he decided that she was right. Crazy Conway had moved his family in here and left a fine house empty. As he stood looking at the house where he knew a lot of family trauma had been endured, the seed of an idea ignited in Jack's mind. But because the idea was so impractical, he was reluctant to let it come to the surface.

He continued onwards to the adjoining cow houses, where he decided that a few slates here and there was all that was needed, and again a rebuilding of sagging walls. But there was no proper calf house, and they were wedged in behind the cows, overcrowded and uncomfortable, which was a far from healthy situation. When they saw him they pushed and struggled with each other to try to reach the door, but there was very little room to even stand. Strong healthy calves could not be produced in such an environment, and that was good money going down the drain.

At right angles to these stalls were the stables, which he decided were not fit to house any kind of horse. Next was the hay barn with its rusty sagging roof in which well-saved hay was bound to rot. He was now back to the gate, having gone all around the square yard. Then he retraced his footsteps to a hidden archway that stood between the barn and the stables. This archway told the story of how things used to be in Furze Hill. Through this archway, the Barrys had come into their farmyard from the walled garden that surrounded their old family home. Now the whole archway was overgrown with bushes and briars, and there was no sight of the house that must be buried inside. He remembered hearing that old Conway had fenced the entire place in with thorny wire to keep his own family and everyone else out. Few could understand his reasoning. He had proclaimed that he wanted to avoid paying the high rates on the big house, but most of the neighbours felt that he wanted to get back at Molly for a marriage gone sour.

Having calculated that he could not get in through the archway, Jack walked out the yard gate and a little way along the road by the high stone wall to what used to be the entrance to the old house. The rusted gates were smothered in briars blinding any sighting of what might be inside. He stood there trying to imagine the way it used to be. Then slowly, in the deep recesses of his mind, a buried memory began to stir. He was a little boy holding his mother's hand and staring across a flower garden at a blue door of a big house clothed in ivy. The picture must have imprinted itself on the back pages of his mind. But now all was changed, buried in a scene of choked abandonment.

He returned to the yard and found a slasher, a hatchet and saw, and bringing them back he reached up and put them on top of the high wall. Having levered himself up by digging his toe caps between the stones, he sat astride the wall and began

71

to slash a hole in the thick undergrowth beside the stone pillar. When he had finally made an opening, he eased himself down inside the wall and arched his back low to get between the strands of thorny wire. It seemed like an impenetrable jungle, but he began to cut his way through. Briars tore his face as he wielded the slasher to create an opening through them. He used his saw and hatchet to remove the many interwoven branches that barred his way like a hedge. At times he wondered if he was ever going to get anywhere and occasionally had to sit down on a sawn-off branch to get his breath. His shirt clung to his back with perspiration, and the thought crossed his mind that if his dodgy heart decided to give up that he would never be found in here. But he kept on determinedly and finally, when he was beginning to think that his energy was not going to see him through, he reached what he judged to be the wall of the house. He leant against it in relief. Guided more by touch than direction, he inspected the wall and reached what could be a window, but he was not sure because it was sheeted over. *By God*, he thought to himself, *this place was left well protected by old man Phelan*. He kept walking in what he hoped was the general direction of the front door and was proved right when the wall suddenly disappeared and he stepped back into a alcoves. The front door was recessed back under an archway that had saved it from the worst of the elements. The thought that had come to him earlier kept floating into his mind, and although he would not allow himself to entertain it, it kept coming back.

He realised that he was exhausted and decided that it was time to go home. He needed to sit down and with the calm light of reason slowly think the whole thing through. He retraced his way back through his burrowed pathway and replaced the tools in the barn and cycled home. As he passed by the village, he heard cheering from the pitch and wondered how the boys were doing. He hoped that Danny was having a good game. No doubt he would hear it all from Shiner and Peter in the morning.

After he had his tea, he sat looking out the window at his much-loved view, but he was not seeing Nolan's cows in the field in front of his cottage or the village in the valley with its elegant steeple glinting grey in the early March sunlight. Instead his mind was across the river in Furze Hill. He was rearranging the farmyard and planning the best strategy with which to approach the entire project. But despite his best efforts to quell it, there was growing determinedly at the back of his mind an idea that he had already decided was not feasible. Finally he went to the drawer of his dresser and took out an old writing pad and rooted around in the bottom of the drawer until he found a pencil.

"Jack lad," he told himself, "it's tough lines when you are turning to pencil and paper to straighten out your thinking. Bad sign of the head!"

He made a list of expenses, but he was not too worried about these as Kate had said that Danny had shown her a list of what he had envisaged everything would cost him, and the lad was bound to have got all that right down to the last penny. At the same time, he would feel more on top of the job if he had his own costings, though it was the overall plan that was really bothering him. Old man Phelan had always advised having a planned strategy and doing it step by step rather than working in starts and stops. With no plan, he had warned, you spent much more and ended up with a higgledy-piggledy conclusion, that was if you ever really reached a conclusion. So Furze Hill needed an overall plan, and that was why all ideas, feasible or otherwise, had to be incorporated from the beginning or not at all.

He was so immersed in his thoughts that he did not see Kate pass by the window, so when she pushed open the door she took him by surprise.

"Good God, Kate," he told her in a startled voice, "you frightened the life out of me."

"Jack, I looked in passing the window and it was as if you were in another world."

"I was," he smiled, "over in Furze Hill."

"Oh," she said with delight,"so Danny called."

"No, but I'm getting ready for him," he told her.

"But how?" she asked doubtfully.

"Well," he told her slowly, "I went over there this evening and. . ."

"But Danny was playing a match today," she broke in.

"I knew that," he told her. "That's why I went over, because I wanted to think things out in my own time."

"Oh, I see," she smiled in understanding. "That's you all out, Jack; do it quietly in your own way, take your time and iron out all the wrinkles in advance."

"Only this time I think that instead of ironing out wrinkles I might be creating a very big one, and I'm not sure if I should go down that road or not."

"Oh," Kate said in a surprised voice, "that's not like you. Do you need a 'Johnny sound all'?"

It was an expression they had picked up from David that he used in the classroom to test if something had got through to the entire class. There would be one student who was neither too bright nor too slow, and if he got it the chances were that most of them had it.

"Well, I suppose you're as good a 'Johnny' as I'm going to get," he said heavily.

"Thanks for nothing," she told him smartly, seating herself in the rocking chair in front of the fire and patting his own armchair. "Come over here to the fire. It's getting too dusky now to be peering out the window, and anyway you always say that you think better looking into the fire."

He sat into his chair and took out his pipe as Kate poked the fire and put on extra logs and, having settled herself comfortably, turned to him questioningly.

"Now what has you in such a quandary?" she demanded.

"Well," he told her, "I went over to Furze Hill today with a certain plan of action in my head."

"Not a good thing," she assured him. "Perceived ideas blind you to new possibilities."

"That's just it," he told her in surprise, "but this new idea that has forced itself into my mind is a bit preposterous."

"Spit it out, as you say yourself, and I'll soon tell you."

"Well, Kate, when I stood in front of the Conway house, a thought came into my head from the Lord only knows where."

"Jack, will you for goodness sakes just say what it is and stop meandering on about its source and how outrageous it is," she demanded.

"That Danny Conway should move back into the old home," he blurted out.

Kate looked at him in amazement but said nothing for a few seconds, and then she nodded her head.

"Do you know something, Jack," she said slowly and thoughtfully, "that's a bloody brilliant idea."

"But it's the practicalities that I'm worried about," he told her.

"Well, whatever about the practicalities of the matter," Kate declared, "it would be great for the Conways. Give them a whole new sense of themselves. The poke, as Molly called it, can only be full of bad memories."

"You're right there, but you know something, Kate, I was not even thinking along those lines. I was totally taken up with planning the yard as well and economically as I could, and then this idea came from nowhere and. . ."

"Not from nowhere, Jack," Kate asserted smilingly. "That was old Molly Barry. You always had great time for her, and she saw her chance!"

"Could be," he agreed ruefully. "I'm around too long now to question the power of unknown elements at work."

"Would it make things that much more expensive?" Kate asked.

"I've been doing my sums, and it might not, you know. Because he badly needs a new calf house, and that would solve that problem because he could use the poke, so he would be saved from building that. Of course, it will all depend on the condition of Furze Hill itself. It has been locked up for years."

"I never even saw it," Kate told him. "Never knew for years that there was anything inside in that grove of trees."

"The whole place is completely closed in," Jack said, "but when I was over today I got as far as the front door with the help of a slasher, and do you know something? I was pleasantly surprised at the condition of the place."

"But it must be in a bad state having been locked up for so long," Kate mused.

"My only reason for thinking that it might be all right is that it was your grandfather who put on the roof and boarded up the windows, and he would do a great job."

"But why did Granda help him to close up that house?"

"Conway was hell-bent on going ahead with his mad idea, and your grandfather wanted to make the house as secure as possible against whatever might come its way. He wanted to help Molly and make her feel that one day the family might be able to go back," Jack told her.

"And now that day is here," Kate said.

"So you think that's the way to go?"

"Without a doubt," Kate assured him. "It makes all the sense in the world."

"Whatever about the financial world," Jack smiled.

"Jack, you once told me that there were some problems that nothing could solve, but that there are others that money can solve, and that these were not real problems at all because the money will always come from somewhere."

"Did I say that?" he smiled. "I must have been talking about someone else's problems. It's always easy to be philosophical about other people's problems."

"No, you were not," she told him. "You were talking about Mossgrove."

"God bless you, Kate, but you have a great memory. You're enough to make any fellow think well before he opens his mouth. But I somehow get the feeling that you are telling me to grasp this nettle and encourage young Danny along these lines."

"You'd want to have it all worked out now, Jack, before you put this proposition up to Danny. He might well think at first that it's an unrealisable dream," she cautioned.

"And so it might well be," Jack told her.

"Now, Jack, you know and I know that if you put your back teeth into it you will make it work," she told him.

"Kate girleen, my back teeth are getting a bit worn down now for big projects," he warned.

"Yerra go on, Jack, you know that you love a challenge, and I'll be right behind you on this one. Between the two of us we could turn water into wine."

"We might well need a miracle or two along the way," he smiled, but he was secretly glad that Kate was showing such interest in the undertaking. He felt in his bones that he was right about Danny moving back into Furze Hill, but her encouragement made him feel more positive.

"When are you going to meet up with Danny?" she asked.

"I hadn't thought that out yet," he said slowly. "Do you think that I should go to him or wait until he comes to me?"

"You know, it might be nice to offer," Kate told him. "Isn't it always nice when somebody holds out a helping hand instead of waiting for you to ask?"

"You might be right," he agreed. "He wouldn't think that I was putting my nose into his business now, would he?"

"Not at all," Kate assured him. "Poor Danny has his back to the wall, and I'd say that any offer of help would be like manna in the desert."

"Right! I'll walk over there some evening this week after the cows, and we'll see how things go from there."

"Now that that's settled, Jack, I'm going to make tea for the two of us. This farm planning is thirsty work," Kate told him, going to the dresser and taking down two china cups and putting milk and sugar on to a tray. When he attempted to get up to make the tea she told him, "Stay where you are now, Jack, and I'll tend you for a change."

As they sat by the fire in companionable silence, he saw that Kate was not her usual chirpy self. He had been so intent on Furze Hill that he had not noticed until now.

"How are things with you, Kate?" he inquired.

"Thought that you'd never ask," she told him ruefully, "though I should not be bringing you my troubles when you are so taken up with Furze Hill."

"Kate girleen, there are no troubles in my life more important than yours," he told her warmly.

"You know something, Jack, I have always known that," she said, putting her hand over his, "and it has turned you into my father confessor. When I have a problem, the first person that I think of sharing it with is you. Maybe not so good for you but great for me. But this problem is more David's than mine, though of course when he's upset so am I."

"So what's causing this upset?" he asked gently.

"Martha," she told him grimly.

"Martha?" he asked in a puzzled voice.

"Well, maybe not on the surface, but without a doubt she's behind it," Kate said, and she told him about the letter from Rodney Jackson.

"So you think that Martha is up to her old tricks?" he asked. "And we thinking that all that was behind us."

"Could I be wronging her?" Kate asked doubtfully.

"Hard to answer that now," he told her. "Martha and I have

worked side by side with years in Mossgrove, and just when I think that I have her measure, she throws a surprise punch out of the blue. Though since Matt Conway's death I think that she has calmed down a lot. It was as if she buried some demons with him."

Later, when Kate had gone home, he went down into his little parlour and looked across the valley at Furze Hill. The high cliff over Yalla Hole was a pale bite at the bottom of the high field. The old house lay buried in the trees. Bringing it back to life was one half of his plan, and he was glad to have discussed it with Kate. But he had not told her the full story. The time was not right.

CHAPTER SIX

DANNY STOOD INSIDE his kitchen window and looked across the valley at Mossgrove. It was everything that he wished for this place: a fine, well-kept house surrounded by large green fields. He looked around at the small, drab kitchen with its stained walls. From as far back as he could remember, they had had buckets in strategic corners to catch the drop-down when it rained. When the old fellow died, the girls had cleaned it up as best they could, but there was no money to do any more. His mother had been so run down and exhausted that he was glad when the girls had insisted that she go back to Dublin with them, and she had not come home since. Now he kept everything that he needed on the kitchen table, which reduced housework to a minimum. All his energies were directed into the farmyard and the farm. If only he could get going, he had such plans for this place. His aim was to make it like Mossgrove. He felt that he knew every inch of the place across the river because Shiner was always talking about it. Peter and Shiner worked there like brothers, and Peter never "acted the big man", as Shiner termed it. But, of course, Martha Phelan cracked the whip over the two of them, or at least she tried from what he gathered from Shiner. But she did not cross Jack, because as everyone in Kilmeen knew Jack was the real farmer in Mossgrove.

So wrapped up in his thoughts that he never heard the footsteps coming across the yard, he swung around at the sound of the voice behind him.

"Danny lad, can I come in?" Jack said quietly from outside the open door.

Danny could hardly believe that Jack Tobin was actually standing here after all the trouble between the two families. This small, wiry man in his tweed cap was synonymous with Mossgrove and the Phelans, and it had been his father's aim in life to destroy them both.

"Jack," he said in confusion, "I can't believe you came."

For days he had been trying to pluck up the courage to go to see Jack, although he was afraid that Jack would find it very hard to help him after all that his father had done to them in Mossgrove. But now Jack was here.

"Come in, come in," he said eagerly, pulling out a chair.

"I was half afraid that you might think that I was pushing my nose into your business, so it's good to be made feel welcome," Jack said in a relieved tone, coming into the kitchen and sitting into a wobbly *súgán* chair.

"But sure, of course, you're welcome," Danny told him gladly, "because even though Kate said you'd help me, I was afraid that after all that had happened over the years you might not want to."

"All water under the bridge now, lad," Jack assured him, looking out the window, "and do you know, I seldom see Mossgrove from across the river."

"And it looks good," Danny said ruefully. "I couldn't tell you how often I have stood here and envied you all over there."

"Well, lad, maybe we can turn things around here so that in time you will be proud of Furze Hill," Jack told him.

"Even hearing it called Furze Hill makes me feel better," Danny said. "Nobody ever called it that only my grandmother, and she always had such pride in her voice when she spoke of the old days here."

"She was a great woman," Jack assured him. "Went through rough times with your grandfather, but she never lost her spirit."

"She was too good for him, wasn't she?" he asked.

"She was," Jack told him. "She fell from a high rookery, as old man Phelan used to say."

Since his father's death Danny had a growing need to know more about his grandmother and how things had been in Furze Hill in her day. It was as if the roots of his own story stretched back to hers. Now here was a man who must have known her in her younger days and might even remember Furze Hill before it got swallowed up in briars and furze bushes. Jack was sitting at the side table looking out the window; Danny stacked some of the ware out of their way and took the chair at the head of the table. This had been his father's chair, and since his death Danny had found that if he sat in any other chair, the image of his father was still in this chair.

"Have you any memory of Furze Hill before it got grown over?" he asked Jack eagerly.

"Strange thing is that if you had asked me that a week ago I would have said no, but when I was here last Sunday. . ."

"Were you here last Sunday?" he asked in surprise.

"I was, I'm ashamed to say," Jack told him, "but I wanted to walk around and try to work out some kind of a feasible plan before you came to me. The peculiar thing was that when I stood outside the old gate down there a memory came back to me of standing in the same spot with my mother when I must have been a garsoon and looking in across a lovely garden at an ivy-clad house."

"God, imagine that!" Danny said with delight. "So it was lovely. Nana always said that it was a beautiful place, but I sometimes wondered if it was wishful thinking on her part."

"Oh, it was no wishful thinking," Jack assured him. "Your grandmother was not one for wishful thinking. She was a strong, factual woman who weathered some storms in her day."

"What was she like when she was younger?" he asked curiously.

"A beauty, with red hair like Kitty. But she was completely spoilt and stubborn as a mule. Molly was an only child and there was no shortage of money, so she got everything that she wanted. She was born when your great-grandparents were pushing on a bit, so when she began to go a bit wild she was more than they could handle. But, of course, marrying your grandfather turned her whole life upside down."

"He was very mean to her?" Danny asked hesitantly.

"Dog rough! The Barrys were fine people and the Conways were rough," Jack proclaimed, and then as if to soften his pronouncement, he continued, "but don't you ever forget, Danny, that the blood of the Barrys runs through your veins."

"And what about the Conway side of the house?" Danny asked.

"You're a Barry," Jack told him firmly. "You even look like them. The same fine, tall cut of them with the same rich, red hair. But Rory is all Conway — swarthy, black and mean. Some of the others are probably a mixture, but you are a Barry; always remember that."

"Jack, are you very interested in bloodlines?" Danny asked tentatively.

"I suppose I am," Jack admitted, smiling ruefully. "Comes with the territory, because in farming you are for ever watching pedigree and breeding in pure-bred cows and horses, and it always tells in the end. You can't make a racehorse out of a donkey, Danny. If it was Rory was here now, I would not even bother to cross the river, because it wouldn't be worth my while. It would be your father all over again."

"Rory is my other worry," Danny told him, "because, as you probably guessed, I don't own this place, and he is the only one who wants to make trouble. All the others have signed off their claim, but not him. So I'm going to have trouble with Rory, and because he's the oldest he feels that he is entitled to the place."

"Well, laddie, let's take it step by step. As old man Phelan used to tell me, 'Worries are often overcome by events.' So the first step is to get this place up and running."

"No small job," Danny sighed. "I seem to be crawling at a snail's pace here, and I look across the river and see you all galloping ahead over in Mossgrove. Though Kate said that there were hard times over there as well and that you pulled them through."

"Sometimes Kate thinks that I'm better than I am, but the truth is that old man Phelan had solid foundations laid in Mossgrove, and when things collapsed they were always beneath us."

"No such foundations here," Danny told him bitterly.

"You are wrong there, laddie," Jack said quietly.

"I am?" he asked in surprise.

"The Barrys laid foundations, and we must take Furze Hill back to the Barrys' time," Jack told him.

"But how?" he asked in a puzzled voice.

"We must begin by opening up the old house," Jack said.

"What!" Danny gasped. "But that would cost a fortune, and I don't even have enough to buy galvanised iron for the barn roof."

"You might not even need to buy it," Jack told him.

"What are you talking about?" Danny demanded in frustration.

He was afraid to grasp the hope that Jack was dangling in front of him. Since childhood it had always been his dream to open up Furze Hill, and in her later years his grandmother had fuelled that dream. But in the struggle of recent months, reality had reared its head and the dream had died. Now practical Jack, of all people, was proposing what to him seemed impossible.

"At first," Jack said quietly, "I never even thought of going down that road either, but here last Sunday evening the idea came into my head, and the more I thought about it, the more feasible it became. Let me start at the beginning of my plan. You need a new calf house; this one where we are now would be just right, so that would eliminate the building of a new calf house.

Then we could resheet the barn with the iron off Furze Hill and reslate the old house."

"But with what?" Danny demanded.

"The slates are stacked up behind it."

"How do you know that?"

"Because it was old Edward Phelan who stacked them there, and he told me."

"I can't believe!" Danny gasped.

His head whirled as Jack outlined his proposals. Was it possible that it could happen? He was almost afraid to allow himself to consider the possibility. But if Jack had worked it out, it must be possible, because Jack was no fool. A little spurt of joy kindled in his heart, and for the first time in years he felt the excitement of anticipation.

"Come on, lad, and we'll walk around outside," Jack said, rising from the battered chair that rocked on its uneven legs as he got up. He went out into the yard, and when he walked as far as the gate, Danny knew that they were going to go through the yard in precise detail.

"Now, laddie," Jack said, looking at the piggery, "you're getting this right anyway, and that's a beginning."

"I love working with stone, but I'm no stonemason," Danny said ruefully.

"Maybe not," Jack told him smiling, "but then neither are pigs, and as long as they are dry and comfortable they are not too worried about stonework, but that door must be a nightmare at feeding time."

"That's for sure," Danny told him, "but it's one of the things that I can manage to do without."

"I can understand that," Jack said, "but it all adds hardship to the daily grind, and we must try to ease that." They were standing outside a dilapidated building with a sunken roof and a rotting door. "Now this hen house needs a major overhaul and extension."

Danny nodded in agreement, and then they came back to the poke. Up to now Danny had not looked at it with a view to doing anything with it, but Jack's plan gave it a whole new aspect. Now he saw it as a potential house for the young calves, and straightaway he could see how suitable it was with its low ceiling and small windows. It could be made dry and the doors cut to make half doors dividing the older calves, and, of course, moving the calves in here would give more space in the cow stalls. That, too, needed an overhaul and extension if he was to increase the herd. Increasing the herd was his priority; a more a substantial milk cheque would be the lifeblood of the farm.

When they reached the barn, Jack declared, "This barn cannot face another winter in this condition, so that must be the first step."

"Hard to know where to begin," Danny said, scratching his head.

"I think the place to begin is with the old house," Jack told him thoughtfully, "because we must find out if the sheet iron off that is good enough for this barn. If it is, well, then that's where we must begin. If it's not worth moving, well, then that's a different story."

"God, I hope it's good enough," Danny said fervently, "because I think that if moving into Furze Hill was part of the equation, it would make any hardship worthwhile. It has always been my dream."

"Well, laddie, we all need dreams," Jack told him as they walked back to the old arch, "so hold on to that one and we might make it happen."

They stood in front of the stone arch. To Danny it was an entrance into another world that had always been beyond his reach. His father had tried to make them feel that it was a locked-up hell in there, but he had always felt that it was a lost birthright. Matt Conway had put it out of bounds, and none of them ever disobeyed, terrified of the consequence. But he had often wondered how his grandfather could have so poisoned his father's mind against his own mother and the Barry family. She, in turn, had despised both of them and must have seen in himself her only chance to redeem the situation. Now he felt the responsibility of her trust.

"Well, lad, some day you'll walk through that arch, but at the moment it's easier to get in the front way," Jack said and headed off out the yard gate with Danny following. When they reached the old gate, he was surprised to see Jack climb up by the pillar and then disappear in over the wall. He followed, wondering how someone of Jack's age could have climbed the high wall so quickly and got through the thorny wire. The briars and bushes were almost an impenetrable barrier, but he forced his way along the narrow opening that Jack had created. Jack must have sweated here on Sunday. Laurel leaves slapped his face, and having tripped over a tree stump he kept a watchful eye on the ground; there was no trace of Jack up ahead, but he followed on. The dense shrubbery seemed endless, and overhead trees clothed the whole area in semi-darkness. As he shouldered his way through, long sinuous briars scratched his face. Finally he caught up with Jack just as he reached the wall of the house. It was a strange feeling to be able to touch the house that for so long had been out of bounds. With Danny following, Jack edged along by the wall and then stepped back into an opening that was smothered in streams of ivy pouring down in front of it like dark curtains. He followed Jack into the alcove to the old door, weathered to a soft grey, but when he touched it the wood was firm beneath his fingers.

"I remember this door," Jack said quietly. "It was painted blue then."

Gently Danny moved his hands over the door. Behind this door was all that Nana Molly had lost and had pined for right up to the day she died. Many times she had told him stories about this house. Now at last he was here, and he was not sure if it was the memories of the past or the hopes for the future that were causing the tumult of emotions churning in him.

"He is dead almost a year now," Danny whispered, "but I never came in here since he died. I could have come, but I didn't. Was it guilt?"

"The time was not right," Jack assured him. "You have gone through a lot, lad, and the mind can only cope with so much at one time."

"You knew that she did it?" he asked.

"I thought that she might have," Jack told him.

"I could have saved him," Danny said.

"But sometimes life steps in and we can only stand back and allow things to take their course."

"She had nerves of steel," Danny said quietly.

"He went a step too far when he attacked Nora," Jack told him, "and sooner or later she would have got him. You could not have prevented the inevitable."

Now Danny dragged away some of the overhanging greenery and viewed the heavy old door with a hundred questions running through his mind. This was the door that his grandmother used every day when she was his age, and from all the stories that she told him, he knew that she had loved this place and been happy here. When she had had to lock it up and walk away from it, she had left the best part of her life behind her. He stood back and looked up at the arched fanlight.

"There is not even a crack in the glass," he whispered in an awed voice.

"Nobody would dare come near this place with your father and his dogs," Jack told him, "so everything will be just as it was left, with only the passage of time doing any harm."

"Everything will probably have rotted with damp and dust," Danny decided.

"Maybe not," Jack told him. "This was a fine, sound, well-built house."

"But, Jack, it's been closed up for years," Danny protested.

"Well, we'll find out when we get inside," Jack told him.

"It seems to be locked up solid," Danny declared. He gave the door a firm push but it remained motionless. They went back to a window that was boarded up on the outside. When Danny prised away a piece of the weathered timber and peered in, he discovered that the window was boarded up on the inside as well.

"We will go around to the back," Jack decided, "because there is no hope of getting in the windows without damaging them, and that would be a shame."

"The place is like a bloody fortress," Danny declared. "'Twas locked up with the intention of it never again being reopened."

"Don't think so," Jack said thoughtfully. "This place was locked up by two very different men. At the time they were friends, but they had very different reasons for turning this place into a fortress, as you call it. Your grandfather Rory Conway wanted rid of the place and could not lock it up tight enough, but his friend Edward Phelan wanted to preserve it. He had tried to persuade your grandfather not to leave this house, but when he failed in that he wanted to preserve it for your grandmother's sake because he knew she dreamed that one day she would return. In later years, of course, the split between the two men happened and Molly turned against the Phelans, but she never gave up on her dream of one day coming back here."

"But though she fell out with the Phelans," Danny said, "in another way she admired them, especially Kate."

"You're right there," Jack said breathlessly as they forced their way through briars and branches along the side of the house. They finally rounded a corner and found the back door, but that too was as impenetrable as the front and had sheets of corrugated iron nailed to the outside.

"By God," Danny declared, "there is no getting in this way either."

"I can see old Edward Phelan's hand at work all over the this place," Jack said with a smile on his face. "No short cuts were taken with this job. It was done to mind the house and to stand the test of time, and it has done all of that."

"How the hell are we going to get in?" Danny wanted to know.

"Well, we're not going to break in like common thieves," Jack declared. "The man that took such care in the closing up of this house deserves that we take the same care in getting back in."

"But how?" Danny demanded.

"There must be a key," Jack declared.

"A key after all these years," Danny gasped. "Sure, that's daft."

"Not so daft," Jack told him. "I'd say that your grandmother locked that door and took the key with her."

"But where the hell could it be now?" Danny demanded.

"Did your grandmother have anything belonging to this place over in the poke?" Jack asked.

"I don't think so," Danny said, slowly trying to think back over the years of all his grandmother's stories. Sometimes he was only half listening to her, but he felt sure that she had never mentioned a key.

"Are you sure?"

"Well, I'm not, but I think that I'd remember if she ever mentioned a key," Danny said slowly.

"I'm not talking about a key," Jack said impatiently. "I'm talking about a press or furniture or anything like that."

"Oh," Danny said with surprise, "there was the bed. A big monstrosity of a timber bed where we all slept with her at different times when we were small. It was in that bed she died."

"So the chances are that the key is stuck somewhere in that old bed."

"Holy God, Jack, it couldn't be, because after she died my father tore it asunder looking for money, and all he found were diaries, and then he burnt the diaries and the mattress because he said that it smelt of piss. Not that it was the real reason because, as you probably know, bad smells did not exactly bother him, but he burnt everything."

"And probably the history of half the parish with them," Jack concluded, "but that key is somewhere, and we must find it, because that was the way she would have wanted it."

"How do you know?" Danny asked, mystified.

"Because my old bones tell me, and I always listen to my bones," Jack told him.

"Well, I'll listen to your bones as well," he decided, "because from what I can see they have never led you astray."

Later, when Jack had gone home, Danny walked slowly back into the yard. He looked around at the dilapidated farm buildings, but in his head there was now a different picture. Jack's plan had taken shape in his mind. This was all going to be transformed. There was no more money now than yesterday, but he had a plan and a belief that it was possible. A new sense of excitement was throbbing through him. He was going to turn the tide of bad fortune that had flowed over Furze Hill since his grandmother had left the old house. Now they were going to go back there and have a whole new beginning. His mother would have a new life. It was good to feel that the tide was about to turn. He whistled happily to himself as he approached the open kitchen door. But as he came through the doorway, the tune choked in his throat. Rory was sitting in his father's chair.

CHAPTER SEVEN

KATE SAT IN the ticket office of the village hall. The small, cramped corner where forgotten coats and cardigans had accumulated over the years hardly deserved the title ticket office, but it occupied one side of the short passage into the main hall, from which it was divided by a timber partition incorporating a small sliding perspex door and through this opening tickets were doled out and money taken in for any functions in the hall, which were mostly local concerts or travelling shows. The one advantage the ticket office had was a raised floor and a window running the entire length of the side looking down into the hall, so that the occupants had full view down over all the activities going on inside. This was a compensation for long hours doling out tickets to latecomers. It was Kate's first time in charge here for a dance. She was still a bit surprised that she had let herself be talked into it, but Rosie had coaxed and conjoled, assuring her that it would give the first effort of the youth club an air of mature responsibility to have herself and Fr Brady at the door. It would reassure parents who were dubious of this new enterprise run solely by the young teenagers. With this Kate had to agree. On her rounds of the parish she had to reassure many doubting parents that this was going to be a well-run club that would be of great benefit to their sons and daughters, who had often complained of the lack of entertainment for their own age group. Many of these parents were prepared to go on listening to the complaints, believing that what was good enough for them was good enough for the young ones, but Rosie had no intention of listening to them.

Kate had been impressed as Rosie had taken the idea of the youth club on board with enthusiasm. Even at the very first meeting, she had stage-managed the whole thing so that she had been nominated and voted in as chairman before most of the others had settled into their seats. Kate suspected that Rosie had lined up her brother Jeremy, Nora, Peter and Davey to get her into the chair as fast as possible, from where she could mastermind her strategy. She had planned this dance with meticulous detail, putting up posters all over the parish. A local band who normally played for parish events was set aside, and an outside group with more appeal to the young, but costing double the price, was engaged. Rosie was prepared to take her chance that the more trendy band would bring in a bigger crowd and so cover the higher expenses. This had raised a few disapproving eyebrows, but Rosie backed off the opposition in her determination to make life more exciting in Kilmeen.

Now she was busy in the middle of the dance floor scattering crystals around. Kate smiled as she watched her waltz in a circle by herself, testing the smoothness of the floor, and then, not satisfied, gave it another swish of crystals. Kate drew back the shutter and called down, "Easy on the crystals, Rosie, or you'll turn it into a skating rink and they'll all crack their necks slithering around on it."

"I'm not worried about that," Rosie called back. "Once we have a crowd in I don't care. If I can't make the price of this band, I'll be listening to 'I told you so's' for the rest of my life. Will we have a crowd, do you think?" she finished worriedly.

"You will," Kate assured her. "They'll be hanging off the rafters."

"God, I hope you're right," Rosie said grimly, "but where the hell are the others? They were all supposed to be here before nine to get everything ready before the band came on stage."

"They're coming, they're coming," Kate called down to her as Nora and Peter appeared in front of the hatch.

"I suppose you're free," she asked them, "as you're on the committee?"

"No such luck," Peter informed her. "Madam Chairman passed a resolution at the last meeting that everybody pays, and you're lucky if it does not include you for the pleasure of collecting the money."

"At least, Aunty Kate, you'll get to see all the action from your little cubby hole," Nora grinned in at her.

"I doubt that there will be much action," Peter said dismissively, opening the door into the hall. "This is Kilmeen, you know."

When he had gone through, Nora looked at Kate anxiously. "Do I look all right, Aunty Kate?"

"Stand back a bit so that I can see you properly."

Nora stood back against the wall holding out the sides of her flowing skirt. In her white dress scattered with pink roses and its little standing-up collar and puff sleeves, she looked so young and vulnerable that Kate felt a lump in her throat.

"Do I look like a bit of a baby?" Nora wanted to know. "Mom made the dress, and I know that it's perfect, but is it too childish for a dance?"

Kate wanted to run out and put reassuring arms around her but knew that it would be the wrong thing to do. Tonight Nora wanted to feel grown up, and the last thing she would appreciate was to be treated like a little girl.

"You look just right: cool and inviting like a breath of fresh air," Kate assured her, and a more relaxed Nora followed Peter into the hall where Rosie immediately had them dimming lights and testing the crystal ball that she had procured in Ross during the week. She had confessed to Kate that it had cost more than she had dared mention at the meeting. She would tell them that when they had made a profit at the dance. If they made a profit!

"For God's sake, Rosie, we can't keep the lights that low," Peter protested, "or we'll be all falling over each other. At least give us fellows a chance to see what we are dancing with."

"Peter, I'm trying to create an atmosphere," Rosie wailed.

"There is atmosphere and there is half dark," Peter complained.

As Kate listened to them arguing back and forth about lighting and angles, she heard a screech of brakes outside the hall and looked out to see a black van with orange writing along the side screaming "The Vikings". The band had arrived. They poured out of the van with a clatter of instruments and black boxes. Kate smiled as she viewed their quiffed haircuts and white satin suits. Kilmeen had never seen anything like these.

Where had Rosie found them? But knowing Rosie, the chances were that they were super musicians. These were going to be a big change from Tom Murphy and his middle-aged group of violin and accordion players. There appeared to be about six of them in all, and as they came towards the hall they were almost obscured by their large instruments and leads draped over their shoulders and the heavy black boxes they carried between them. Kate dashed out to hold the inside door open for them. They packed the narrow corridor with their gear, and she breathed a sigh of relief when everything seemed to fit and they made it through into the hall where they were able to spread out and approach the stage like a tidal wave.

It took about an an hour to get all their gear up and do test runs on the stage, and during that time Rosie made several visits to the door to see if there was any activity outside. She was not reassured by what she saw, and in her desperation she confessed to Kate what the band was costing and the minimum number she needed in the hall to clear all her expenses. Kate was gobsmacked by the price of the band but did her best to hide her dismay from Rosie.

Finally the band were ready, and the first blast of sound hit the hall. Kate felt the walls shudder around her and thought that she could be blown across the road by the force of the music. Were they a good band? She honestly did not know. All she knew was that she had never heard the likes of it before. But it had some magic, because faces began to appear in front of her, and soon a queue filled the little corridor and quickly backed out into the street. She was glad when Fr Tim arrived, and the two of them doled out tickets and took in money so fast that there was no time to do or think of anything only keeping the queue moving. Finally there was a lull and they looked at each other in disbelief.

"Phew," Kate grinned, "that was some avalanche! Where the hell did they all come from?"

"Apparently the Vikings are a big name out there with the young ones," Fr Tim told her. "I've asked around, and they are the new rock and roll wonder band."

"Well, Rosie got it right," Kate said, "and I'm delighted for her, because she took a big chance."

"I think that Rosie will always take chances," Fr Tim smiled. "That girl likes excitement and challenge."

And with that the door out of the hall burst open, and Rosie was dancing around in front of their little office. She was glowing with achievement, and her blonde hair that had started the night in an elegant knot on top of her head had now fallen down around her shoulders, and her bright red dress showed patches of perspiration under her arms. She was a picture of vibrancy and delight.

"We made it! We made it!" she chanted. "We're home and dry with money to spare."

"Well done," Kate said warmly, "and now we must make sure that everything goes well and that they all go home having had a great night. That will send out the right signal about the new club."

"But why wouldn't they?" Rosie asked in surprise, looking down through the glass partition into the hall. "They're all having a ball."

Kate had to agree with her as she looked in over the scene of swirling young bodies who seemed to be able to achieve any conceivable dancing angle a supple body could master.

"I'm glad that they stopped coming," Kate said, "because you would not like to refuse anybody, but to let in any more could be dangerous."

"Oh, I never thought of it like that. I just thought that if the crowd got any bigger that we wouldn't have enough room to enjoy the dancing," Rosie told her happily, pointing down to where Nora and Danny Conway were clapping their hands in the air and dancing in an energetic circle of movement. "You need space to dance properly to the Vikings. They are an art form in themselves," she enthused, "and whoever would have thought that Danny Conway could move like that? He is full of rhythm. It's so good for Danny to forget that bloody farm for a change; he was turning into an old man before his time. And now I must test Peter Phelan's rhythm," Rosie declared and disappeared back into the hall.

"I've a feeling," Kate told Fr Tim ruefully, "that I'm gone over the hill. The energy that's being expended down in that hall makes me feel old just watching it."

"They're great, aren't they?" he said enthusiastically. "You know, I really miss dancing. I just loved it. That crowd in there are having the time of their lives, and I don't think that we'll have a bother in the world with them. I'd say that they're all in now so we can relax. One of us should take a break. Why don't you walk down home and have a cup of tea with David, and then I'll go when you come back."

"That's a good idea," Kate told him, but just as she got up from her chair there was movement outside the hatch. She heard Fr Tim's quick intake of breath and she opened the door to find Kitty Conway smiling up at her. Kitty's rich auburn hair fell in profusion down around her small golden-brown elfin face, and her green scanty dress matched exactly the colour of her green eyes. The short clinging dress displayed her beautifully shapely legs, and her golden strapped sandals were the most elegant that Kate had ever seen. She was stunning.

"Kitty, how lovely to see you," she said warmly. She knew what Kitty had endured as a young girl and was glad to see her looking so beautiful. Kitty Conway was going to create quite a stir when she made her entrance into the hall, and Kate had a tiny suspicion that Kitty had come late with just that in mind. She was delighted that Kitty was here, but her delight was short-lived when a dark form came in the door behind her and she turned around to be confronted by Rory Conway.

"Hello, Rory," she said quietly.

"Huh," he grunted at her, and she could smell drink from him.

"Well, go ahead and enjoy yourselves," she told them, and she noticed that it was Kitty who paid for the two tickets. When they had gone in, she returned to her seat by Fr Tim.

"I think that I'll stay put," she told him grimly. "Why do I always smell trouble when I see Rory Conway?"

"I don't think that he can cause any trouble here," Fr Tim assured her.

As Kate had expected, all eyes in the hall turned towards Kitty Conway. She stood alone and composed just inside the door. Rory disappeared into the crowd of men at the other side of the hall. Kate had thought that when the music started up there would be a rush in Kitty's direction, but it did not happen. She realised that many of the young fellows were too self-conscious to break ranks, and Kate was just beginning to worry about her when Peter strode forward, and after a short chat they danced into the crowd. *Good for you, Peter*, she thought. But her satisfaction was short-lived when, after succeeding dances, they stood side by side, then danced again, and it looked as if they were going to spend the entire night together. If word of this got home to Martha, there would be hell to pay. She had been so intent on Kitty and Peter that she had forgotten the other dancers, and suddenly her eye was caught by Rosie, who was looking daggers at the pair in the middle of the floor. Poor Rosie, who had decided that Peter was going to be the love of her life. Kate turned to Fr Tim and surprised him by singing, in Maurice Chevalier tones, "I'm glad I'm not young any more."

"You've changed your tune pretty fast," he told her.

"You know, when you look at the young enjoying themselves you forget about the accompanying pain, but looking down there I can see Rosie suffering," she said.

"Nora and Danny seem to be having a great time," he remarked.

"Nora loves dancing," Kate told him, "and I'd say that she is delighted with Danny's skill on the floor. At least I hope that's all it is, because one complication is enough not to mind having two to cope with."

"You're probably right about Nora, though I'd not be so sure about Danny," Fr Tim said.

"Oh, thank goodness, Davey Shine is after asking Kitty to dance," Kate said, watching the action down on the dance floor. "It might break that up for a bit anyway."

"Shiner is always on the lookout for Peter," Fr Tim smiled. "Maybe he thought that Peter needed breathing space."

"Peter is gone over now to dance with Rosie," Kate reported.

"Kate, you're like a match commentator," Fr Tim, who was busy counting the money, told her.

"This is the most entertaining night that I've had with a long time, and to think that I nearly passed up on it," Kate smiled. "Danny is now dancing with that blonde girl from the bank in Ross. This is the first time that we ever got a crowd in here from Ross. The Vikings must have pulling power. I can't see Nora at all at the moment. Oh, there she is, coming out of the ladies. Oh my God, Rory Conway is watching her come out. I bet that he saw her going in and he lay in wait."

"Kate, you make him sound like a fox watching a rabbit," Fr Tim protested.

"That's what it feels like," she told him grimly. "I'm not sure that Nora is going to be able to handle dancing with Rory Conway if he asks her. And that's just what's going to happen because he is coming up behind her, and he is going to take her by surprise so she'll have no excuse."

Kate watched with a feeling of apprehension as Rory Conway asked Nora to dance, and even from a distance Kate could sense her reluctance. The vibrant laughing Nora who had earlier danced around with Danny and Shiner was gone, and a wooden figure moved across the floor. The band were playing what Rosie termed a slow smoochy number, and as Kate watched she could see Rory Conway draw Nora closer. She tried to push him away and Kate saw him stagger. He was quite unsteady on his feet and he tried to hang on to Nora. Then he wrapped his arms around her and what Kate had dreaded happened: Nora thumped her fists off his chest and started to scream. Then she slapped his face and bolted, ashen-faced, for the door.

Quick thinking Fr Tim was there to put his arms around her,

calling to Kate, "I'll take her down home to David. You stay here in case there's trouble." And they were gone out the door.

When Kate's horrified gaze swung back to the dance floor, Peter was running across the hall towards Rory. Kate knew that Nora's scream had brought back that terrible night in the wood and that Peter was out for vengeance. He came at Rory like an avalanche and Rory crashed to the floor. But Rory Conway was big and strong and used to fighting his way through the pubs and dance halls of Camden, and despite being drunk he was up like a shot and going for Peter with deadly intent. Shiner rushed over to help Peter take him on, but Rory had come prepared for a fight. Kate froze when she saw the glint of a knife in his hand. *Jesus*, she prayed, *don't let anyone get hurt.* She was too far away to move, but someone else was not. Kitty, quick as lightning, stood in front of her brother and confronted Peter and Davey.

"Get your dirty hands off my brother," she yelled, and Kate from her vantage point saw her reach behind her back and cover the knife with her hand. "Come on, Rory, let's get out of this one-horse dive of a place." She walked a surprised and unprotesting Rory out the door. As she passed the ticket office, she threw the knife on the table in front of Kate, and looking up Kate saw tears in her eyes. When she looked down there was blood on the blade of the knife. Kitty must have nicked her hand when she grasped the knife!

There was mayhem in the hall, and Kate was angry that the band had stopped playing and were letting the chaos continue. The faster that they all got back dancing now the better. Rosie had the same idea, and suddenly she was up on the stage and had taken the microphone from a surprised Viking.

"No extra charge for the sideshow," she announced smilingly, and after a few nervous laughs she got a round of applause.

"Now we are going to try a new dance. Some of you may have tried it before and you'll know what fun it is. So come on now and we'll do Simple Simon. Put your hands in the air." She beckoned to the bemused band to start up, and soon the entire crowd were back in action and the disruption forgotten. Now that Rosie had got the crowd going, she was loath to give up on them. She led them on from one action-packed dance to another and they loved it. She was totally at ease on the stage and with the microphone. The Vikings, with their white suits and red shirts, were the perfect backdrop to Rosie's red dress, and she had whipped off her bolero top and caught her hair up in a pony tail. *There is no doubt*, Kate thought, *but she has got stage presence.* Until then Kate had never been quite sure what that was, but she recognised it when she saw it. The crowd loved Rosie and did not want to let her go, so she stayed singing with the Vikings until the last dance. After the national anthem, the crowd thinned out slowly as everybody stood around discussing the band, but most of all Rosie.

· During the last few dances, Kate had noticed a suave-looking man watching Rosie from the side of the hall, and when the last dance was being played he came back to Kate and inquired, "Who's that girl?"

Kate told him and asked why he wanted to know.

"I manage the Vikings," he told her, "and I'm looking for a lead singer. She is just the chick to fit the bill."

Kate was not too sure that she liked his way of putting things. Rosie would be delighted, but the last thing that Betty and Con Nolan would want for their only daughter was to go off singing with a showband before she had even done her leaving cert. Then Rosie rushed in and Kate did the introductions. When he told Rosie about his plans, she took Kate by surprise by cooly telling him, "We'll settle the charge for tonight first."

"But that was agreed in advance," he told her.

"That was before I sang for half the night with them," Rosie asserted, and she argued and bargained with him until she got a good knock-down price. Kate was impressed.

When the band had finally got all their gear packed into the van and departed, Kate helped Rosie, Peter, Shiner and Danny to tidy up the hall. Then she told them all, "Let's go down to my place for tea."

She saw Danny look at her uncertainly and she smiled reassuringly at him.

"You, too, Danny," she told him.

Back at the house Nora, David and Fr Tim were having tea, and before anyone could ask Nora said, "I'm fine, and maybe Rory meant no harm, only he was drunk and I was scared."

"Well, that's understandable," Fr Tim told her, and to lead the conversation away from what was a touchy subject in the present company, he continued, "That was one enjoyable night."

"A great time was had by all," Shiner declared.

"Tell them your news, Rosie," Kate told her.

"Well, now," Rosie began dramatically, "tonight something happened that might change my life."

"Did you propose, Phelan?" Shiner asked Peter.

"Davey Shine, you are one thick eejit," Rosie told him in exasperation, knowing that Shiner always aimed to take the wind out of her sails when she wanted to hold centre stage.

"Don't mind Shiner," Peter told her, "he's only setting you up."

"You've no sense of occasion, Shiner, that's your problem," Rosie informed Davey, who was about to retort but he got a kick in the shin from Peter under the table.

"Well," Rosie began again, looking daggers at Shiner, "now that all the fools have had their say, I am delighted to inform you that the manager of the Vikings wants me to become their lead singer."

There was a combined gasp of astonishment from around the table which brought a look of intense satisfaction to Rosie's face, and even Shiner had the grace to be impressed. He slapped her on the back saying, "Well, fair play to you," but then had to spoil it by adding, "my roundy girl."

But she decided to ignore the last remark because, as she told Nora later, she had always considered Shiner to lack a certain sense of finesse. Peter's reaction, however, was all that she could have hoped for as he looked at her with eyes full of admiration. But Nora was staunch in her rejection of the idea.

"Rosie, you must do your leaving cert, otherwise you'll have five years of study gone down the drain."

"But if I pass this up now, I may never get the chance again," Rosie protested.

"It's a bit late in the night to be making life-changing decisions," Fr Tim told them, "so maybe tomorrow might be a better time to discuss all of this."

"You're right," Kate agreed as she poured out more tea.

"Kate," Fr Tim began tentatively, "your car is gone until morning."

"What do you mean my car is gone until morning?" Kate

demanded, putting down the teapot with a bang and looking in amazement at Fr Tim.

"Rory wanted to get to the railway station," her husband put in quietly, "and it was the only way we had to get him there."

Now everybody was staring at David and Fr Tim.

"What the hell happened?" Peter demanded.

"Kitty insisted that Rory leave and go back to England tonight," Fr Tim began.

"But how come he agreed?" Danny asked in amazement.

"She threatened that we would report him to the guards, that he pulled a knife on you, Peter, and that Kate had the knife as evidence and that he would finish up in jail."

"Good God," Peter breathed, "how did he fall for that?"

"He was pretty mixed up, so it worked," David said quietly.

"But why did he take my car?" Kate demanded. "Why didn't one of you drive him?"

"Because that was the way he wanted it, and we were afraid to push him too far in case things would backfire on us," Fr Tim told her. "He's going to leave it at the station in Ross, and David will drive you in early in the morning to collect it."

"I hope 'twill be there and fit to drive," Kate said grimly.

"I feel that it will be," David assured her. "Kitty seemed to have him on the run."

"And where is Kitty?" Peter asked.

"Gone with him to get the late train back to Dublin. So that's why I'm so sure that the car will be at the station," Fr Tim told them.

"Was her hand all right?" Kate asked.

"It wasn't cut very deep, and I did a bit of first aid on it," Fr Tim said.

"What a strange finish to the night," Shiner decided.

"A simply great finish," Danny declared in a relieved voice, "and now I had better head for home."

"Will I drive you all home?" Fr Tim offered.

"No, no," Peter put in quickly. "Norry is staying here, and Rosie, Shiner and myself will be with Danny as far as the bridge. The fresh air will do us all good."

"Peter is a great believer in fresh air all of a sudden," Shiner observed to no one in particular.

Kate looked around at these young people and felt immensely proud of them. They had done a great job tonight, and with the exception of Nora's upset, it had all gone without a hitch. But even Nora's little episode had a bright side to it in that it had sent Rory back to England, at least for the time being. Kate knew that when he had sobered up he would figure out that Kitty had pulled a fast one on him and that it would not be that easy to get rid of him the next time. But at least it gave Danny breathing space for another while. She was delighted that Peter had included Danny in his group walking home together, even though she realised that Peter's real reason for the walk was to have time alone with Rosie at the end of it. But at least Danny was part of the little circle, and she knew that this was very important for him as the Conways had always been outsiders in Kilmeen, or rather Matt Conway had made sure that they were kept apart.

When everybody was gone home and Nora gone to bed, herself and David sat discussing the night. But after a while she realised that David's mind had wandered to what had been worrying him since they had got Rodney Jackon's letter.

"The future of the school is taking the good out of

110

everything for you, isn't it?" she asked, taking his hand and laying it against her face.

"It's like a shadow hanging over me," he sighed.

"Well, he'll be here soon, and then we'll know exactly what is going to happen. Everything might be fine," Kate assured him.

She felt confident that Rodney would act honourably, but the thought of Martha controlling things in the background worried her.

Chapter Eight

Nora was struggling to get to sleep. Every time she dozed off, Matt Conway's face leered up in front of her, and then he was Rory Conway. When she finally drifted off, she was back in the wood, and a naked Matt Conway, who kept turning into Rory, was laughing and dancing beneath the trees, and she was climbing up a thorny tree trying to get away. The thorns were digging into her hands, and he stood below laughing up at her. Then he started to climb. She woke up sobbing, with her legs drawn up as close as she could get them to her chin. Her heart pounded and she was stiff with fright.

The house was so quiet that she thought that Aunty Kate and Uncle David must hear her heart pounding. Her body was rigid. She made herself breathe deeply and stretch out her cramped legs. Slowly the terror eased and she could breathe easily again. It was a long time since she'd had this nightmare, but every so often something would happen to trigger it off.

Tonight, of course, it was Rory Conway at the dance. He was so like Matt Conway. She had seen him early in the night and had kept him at a safe distance. It was easy to do this because he had sat in a corner and not moved, but she had felt his eyes following her around the hall. She had decided that he was probably too drunk to dance, but when she came out of the cloakroom and he had taken her by surprise, she knew that he had been lying in wait for her.

She was glad that the whole thing had ended in him leaving Kilmeen. It was good to be rid of him, and it would give Danny a chance. She had enjoyed dancing with Danny. It had been a surprise that he was such a lovely dancer, and he had told her that Mary and Kitty had spent hours teaching him when he was younger. Dancing with him had been exciting. It was hard to think that he and Rory were brothers, but it was hard to forget it too. She knew that Mom would be very annoyed if she heard that they had danced together so often, and would have been even more annoyed if she had seen Kitty and Peter. 'Twas luck Kitty had had to go. She had never liked Kitty since their days together in the Glen school, but it was very good of Kitty to have managed things the way she had and surprising that Rory had done as she had told him. Danny had said that she was the one who could best handle Rory.

If Kitty had stayed on at the dance, Nora wondered how things would have worked out between Peter and herself. The chances were that Rosie would have come up with some strategy to torpedo what had looked like a promising situation. It was probably Rosie who had got Shiner to intervene by asking Kitty to dance. Rosie was a firm believer in giving fate a push in the right direction. A romance between Rosie and Peter would certainly be a lot less complicated than between Kitty and Peter. It might also stop Rosie from going off singing with the Vikings. That would be just great! As she drifted off to sleep, she wondered how Danny had enjoyed the dance.

When she woke, the late morning sun was streaming in the window. She stretched out in the luxury of Aunty Kate's comfortable bed. Sleeping late was something that Mom did not allow. No matter how tired you felt, she insisted that you get out of bed early in the morning. Now it was just great to lie here in comfort and not have anybody calling from the foot of the stairs. The white dress was thrown across a chair beside the bed. She had had such doubts about that dress for the dance, but Kate was reassuring, and it must have looked good because she had such a great night in it. That was, until the episode with Rory. Thank God he was gone!

Now she decided that it was time to get up and have a slow, leisurely bath. She slipped out of the soft, bouncy bed and eased Kate's white lace nightdress over her head. On the dressing table over by the window, Nana Nellie's silver-backed hairbrush glinted in the sun. She waltzed across the bedroom and stood in front of the long mirror. There was no mirror like this in Mossgrove, so there were few opportunities for critical appraisal. She liked her long legs and slim body, but she wished that she had bigger breasts. Maybe she was not as beautiful as Mom, but on the whole she liked what she saw. She let down her curly blonde hair from the knot on top of her head and brushed it streaming down her back. She had often wished that her hair was straight like Rosie's, but looking at it now, maybe it suited her better this way. When she was a little girl, she had brushed her hair with this brush, and after Nana Nellie had died and left it to Aunty Kate, she always used it when she came here. Aunty Kate put it on the dressing table whenever she stayed overnight.

She danced around the room humming one of the tunes that the band had played last night. Looking back now, she thought that dancing with Danny had been the best part of the night. Was it because she knew that he had always fancied her? But could it be more than that? Whatever it was, she was feeling good this morning. She waltzed across the corridor to the bathroom, and having splashed some of Aunty Kate's gorgeous smelling oil into the bath, she turned on the two taps to full flow. Aunty Kate had always told her to feel free to help herself. She was going to have a foaming bath and stay in for as long as she liked. At home Mom was always hurrying you out of the bath, and the bathroom was so clean and functional, a bit like Mom's dairy. Aunty Kate had a gorgeous blue bathroom with big jars of bath oil and soft fluffy towels. As she soaked in the soft, scented water, she hummed a Viking tune.

It was as if the scene with Rory last night and the following nightmare had washed away the trauma in the wood. She would put it all behind her now, study hard for the next two months and hopefully get into university, then come home to Kilmeen and teach with Uncle David. When her thoughts turned to Uncle David, she felt a slight sense of unease. She wondered if everything was all right with him. He was not himself with the last few weeks. But she was not going to think about anything like that now; she was going to have a lovely hour all to herself. After she had soaked for an hour, she stepped out of the bath feeling that she could take on the world and wrapped herself dry in Aunty Kate's big soft towels.

As she came down the stairs, the front door opened, and Kate came in looking crisp and fresh in her white coat.

"Did you get your car," she asked worriedly, "and was it all right?"

"Fine," Kate told her. "David dropped me over to the station on his way to a meeting, and I got some of my calls done on the way back."

"You look and smell like a nurse," Nora said, hugging her.

"Which is exactly what I am," Kate smiled, returning her hug, "and you smell and look like a lovely princess, but to what do I owe this big hug?"

"Just for being the most wonderful aunt in the whole world," Nora declared.

"Well, that's a good start to my week," Kate smiled. "How did you sleep last night?"

"The nightmare came back, which I suppose was to be expected after the episode in the hall, but then I went to sleep again and slept like a log, and do you know something, Aunty Kate? I feel this morning that I have put it all behind me at last."

"Good for you," Kate said thoughtfully. She was never one to probe. She had often told Nora not to ask too many questions because if people wanted you to know something they told you in their own good time. Anyway, Nora could not explain to Kate why she was feeling so good because she was not quite sure of the explanation herself.

"Put on the kettle," Kate told her, "and we'll have something to eat before you head back to Mossgrove."

"Will we have it out in the garden? I love the way you and Uncle David eat out there so much."

"Of course," Kate told her. "Put whatever you feel like having on a tray and carry it out there while I go upstairs and have a bit of a tidy-up."

Nora put on the kettle and went to Kate's fridge to collect anything that looked inviting and headed out to the table under the tree at the bottom of the garden. She came back into the kitchen and collected a tablecloth from Kate's supply in the dresser drawer, and when she had covered the old table in the garden, she laid out the tea things and stood back to appraise her work. She knew that Kate liked her table nicely set. When she came back in, the kettle was boiling, and as she made the tea Kate came into the kitchen minus her white coat.

"You look less like the district nurse now," Nora smiled.

"I feel less like one too," Kate told her.

"This is so good," she declared as she bit into the crunchy sandwich that Kate had whipped together.

"That's because you're hungry," Kate told her. "Hunger is a great sauce."

"Nana Nellie used to say that," she remembered.

"She did indeed," Kate agreed, and then, looking at her appraisingly, "You are so like her that sometimes it's uncanny to watch you."

"Jack says that too," she said.

"That's a big compliment coming from Jack," Kate told her, "because he loved Nellie."

"You mean really loved her?" she asked in surprise.

"Yes, really loved her. You're old enough to understand now. Your grandfather was an alcoholic who gave her a hard life and, I'd say, slowly killed whatever had been between them. Jack, I think, had always loved her, even before she married my father, and when Dad died it is easy to understand that over the years

117

of being there for her and working with her a huge bond formed between them. As I grew up I was always aware of it and knew that they loved each other deeply."

"Did you mind?"

"No, not at all. As a matter of fact it made home a more warm, loving place," Kate told her.

"But they never did . . . well, you know what I mean," she finished in confusion.

Kate leant across the table and gently stroked her face.

"I think that being there for each other was enough. When my father died nothing changed, and by then Mossgrove was in such a state that all their concentration was on saving the place, and by then as well we were growing up and became the centre of their universe. We were Nellie's children, but in some way we were Jack's as well. Jack and my father had gone to school together and were best friends, and despite all the my father's shortcomings, I think that Jack understood him."

"Jack understands us all," Nora marvelled, "and now he is looking across the river and is going to help Danny Conway."

"That's the beauty of Jack: there is no bitterness in his heart. All his energies are channelled into his love of the land."

"Do you think that he'll be able to help Danny?" Nora asked.

"Well, if anyone can Jack can," Kate told her. "Is it important for you?"

"I don't really know," and she could feel her face warming, "but I always liked Danny, and now I feel such admiration for him that he is so enthusiastic about getting across the river up and running. But that place is so run down that I cannot imagine it ever looking good. It somehow seems like an impossible dream."

"Don't underestimate Jack and Danny," Kate told her, "and as well as that, Jack feels that they have old Molly Barry on their side. He feels it in his bones."

"Oh, Jack's bones," Nora smiled. "I sometimes wish that I had bones like Jack, and then I'd know what was around the corner."

"Sometimes 'twould be handy," Kate agreed, and something in her tone alerted Nora that Kate was worried. So she had been right in thinking that Uncle David had something on his mind, because if Uncle David had a problem, then so would Kate. She decided that she was not going to follow Kate's advice about not asking questions.

"Are you and Uncle David worried about something?" she asked bluntly.

"Does it show that much?" Kate said in alarm.

"No, no," Nora assured her, "but I've been watching Uncle David, and I sensed that he is not himself. I know that he is always under a bit of pressure when we are coming up to exam time, but this year he is more preoccupied than worried. As if he had something else on his mind."

"You are a very perceptive young lady," Kate told her, and Nora felt a twinge of guilt, because where Uncle David was concerned she watched his every mood, "and you are right that he has something else on his mind besides the exams. There was a letter from Rodney Jackson, and we can't have the Jackson house for the school after the summer."

"What?" Nora exclaimed. "But why?"

"Because apparently he wants to turn it into a hotel," Kate told her.

"A hotel. But that's crazy. What would we do with a hotel in

Kilmeen, and what about the school?" she demanded in a shocked voice, realising that this could destroy her own future plans.

"We don't know," Kate said bleakly. "At the moment it's all a bit up in the air, but Rodney is coming soon so we'll know then. He was supposed to be here for Easter but he got held up."

"But where did this idea of a hotel come from?" Nora demanded.

"You are as wise as I am," Kate told her.

As she walked home to Mossgrove, Nora had planned to call in to Rosie to discuss last night, but Kate's announcement had changed her mind, and luckily Rosie was not out at the gate. She was dismayed at the prospect of no school in Kilmeen. She wanted to get home and discuss things with Peter. If Rodney was not going to give them the Jackson house for the school, what were they going to do? It was the only house in Kilmeen big enough to house the school, though she had to admit that there had been times when she had thought that it was too grand for all the running and thumping that was done up its lovely curved staircase. But Uncle David was very concerned about the care of it and was for ever telling the students to be careful and not to be banging the old doors or scratching the woodwork. Now she wondered what the future was for the Jackson school. Where would they go? They just could not close down. But she felt that Rodney Jackson would not do anything as drastic as telling them that they could not have the school without offering them an alternative. But what! And what put the notion of a hotel into his head? With all his visiting back and forth, did he feel the need for a hotel in Kilmeen? Nora could find no answers, but when she got home Peter was not long putting his own slant on the whole thing. She found him sitting on the old sofa in the kitchen looking through the newspaper that Jack had brought from the creamery that morning.

"Where's Mom?" she asked.

"Outside somewhere," he told her without even looking up.

Nora settled herself on the sofa beside him, which caused him to turn an amused face in her direction.

"No post mortem about the afters of last night now, Norry," he cautioned.

"Would I?" she smiled innocently.

"You would so," he told her. "Yourself and Rosie nearly discuss what you had for your breakfast."

"Well, you're on the wrong track now," she told him dismissively. "I have a more serious matter to discuss."

"Oh? Let's hear it," he said with interest, putting down the newspaper.

He listened intently, nodding his head occasionally, as she filled him in on the details about the school and the hotel.

"It's Mom," he declared without hesitation.

"But why would it be Mom?" Nora protested, even though the thought had crossed her mind.

"Because it all adds up," Peter declared.

"How does it all add up?" she demanded, wondering how on earth Peter had figured that out.

"As soon as she eased off trying to run this place, I felt sure that there had to be another agenda, and as well as that she was getting fed up here when she did not have it all her own way. She was looking for more challenging horizons, and a hotel would be right up her alley. She'd just love getting it up and going, and having staff to manage would be her notion of heaven. It has to be her idea," Peter declared with certainty.

"But what about the school?" Nora protested.

"The school wouldn't cost Mom a thought as long as she was getting what she wanted," he told her.

"But that's not fair," Nora asserted angrily.

"When did Mom ever play fair?" Peter demanded.

"You always see the bad side of her," she told him.

"I see the real Mom, and you always think that she is other than she is," he declared.

"And anyway," Nora said triumphantly, "you said that she had no notion of marrying Rodney Jackson, so how is she going to take over his old home?"

"You must have come down in the last shower, Norry! Didn't I tell you Mom was going to use this situation to her advantage. She is not going to marry him, but she is going to use him."

"You could be wrong. . ." Nora broke off in confusion as a slight movement by the back door caught her eye and she looked up to see her mother viewing the two of them coldly. Nora felt her face transfuse with guilty colour, but Peter was unruffled.

"Listening at doors is not a good idea, Mother," he told her cooly.

"Well, it's nice to know what a high opinion you have of your mother," she challenged him, striding across the kitchen and glaring down at him.

"Can you contradict me?" Peter challenged.

"You'll have to wait and find out, won't you?" she informed him icily and swept out the front door.

CHAPTER NINE

AS DANNY CAME in the door, he saw the two letters on the kitchen table. Johnny must have called while he was at the creamery, and now the letter with the creamery cheque was there on the table. He had been waiting for it for days. It came at the end of each month, but it could be a few days early or late. This month it was late. Most of his neighbours probably did not even notice that it was late, but for him every day was vital. This cheque was his lifeline. It was his only income during these months. Other farmers had calves to sell in the spring, but he did not want to sell because he needed to build up his herd, and because he was feeding them with some of their mothers' milk, the supply to the creamery was not great. As a result the cheque was small, but at least it was something coming in. He was hoping that this month might be a bit up on last month, though he knew in his heart that it was highly unlikely. He did not want to consider the possibility that it could be gone down.

The brown envelope made a crinkling sound as he picked it up, and it gave him a little glow of satisfaction to see the name "Danny Conway" printed inside the transparent flap. The creamery had changed the account to his name, and it was the only semblance of ownership that he had to the farm. He picked a knife off the table, slid it under the flap and ripped the envelope open. Holding his breath, he eased out the flimsy statement with attached cheque and the figure "30" danced up at him. Well, at least it had not gone down and was actually up a few shillings. Next month he knew that it would be better, because two more cows would have calved and the bigger calves were graduating on to sour milk, which meant more fresh milk going to the creamery. So he was over the milk slump for this year.

All of this thirty pounds was already accounted for. He had to pay something off the grocery bill, and there was a sizeable bill for pig feeding, and he owed the vet for the last call. He hated owing money, but there was no other way to survive at the moment. The spending of every penny was weighed up before he finally decided. He would not have gone to the dance last week only Kitty had insisted and given him the money, and it had been great! For just a few hours he had forgotten about the bills and the money. There had only been music and dancing and feeling good. Nora and himself had such fun together, and she seemed so happy to be dancing with him that it made his night. The day after, his troubles did not seem so overpowering. But now that euphoria had worn off, and he sat at the table trying to figure out ways that he could stretch this thirty pounds further. He had to feed the pigs, and his own food requirements were already cut to a minimum. Sometimes he just had to get the vet;

if he had not got him for the cow she could have died, and that would have been a major catastrophe. So there was no way that he could spend less. He never bought meat except an occasional pound of sausages, which he made last the whole week. When the girls came home, they always brought a big roast that lasted for days and days. Mary was great! Sometimes he got a letter with a five pound note inside, which he put away to buy something to help improve the buildings or fertilizer for the land.

He knew that the girls were keeping his mother in Dublin to build her up after all she had gone through, and he felt from her letters that they were succeeding. But as well as that, they understood that he could live more cheaply on his own and that he was young enough to survive hardship. They knew how hard the struggle was, but they had no idea that he had it in mind to restore the old house as well. To them that would have been totally beyond what was possible. Maybe they would be right. When he looked at his meagre cheque he was inclined to agree with them. He was hardly able to survive and do what was necessary to improve the farm buildings, and here he was with crazy notions of restoring the old house. Maybe he should forget about the house. As it was he could not even get into it!

Then his eye fell on the other letter and he recognised Rory's writing. Now what did he want? He felt a certain sense of apprehension as he took up the letter. Typical of Rory, it was even grubby on the outside. It was brief and to the point:

If you want the bloody farm I will sign over my claim for five hundred pounds. There is a business here that I could put the money into and stay where I am instead of going back to that cursed hole.

He smiled ruefully. Five hundred pounds was about as far from him as the sun that was trying to break through and shine in the window. It would be impossible to lay his hands on it. His life seemed to be all about impossibilities at the moment. And yet a few weeks ago, when he had discussed things with Jack, he had been full of hope. What was wrong with him this morning? But at the back of his mind he knew that it was the sight of Peter Phelan at the creamery earlier with his new tractor and trailer full of shining churns. Peter Phelan was already on the top of the ladder, and he was struggling to get his foot on the bottom rung. Life was not fair!

A restless scraping of hooves out in the yard reminded him that Bessie was still under the creamery cart and protesting as well that life was not fair. With a sigh he left the letters on the table and went out to attend to her and the churn. After leading her to the milk stand, he poured the skim milk into the old tar barrel that had served that purpose for years. He untackled Bessie, and when he opened the gate into the haggard, she galloped off in delight to join Rusty, the old mare who was almost as old as himself. He would have to round the two of them up again later, because he intended to finish ploughing the high field after he had done the yard jobs. His father had never gone into ploughing or the setting of grain of any kind but had depended solely on the cows, and he had not looked after them very well either. The farm supported only fourteen cows, but Danny knew that, managed properly, it had the feeding of forty. Well run, Furze Hill could be a good, viable place, better even than Mossgrove.

Over the winter he had attended farming classes that the local Macra branch had put on in the village hall. The instructor, seeing his intense interest, had given him books to read, and late into the night he had studied all aspects of farm improvement. He had got his soil tested and he knew that the land here was top class and that he had no wet field as they had across in Mossgrove. It was ironic that the two fields of Mossgrove that had caused all the bother were wet and coarse and subject to flooding from the river and the two that his grandfather had bought beside the village were fine, flat, dry fields.

As he washed the churn and scalded it clean, his sense of well-being began to return. His determination surfaced when he thought of Nana Molly and all she had suffered and her lost dream of Furze Hill. His mother too deserved a break, and he could just imagine the delight of the girls if ever the old house emerged from the grove that smothered it at the moment. He had a lot to fight for, and he was not going to let the immensity of the task get him down. When the farmwork was done in the evenings, he had started to clear around the old arch, and though it was slow, painstaking work, it was giving him great satisfaction. Now, however, he needed to turn his attention to the job on hand, so he brushed out the cow stalls and the stable and checked the hen house for eggs. He made a bran mash for the cow who had calved the night before and looked in on the baby calf who had already got his legs under him and was standing up for his rights in the crowded calf house. The pigs as usual were hungry, so manoeuvring the intricate door he got in to feed them. In another few weeks they would be ready for the factory, and that would be more money to oil the wheels of his hardship. The thought of that made him feel better.

When he went back into the kitchen to have something to

eat before he went ploughing, he reread Rory's letter and smiled grimly to himself. Trust Rory to ask for enough anyway! But at least it was good to know that money could get him out. For himself the land would have been more important than the money. It was Nana Molly who had passed on that love of the land to him, but Rory had had no time for Nana Molly and no such attachment to the place.

Danny rounded up Rusty and Bessie, who was reluctant to come as she thought that having gone to the creamery she had her bit done for the day. But when she was lined up with Rusty behind the plough, she settled down happily. Ploughing was new to him, but when he had put his hands on the plough for the first time, there was an awakening of a connectedness to the brown earth. Jack had told him that ploughmen were born with the love of the earth in their blood. Jack was right. Now he lined the horses up beside the last furrow, and after a little while the three of them moved together in harmony. All day he guided them up and down the hilly field, and though clods of earth clung to his boots and his shoulders ached from balancing the plough to create straight furrows, a deep sense of satisfaction grew in his gut. As the hours passed, the ploughing soothed him, but when the shadows started to lengthen across the furrows, he decided to call a halt. There was the milking and the yard jobs yet to be done, and Rusty was beginning to tire. She was nearly too old for ploughing, but he could not afford to retire her. He looked after her well, and because she was a great-hearted horse, she continued to give of her best. He untied them from the plough, and they led him home across the fields into the haggard. When he had the tackling taken off them, they galloped away, glad to be free.

The yard was full of noise as the pigs squealed with hunger and the calves bellowed to be fed and the hens cackled for attention. But the first on his agenda were the cows, and it was here that he missed his mother, because while he was milking she would look after the yard jobs. He knew that there was too much work for one person in the day-to-day running of the place, not to mind the work of reclamation that he did every night. But he had been ground down for so long that now, when he had the freedom to get things done, he was energised by the challenge. As yet he could not see light at the end of the tunnel, and there were days when he wondered if he would ever see it, but an inner drive kept him going. He held on to the belief that one day the farm would be a thriving concern and that the house in the trees would stand tall and free and that he would have made good Nana Molly's faith in him.

When he was finally finished and all the animals were quieted down for the night, it was dusk, but he decided that before he went in to have his supper he would spend a little time clearing around the arch. He had been working at it by night for a few weeks, and every morning he had to restrain himself from resuming the clearing of the night before, but he knew that the farmwork had to take priority over anything else. Tonight he might finally get to the other side, and this would eliminate the need to go out into the road to get in over the wall beside the front gate.

He picked up his slasher and saws from where he had tidied them away the night before and started to cut through determinedly. The growth was dense, and he could feel the briars catch at his sleeves as he slashed in around them. Nature when left to herself soon wrapped her arms tightly around everything. But slowly his hacking began to have an impact, and then suddenly when he cut the leg of one scrawny tree, a huge wad of ivy came free from around the arch. Standing well back he pulled at the ivy. It came away like a trailing cloak, and gradually the whole arch was revealed. He whistled in appreciation: it was a solid arch of red brick in perfect condition. A glow of satisfaction suffused his whole being. These Barry ancestors certainly knew how to build! Careful in case he would loosen the brickwork, he eased away the blanket of surrounding ivy.

It was now too dark to do much more, but he was determined to burrow his way through to the front door, which was not far away from this angle. He cut on determinedly and rammed his way through the undergrowth in what he hoped was the right direction. When he hit a wall he knew that he had arrived somewhere in the general direction of where he had intended. Then he worked along by the wall and found that he was just to the left of the front door. At last the path through the arch was open. Tomorrow evening he would clear it properly. He put away his tools carefully and headed back into the kitchen.

Inside it was cold and dark, and after lighting the oil lamp he rekindled the fire with dry sticks and bits of broken turf. Soon the flames were licking the bottom of the kettle, and he put two of the eggs that he had collected earlier into a black saucepan and rested it beside the kettle. He pulled up the only half-comfortable chair in the kitchen and sat down. A wave of exhaustion swept over him, and though he tried to resist it, sleep overpowered him. A grey mist swept him over to the door of Furze Hill, where he was trying one key after another. He could hear Nana Molly's voice urging him to keep trying. She had to get in, she cried, because someone was trying to hold her back. Every key he tried disappeared into the keyhole; Nana's voice was getting more agitated and he was getting more desperate.

He jumped up in fright as a gentle hand on his shoulder woke him. Fr Brady was standing behind him.

"Sorry to wake you, Danny, but I've the tea made and the eggs are boiled, and you probably need something inside you," he smiled.

"God, thanks, Father," he said gratefully. "I'm glad to wake up because I was having a strange dream."

"Well, I'll join you for supper," Fr Brady smiled as he sat to the already laid out table, "because Kate gave me an apple tart for you, and I can't let you have all that to yourself."

But when Danny looked at the table there was cheese and brown bread on it as well.

"You're feeding the hungry, Father," he said ruefully.

"Not really," Fr Tim told him lightly, "just helping a friend who is struggling gallantly up a high hill and who is almost within sight of the summit."

"The summit could be quite a distance yet," Danny said as he joined him at the table.

"The secret is to remember that even in the bad days, when you cannot see it, it is still there. The trouble is that with you working such back-breaking hours things could get on top of you."

"It has happened," Danny told him grimly.

"You need help," Fr Brady declared.

"Help costs money, and as the whole parish probably knows by now, I've no money," Danny told him.

"Help does not always have to cost money," Fr Tim said.

"Well, that's news to me," Danny began, but changed his tone and continued, "but that's not strictly true, because Shiner has been great and comes every chance he gets to help me, and there is nothing in it for him only he is such a good old skin."

"There are more like Shiner out there," Fr Tim told him quietly.

"Like who?" Danny demanded incredulously.

"My father," Fr Tim said evenly.

"Your father?" he exclaimed in amazement.

"Yes, Danny," Fr Tim said, "and now just hear me through. When you are young and challenged like you are, you might be sometimes overburdened, but still life is full of excitement and vibrancy. Now, when you come to my father's age and you have your family reared and you are no longer absolutely necessary for their survival and sometimes they wish that you might just get lost for a while, well, then it's a different story altogether. As a young man my father worked on the buildings in England where he made good money. He was smart enough to get out while he was still young, and he came home and bought a pub. He did well, but he had hard times too because my mother died when we were all young, but he got through it and reared six of us and put us out in the world. My brother who is at home in the business got married last year, and my father now finds himself surplus to requirements in his own house and business. He is beginning to think that he has nothing to look forward to but old age. In other words, he needs a project. And this is where you come in. He would reroof Furze Hill with the slates that Jack says are stacked up at the back, and then he could do the barn. At least it would be a start."

Danny listened in growing amazement. Could this really be happening? A hundred questions ran through his mind.

"But how old is he?" he blurted out.

"Sixty next year and as fit as a fiddle," Fr Brady assured him, "and the great thing is that he has all his tools in perfect nick, and my garden shed is like a carpenter's workshop. That is his burning interest: carpentry, building and gardening.

"I can't believe it."

"He's probably just what the doctor ordered," Fr Tim quipped.

"He's a godsend," Danny declared in amazement.

"He's been called worse. You're on then?" Fr Tim asked.

"Well, of course I'm on! Wouldn't I be a bloody fool not to be?" Danny gasped, hardly able to take it in.

"Any move on the ownership problem?" Fr Tim asked.

In answer Danny handed him Rory's letter. He read it slowly, nodding his head, and then asked, "Can I take this with me?"

"You can, of course," Danny told him in surprise, although after the last few minutes he felt as if he was gone beyond being surprised. From his experience of training sessions, he knew that Fr Brady moved fast, but tonight he was passing himself out.

The following morning as Danny let out the cows after milking, Fr Brady's car whipped into the yard, and as he unfolded his long legs from beneath the steering wheel, a much smaller man with a thatch of greying hair jumped out of the passenger seat. Danny felt a jolt of surprise. He was not quite sure what he had expected Fr Brady's father to look like, but certainly nothing like this youthful, solidly built man who strode forward and caught his hand in a warm, firm grasp and announced, "I'm Bill Brady."

"Thanks for coming, Mr Brady," Danny stammered in confusion.

"Forget the Mr," he was told with a friendly smile.

"Nothing like the geriatric you were expecting?" Fr Brady grinned in amusement at Danny.

"Well, no," Danny admitted wryly.

"Dad, I think that Danny was expecting a much more senior citizen," he told his father.

"Well, that's probably on the way, but hopefully this job will postpone it for another while," he said with enthusiasm, rubbing his hands together in anticipation. Almost like a magnet, his eyes were drawn to the arch. "Oh boy," he breathed, "look at that for workmanship."

"Would you like to see the house?" Danny asked, sensing his enthusiasm to size up the whole situation.

"Lead me to it," Bill Brady instructed.

Danny led them under the arch and through the tunnel that he had created last night. When they reached the front door, Bill Brady stood back silently appraising it and then ran his fingers lovingly along its surface and outline.

"We don't make doors or entrances like this any more," he breathed. Turning to Danny with a face full of admiration, he declared, "Young fellow, your grandmother's people could certainly build a house."

Danny felt a glow of appreciation for this warm exuberant man. This was the kind of father to be proud of and love. For no reason that he could understand, Danny felt tears in his eyes. The older man put his arm around him and hugged him.

"Young Danny," he told him, "you and I are going to do wonders here. Tim, you go about your business now and, Danny, you look after your farm jobs. I need a few hours here to get the feel of things and form a plan of campaign."

CHAPTER TEN

AT FIRST JACK thought that he was imagining it when he saw movement on the roof of Furze Hill. He was walking down to Mossgrove, his eye wandering along the valley. As his gaze rose to the distant hills, a sudden movement on the roof caught his eye. He was so familiar with every inch of the landscape that anything different struck him immediately. That someone was on the roof of Furze Hill brought him to a standstill. He had no clear view as the roof was partly submerged in trees, but some had not yet leafed, so through bare branches he could see a figure move carefully along. He was too far away for recognition but knew from the outline that it was not Danny Conway. Who on earth could it be? Then, as he watched, two other men came across the roof. They were carrying tools and began to remove the sheeting and slide it down off the roof. The other man, the one he had noticed first, had some kind of a pulley system bringing up what must be slates on to the roof. He was carrying them slowly along and carefully placing them beside the stripped section. Then he began to reroof.

Jack could see that these men knew exactly what they were doing; they had the look of men at home on rooftops. Where on earth did they come from? *By God,* he thought, *miracles do happen, and Molly Barry is getting her roof back on!* He stood watching them, impressed by the methodical way they were working. It was only when Bran came panting up the boreen and began to lick his hand that he realised he had been standing there watching for a long time and was running behind schedule.

"Good boy, Bran," he praised, patting the dog's head. "What the neighbours are doing does not bother you. Your job is to get the cows in for milking."

He turned in the next gap where the cows were lying in a cluster at the bottom of the field. Bran ran ahead, his paws spattering dew and creating a green path through the silver field. When the cows saw him, they began to lever themselves up, leaving flattened nests in the high grass. Bran circled around them, making sure that they all understood that milking time had come and that there was nowhere to go only out the gap. But that did not hurry them as they slowly came on to all fours and calmly ambled across the field. Long necks craned over big bellies as the entire bawn gently nudged or forced each other through the gap, and then they stretched out into an orderly row down the boreen. Jack smiled to see Mother Legs lead the bawn as usual. She was a long-legged, bawny cow who had great difficulty calving but was a good milker. They had had her for years, and now she had a daughter and granddaughter in the herd, both of them close behind her in the row. The Legs were speedy movers, but then they were not weighed down with large udders of milk like Snow White, who was trailing at the rear. Snow White was a strange name for a red cow, but she had been a pet calf of Nora's, who had named her after her favourite fairy story at the time.

He had two of his cows milked before Peter arrived silently and sat under Snow White across the stone channel from him. They each had their own quota of cows and without discussion went straight to their own. Peter was not a morning person, so there was no salutation, and it would take him a while to make any attempt at conversation. Jack understood this and waited for him to thaw out. Shiner, however, when he arrived a few minutes afterwards, had no such considerations and, full of exuberance, started singing:

"Oh what a beautiful morning,

Oh what a beautiful day."

"Shut up," Peter growled.

"Oh boys, you're a right pain in the arse in the morning," Shiner told him.

"Did any of you notice anything strange across the river this morning?" Jack wanted to know.

"Across the river?" Shiner asked in a puzzled voice.

"Conways', stupid," Peter snapped.

"Well, there's no way you'd notice anything anyway," Shiner told him good humouredly. "You can hardly find your way out here in the morning."

"Shiner, would you ever piss off," Peter said petulantly. "Jack, how could you be watching what's going on across the river at this hour of the morning?"

"Because it was extraordinary," Jack declared and was rewarded when Peter stopped milking and Shiner, who had been heading back the stall to his own cows, stopped beside him and demanded, "Like what?"

"There are men on the roof of Furze Hill," Jack told them.

His announcement had the desired effect, and they both stared at him.

"Jack, are you sure that you are not losing it?" Shiner demanded. "Seeing little men is the first sign."

"Shiner, would you ever cop on! If Jack says that there are men on top of Conways', then there are men on top of Conways'," Peter asserted.

"In other words, Jack, you can't be wrong; you're infallible," Shiner grinned at him.

"Would the two of you ever stop?" Jack protested. "Are ye not amazed as I am that there are men on the roof of Furze Hill?"

"But what the hell are they doing up there?" Shiner wondered.

"Fishing," Peter said sarcastically.

"They're reroofing it," he told them.

"Holy God," Shiner breathed. "How did this get going?"

"No idea. Didn't Danny say anything?" he asked.

"I wasn't over there with a bit because my mother has me building a bloody hen house every evening. But something must have happened to change things."

"Extraordinary," Jack declared.

When they went in for their breakfast after milking, he knew that Shiner would not bring up the subject of Furze Hill, but he was not surprised when Peter looked at Martha and said, "They're roofing Conways' place."

If he was expecting a reaction he got it.

"You mean that old house that's been buried for years?" she

demanded in an amazed voice. "In God's name, what would they be doing that for and all the rest of the place falling down around them?"

"Well, maybe that's only the beginning," Peter said evenly.

"And where's the money going to come from?" she demanded. "Sure, the Conways haven't a brown penny and no way of acquiring it either."

"Well, this morning there are three men on the roof of Furze Hill, whoever is paying," Jack put in.

"So it's Furze Hill now, is it?" Martha said disdainfully. "Are we supposed to think that changing the name is supposed to put a better face on things?"

"Well, it was always Furze Hill in the Barrys' time," Jack told her.

"That was a long time ago before they got mixed up with the Conways," Martha said dismissively, "and since then it's been downhill all the way. I don't think that there is any way back up that slippery slope."

"Stranger things have happened," Jack said quietly, "and I think that Danny Conway could be the one to turn things around."

"I doubt it very much," Martha asserted.

"Well, that's his plan," Jack told her.

"Well, that's his business, and we're not going to get mixed up in it," she said firmly, eyeing Shiner who was studiously ignoring her. "We were long enough tangled up with that crowd, and no good ever came of it."

"Different man in charge over there now," Jack said.

"He's not in charge. Aren't they're all stuck into it?" Martha asserted.

"Well, that could be sorted out," Jack told her.

"Not that easy," Martha asserted. "Not everyone gets things handed to them on a plate."

He could see Peter getting ready to rise to the bait, so he interjected quickly, "Anyway, if it does get sorted out, I think that it will be a different place with Danny in charge. The grandmother had a big influence on him."

"Don't be too sure," she cautioned. "It will take longer than that to dilute the bad blood of the Conways."

"Oh, for God's sake," Peter protested, "you are the one who is always preaching that it's what you are that counts, not what you came from, and now you're singing a different song when it suits you. It's either this or that."

"Well, the Conways are neither this nor that," Martha told him decisively. "They're a mongrel breed."

"Jesus," Peter snapped angrily, pushing back his chair, "I'm getting out of here."

When he was gone there was an uneasy silence, and Shiner got up quietly and slipped out after him. As the door closed behind him, Martha turned angrily to Jack and demanded, "Did you know that our brave Peter spent half the night dancing with that foxy Conway one at that youth club dance?"

"How do you know that?" Jack stammered in surprise, because Martha never took the slightest interest in local gossip.

"I know because this is a small, newsy little hole where people love to tell you things that they hope will annoy you."

"Well, if they do I wouldn't mention one word about it to Peter, because these things blossom in opposition, and from what I hear Rosie Nolan has her eye on Peter, and you don't back Rosie off too easily. So let it with her and she might sort things out for us."

"Is that right?" Martha said her face brightening. "Well, anyone is better than one of the Conways."

Thanks be to God, Jack prayed silently, *that she must not have heard about Nora dancing with Danny or there would be blue murder.* Then before he could think of something to change the subject, Martha looked at him and said, "Jack, I know that we have had our differences over the years, and you are more Phelan than I will ever be, or want to be either, it might surprise you to know. Mossgrove to me is just a farm, though I know that you think it's the Garden of Eden. But the place is in good hands now, and to be honest, when I'm not in charge I don't get the same satisfaction out of it. So I'm looking outside of Mossgrove, and I have a project in mind. This little one-horse village is ready to have its boundaries pushed out. So I'm just letting you know that there are changes coming up."

"Thanks for telling me," Jack said quietly.

So Kate was right and Martha was on the move! He wondered if it was the school that she had in mind, but he knew that even if he asked he would not be told, so he changed the conversation. After a few minutes he left the kitchen and went out into the yard.

He breathed a sigh of relief to be back out in the fresh air. He should be used to Peter and his mother having running battles across the table and Shiner and himself getting caught in the crossfire. This morning, however, it was only a minor squabble and of no great consequence. Now he looked around the yard with pride. He had helped to build many of the fine stone houses, and it gave him great satisfaction that the yearly tradition of painting the old timber doors a dark red had never varied. He had had it drilled into him by the old man that constant maintenance was one of the keys to good farming, and he had passed that creed on to Peter. Peter was smart and not afraid of hard work, but he also had Martha's odd streak in him, which was probably why they clashed so often. If she had other interests, the conflict would probably ease off, but they would miss her around the yard where she looked after the fowl and the calves and kept everything in great order. Then maybe it was time for himself to slow down a bit and come in from the fields and he could do the yard work. It was usually the women who did the yard because the work was lighter and they were better with the young animals, but he smiled to himself as he decided that this role would probably suit him better now, especially when Peter was doing so much work with the tractor out the fields. Inside around the house would be a different story, because Martha was a good cook and housekeeper and the place was immaculate. But then maybe Ellen Shine, Shiner's mother, could fall in there. Shiner was for ever saying that with all of them gone except himself she found time on her hands, and, more importantly, she was one of the few neighbouring women that Martha really liked. She maintained that Ellen kept her mouth shut and minded her own business.

"Well now, Jack," he told himself, "you've it all sorted out, even though you don't have a bull's notion what's going to happen."

He did not notice that he had spoken aloud until Shiner, who was taking fresh straw across the yard to the calves, said good humouredly, "If I were you, Jack, I'd be getting worried about myself – men on the roof and talking to myself."

143

"Well, they were on the roof," he protested indignantly.

"Yerra, Jack, you know I'm only doing the fool. You're as near to losing your marbles now as I am to growing wings and flying," Shiner told him.

"Are they still up there?" Jack asked.

"They are," Shiner said. "I went over to the haggard a few minutes ago just to have a good look across the river, and those boys on the roof know what they are at, wherever they came from."

"I'm going to walk over there after the supper to see what's going on," Jack told him.

After supper, instead of heading up the boreen, he turned in the gate leading down to the river. It was a grand time of evening to be taking a stroll down through the fields. As he walked along by the ditch, rabbits scurried in all directions, and even though they were a scourge in the cornfields, their capers still brought a smile to his face. When he was into the Horses' Field, the horses looked in his direction but were not sufficiently curious to come over to him. He walked on through the next field and climbed over the ditch into the Clover Meadow. Suddenly a hare reared up below him and was gone in a flash of grey and gold. Constantly on high alert for the first sign of human intrusion, he raced like lightening on his long, strong legs. The crows were heading home to the big tree in the haggard. Out here all were settling down for the night, but when he saw a fox he knew that this boy had other things on his mind and was about to begin his nightly prowl. The fox, however, was not unduly perturbed by his sudden appearance and strolled slowly into the bushes.

"You're a beautiful boy," Jack told him, admiring his

gorgeous amber tail; but then, remembering the dead hens last year when he forgot to close the hen house, he added, "But you are also a right bastard."

Then he smiled to himself and thought, *Sure, they all have to survive one way or another. If the bloody fox just took one hen and had her for his supper, but the red divil killed anything that moved when he got into the hen house.* Just in front of him a cock pheasant darted out of the bushes and rose in flight, and Jack breathed a sigh of relief that he had escaped the fox. He was so close that Jack could see the golden red of his magnificent wings as he flew over the field seeking a sanctuary. All around him the ditches drooped with whitethorn, and he stopped to breathe in the wonderful smells.

God, he thought, *May is a great month. Everything coming alive.* As he stood there, the voice of the corncrake from the grove below Mossgrove echoed down to him. He could never be sure if the sound of the corncrake was soothing or grating, but it had a certain haunting rhythm. As a child it had been the background music that had put him to sleep at night. He climbed over the ditch, and now he was into the two fields that had caused all the trouble between the Conways and the Phelans. *Strange*, he thought, *the bother we can create over land or money, and then we have to leave it behind, but the bad feelings fester on.* Hopefully now, with Danny at one side of the river and Peter at the other, it would all be finally put to bed. All the trouble had affected the Conways more than the Phelans. When Danny had found the key, he would tell him the full story, but he would tell Kate first.

By now he could hear the sound of the river, and the grass was giving way to rushes. He knew exactly where the boggy patches were and circled around them. When he reached the river bank, he was glad to see that the water was swirling well clear of the top of the stepping stones. These stepping stones had survived all the trauma between the two families. They were the one link that had never been eroded.

As he climbed Danny's high field, he was glad to see the fine even texture of brown earth stretched out in front of him. He had watched from across the valley as Danny had ploughed and harrowed and had been impressed by the thoroughness of the young fellow. Now the first sheen of green was showing as the young corn sprouted. With God's help, he should have a great crop. *There is no doubt,* he thought, *but farming makes you very aware of your dependence on God and nature,* and he sometimes wondered if there was any dividing line between them. When he came into the yard, Danny was stacking his buckets after feeding the calves.

"God bless you, Danny," he called. "My curiosity brought me over to see the great work that's going on."

"Aren't I delighted to see you," Danny told him as he came across the yard. "Come on through and see the progress."

As they went through the arch, Jack looked at it with admiration. It was a fine, sturdy construction and had been very carefully cleaned down.

"That looks good," he said, nodding in appreciation, and was equally impressed to see that a wide path had been cleared to the front of the house and all around it. Now you could see the fine doorway with the limestone pillars at both sides.

"By gor, there is a touch of ould dacency about that," he commented, and then seeing the neatly stacked galvanised iron at the corner he made a beeline for it.

"It's good enough to resheet the barn, I'd say." Danny followed him answering his unasked question. "At least that's what Bill Brady thinks anyway."

"Bill Brady?" Jack questioned.

"Yeah," Danny said in surprise, "Fr Brady's father. 'Tis he's doing it. I thought you'd know."

"Well, sure, he's the boy for the job," Jack exclaimed in delight. "He has mighty experience after the buildings in England. Shiner's father worked with him there and thought that the sun shone off him. No, I didn't know, but I was bursting with curiosity when I saw men on the roof this morning."

"It was all Fr Brady's idea. Then his father organised the whole thing and contacted two of his old workmates. They arrive with him in the morning in his red van with their flasks and sandwiches and look after themselves, and we don't put in or out in each other."

"Perfect arrangement," Jack declared, clapping his hands. "I heard Kate say a while back that Fr Tim felt that his father needed more to do, and this is just it."

"But, Jack, you know I can't pay them, and I feel bad about that. And I'm sure that Bill has bought things like nails and washers, but he brushes it all off and doesn't tell me half of what he is doing," Danny confessed shamefacedly.

"Now, Danny lad," Jack comforted, putting his arm around his shoulder, "we can't have givers without receivers, and sometimes it's good to be able to receive graciously."

"God," Danny assured him, "I'm more than grateful. Sure, they're life-savers for me!"

"Well, it's suiting everyone, so where's the problem?" Jack asked him, clapping him on the back.

Just then they heard singing in the yard and Shiner appeared in the archway.

"Jack, are you hearing confessions as well?" he grinned, and then looking around whistled in appreciation. "Oh boys, oh boys, but there has been some clearing done around here. Danny, did you get in the army?"

"Just three good men who knew what they were at," Jack told him. "Better than any army."

"But who the hell?" Shiner demanded.

"Bill Brady, Fr Brady's father, and his buddies," said Danny.

"Bill Brady! My father worked for him years ago and thought he was top of the range," Shiner smiled. "By God, Conway boy, you're haunted."

As they walked around the house with Danny leading the way, Jack smiled at the proud possessive way he ran caressing fingers along the wall. Danny was really blossoming with the restoration of this old house, and it was good to see it.

"Bill says that we'll leave the coverings over the windows until the roof is done," he told them.

"That makes sense," Jack agreed.

When they reached the back door, Shiner looked at it in surprise.

"Didn't you get in yet?" he demanded.

"No key," Danny answered.

"But where the hell would you find a key after all these years?" Shiner asked in surprise. "Surely you can get in some other way."

"No," Danny told him. "Jack says that there must be a key and that Nana Molly would have left it in safe keeping and that it's only proper to walk in the front door, not break in like hoodlums."

"That's right," Jack said.

"Well, that doesn't surprise me one bit coming from you, Jack, but what happens if the key never turns up?" Shiner demanded.

"It will," Jack told him confidently.

"Blind faith," Shiner pronounced.

"Or perfect trust," Jack smiled.

He knew that the key of Furze Hill would have meant a lot to Molly Barry and that she would have definitely put it into safe keeping. Sooner or later he felt sure that it was bound to turn up.

Now they returned to the front of the house and stood looking at the overgrowth that entirely cut off the view of the entrance gate and the road beyond. It seemed an impenetrable wall.

"Big job clearing that," Shiner said grimly.

"You are lucky that you were not tackling it, because Fr Brady had the idea of bringing in the Kilmeens on a work night. . ." Danny began.

"Holy shit, sure, some of them would be pure useless and wouldn't know where to start."

"Well, Bill Brady felt that too and decided that he would do a better job even though it might take a bit longer," Danny said.

"Fr Brady, God bless him, has a heart that sometimes runs away with his head," Jack smiled, and then stepping back looked up at the roof. "I wonder how much they have covered up there?" he said, and looking around he saw the long ladders stowed away against the wall.

"Come on, lads," he told them, "get these ladders up and I'll have a look around up there."

"Jack, that's a mighty high perch for an ould fellow," Shiner told him, but as Jack began to rise the ladder he went to help. Jack climbed the ladder, years of experience having taught him to mount slowly, and when he reached the top he peered across the expanse of roof, delighted at the smooth clean job that met his eye.

"These boys certainly know how to do a good job," he called down, and then without warning it happened. The roof spun around in front of him and mist rolled in front of his eyes as his hands went numb. But he held on grimly, waiting for it to pass as it had many times before, and sure enough the fog cleared and the roof settled down and the feeling came back into his hands. *Up here is a bad place for a dizzy head*, he decided and began to back down gingerly step by step.

"Are you all right?" Shiner's voice sounded worried, and Jack did not answer until he was safely on solid ground.

"Grand, lads," he told them in a relieved voice.

"Well, you don't look too grand," Shiner declared, peering closely at him.

"God bless you, Shiner," Jack told him, "but you're full of tact."

"I think that we should all go across to the house and have a cup of tea," Danny intervened.

"Have you something to have with it?" Shiner demanded.

"Shiner, people don't go visiting the neighbours because they're hungry," Jack said indignantly.

"Well, you wouldn't want to be hungry when you visit this fella," Shiner told him, and Jack was glad to see Danny smile in amusement. These two understood each other very well.

"We've apple cake," Danny announced.

"Who came?" Shiner demanded.

"Agnes Lehane came yesterday," Danny told him.

"Conway boy, you wouldn't do at all only for the neighbours," Shiner proclaimed.

"Don't I know," Danny agreed heartily.

As they walked across the yard, Jack felt the strength come back into his legs, but he was glad to reach the kitchen and sit down in the wobbly chair. Shiner piled sticks and turf on the fire and had the kettle steaming in a short time. Danny laid the cups and saucers on the table and cut up the apple tart and doled out three pieces.

"Are we on rations?" Shiner asked in an amused voice.

"Would you ever shut up," Jack told him in exasperation.

"Yerra, Jack, we must keep this lad in line, because when he gets into this grand house, he might start spitting down on us," Shiner told him.

When they had finished the tea, the two lads wanted to accompany him down to the river, but he refused point blank, and when they persisted he told them in exasperation, "Don't be trying to make an invalid out of me," and headed out the door on his own.

As he walked down the high field, the moon came up behind Mossgrove and lit up the whole valley. He looked across at his beloved place and decided that he had never before seen it look so peaceful. When he reached the river, he walked carefully across the stepping stones and on through the two troublesome fields, as he had always thought of them. Then he was across the ditch into Clover Meadow, and it was there that the pain came back. He felt it gripping his chest and knew that this time it was not going to go away. Thank God he had written that letter to Kate. He lay down on the long grass, and between the waves of pain came the knowledge that he was going to die. Now at last he would meet Nellie and Ned again. Then the moon came from behind the trees and filled the whole meadow with light.

CHAPTER ELEVEN

WHEN PETER AND Shiner arrived at the stalls and there was no Jack and no cows, they were instantly alarmed. Shiner, with the memory of the previous night still fresh in his mind, was galvanised into action.

"Run in and tell them inside and I'll go up to the cottage," he yelled. As he ran he called back, "Send someone down to the river, because he came up there late last night."

Sensing that Shiner knew more than he had time to explain, Peter ran into the kitchen where Nora was getting ready to go to school. When she saw his face she froze.

"What's wrong?" she demanded in a frightened voice.

"Something's happened. Jack, he's not down," he gasped. "Norry, run down to the river, because he came up that way last night, and I'll go up to see if he's above with the cows. I'll send Mom up the other way in case he's with the cow that was going to calve."

Peter's panic shot her into action, and with her heart

thumping and her mouth dry with fright, she ran up past the stalls and along the path over to the gate leading down to the river. *Oh dear God*, she prayed, *don't let anything happen to Jack. I can't bear it if anything happens to Jack. Nothing can happen to Jack. Oh please, please, God, let nothing be wrong with Jack.* She ran down through the Horses' Field, and they galloped off in fright at her sudden appearance, but she kept running. She was over the ditch and down the next field, and then through the gap into Clover Meadow. Bran and Toby were down there, and when Bran saw her he came loping across the high grass, but Toby stayed below barking and running around in circles.

"Oh Bran, Bran," she gasped as they ran together towards Toby, "is Jack all right?" Jack had to be down there because the two dogs would not be here otherwise. She had to get to him and ran faster but dreaded arriving. Coming closer she could hear Toby whining as he circled a sunken patch in the high grass. Then she could see the toes of Jack's boots. *Maybe he is only asleep*, she thought desperately. *Maybe he was down the fields and felt tired and is just resting.* She gasped with lack of breath and terror. Then she was looking down at him. The frozen realisation that he was dead struck her with blinding force. She felt her head go light and thought that she was going to faint. Her heart was thumping so hard that she could hardly breathe. She fell on her knees and put her arms around him. His cold face sent shivers of horror through her.

"Oh, Jack, Jack," she sobbed, "you can't be dead . . . you can't be gone like Dad."

She rubbed his face and hands as if she could rub life back into him, and Toby ran between the two of them, licking their faces and whimpering in distress. How could Jack be dead when last night at the supper he had been full of fun and laughing? But then it had been like that with Dad too . . . now the two of them were gone . . . but when it happened to Dad, Jack was here . . . Jack was always here . . . but now it had happened to Jack . . . why did it have to happen to Jack? Just as he was leaving last night he had whispered to her that he was going over to see Furze Hill . . . was he coming home from there when it happened? . . . had he been here all night? Oh God, was he out here all night? . . . while she was up late above in the parlour studying, poor Jack was out here dying . . . *Oh why didn't I know? . . . I could have come down.* But it couldn't be true, he couldn't be dead . . . he just couldn't be dead . . . no . . . no . . . no.

She heard screaming, and it was only when she felt Peter's arms around her and heard his soothing "Easy, Norry; easy, Norry" that she knew that she was screaming.

"Jack can't be dead, Peter," she yelled, thumping him with her fists. "Jack can't die like Dad . . . he can't, he can't."

Then Shiner and Danny were there just staring at Jack with stunned faces, and Shiner began to cry. She reached over and put her arms around him and he sobbed.

"We shouldn't have let him go home alone last night. Jesus, we shouldn't have listened to him."

She didn't know what he was talking about. Nothing made sense. The four of them knelt around Jack in stupefied silence, broken by sobs and the whining of Toby.

Martha arrived and, kneeling at his head, gently closed his eyes and folded his arms across his chest. She put her hand in his waistcoat pocket and brought out his rosary beads and placed them around his fingers.

"We'll say the rosary," she said quietly. "He was a rosary man."

And there in the quiet meadow to the sound of the birds singing and the cock pheasant crowing in the headland, they said the rosary around Jack. Slowly the sobbing eased, and even Nora felt able to say her decade as she had said it with him every night since she was a child in the kitchen in Mossgrove.

When the rosary was over, Martha said quietly, "We will say the act of contrition for him now, not that he needs it because he is gone straight to heaven, but it is what he would do himself if he was here." As they prayed even the dogs were quiet. For a little while they knelt in silence and Nora thought, *I will always remember the pain and beauty of this terrible morning*, and words that she had read in one of Uncle Mark's books floated into her mind: "Where there is sorrow, there is sacred ground."

Then quietly and firmly her mother took charge. Nora marvelled that she could think straight; her own thinking was crippled, and a hard rock of pain was lodged in her gut.

"Peter, will you go into the village and tell Kate, and she will bring Fr Brady and Dr Robert with her. And call to the Nolans and Sarah as well. Maybe if you called to Sarah on the way in, she might go with you to be there to tell Kate."

As Peter headed up the field, Nora looked after him with pity that he had to tell Kate. Kate loved Jack just as much as herself and Peter. Her mother's voice was continuing: "Davey and Danny, will you go up to the old turf house, and there is a little door in there. Bring it down and we will carry Jack up on it later." As the two lads went up the field, her mother came over and, kneeling down beside her, she wrapped her arms around her.

"Norry, he loved you more than if you were his own," and silent tears ran down her mother's face. She had never seen her mother cry. They cried together, Martha quietly while wrenching sobs tore through Nora.

"I'm a terrible crier," she said tremulously. "It erupts up from the bottom of my belly."

"You loved him with every fibre of your being, and now every fibre of your being is erupting," her mother told her. "Would you mind being here on your own, because I might go up and get the parlour ready for the wake."

"No," she said, "I'd kind of like to be on my own with him."

"I thought you might," her mother smiled gently, nodding her head. "Jack was always there for you, and you would probably like to be here with him now. This time together will be blessed time for you."

When her mother was gone, she moved closer to Jack and put her hand on his cold one. She ran her fingers over his rosary beads. He had the same rosary beads for as far back as she could remember. Nana Nellie had brought one each to Dad and himself from Knock years ago, and Dad's one had been in his hands the day of his wake. She could still remember the little piece of string that he had used to repair it hanging between his fingers that terrible day. Dad's had been brown and Jack's was black. Jack's had fared better and was still in "perfect working order", as he used to say, and he had loved that rosary beads. Now, like Dad, it would be around his fingers for his wake.

She looked at his kind face and thought of all the times that he had comforted her and listened to her problems, and even if he had no solution, she always felt better after telling him her troubles. To her as a child he had been the grandfather she never had, but when Dad had died he had become her father. She had always known that he loved her unquestioningly and that to him she was perfect, and maybe it was because she was so like Nana Nellie, but it was for herself too. No one might ever again love her as dearly as Jack. She leaned over and fixed his tweed cap properly on his head and her tears poured over his face. Then she thought of the words of a poem that he had taught her a long time ago as they had looked over the ditch at one of Nolan's fields of barley:

> There's music in my heart all day,
> I hear it late and early.
> It comes from fields far far away.
> It's the wind that shakes the barley.

This would be the last time that she would ever sit with him, and she did not want it to end. Then suddenly she heard a rustle in the grass at the other side of Jack, and she looked up in amazement to see a russet hare on his haunches looking at her. He did not move for a few seconds and then in a flash of golden brown was gone. *Did I imagine that?* she wondered. But it would not have surprised Jack. He had often talked of the mystic world of the hare. *Now*, she thought, *Jack knows everything about everything.*

Bran and Toby arrived with lolling tongues, and Nora saw Kate coming across the field. She ran towards her and they clung to each other in raw grief.

"I can't believe it," Nora whispered between her sobs.

"This shock would blow the head off you," Kate said, and taking her hand they walked back to Jack. The dogs were there before them, nuzzling around him, and Nora wondered how much they understood. Toby especially had never known any other master. Kate knelt and sobbed and then quietly talked to Jack.

"You would have wanted it no other way, my darling, but to die out here in your beloved fields. This was your heaven on earth, and now you are gone into the big mystery, as you called it. You always wanted the old ticker to give up before you started to rust away like an old mowing machine in a dyke. You have your wish, and I wouldn't take it from you, but we are going to miss you . . . miss you . . . miss you," Kate cried in great racking sobs, and Nora just stood helplessly watching her. She knew that there was nothing that anyone could do or say to make this easy. An amputation was taking place; they were letting go of Jack who had been part of them for so, so long. Jack and herself had talked of death many times, especially when they were talking about Dad, and she could hear him now.

"Nora girleen, to grieve is the most natural thing in the world. Death is a pulling up of roots. It rocks our foundations because loving roots are intertwined. All this religion thing about praying and God comforting you is grand when it's not yourself that's bruised and broken. Nothing, girlie, helps only time and nature and the kindness of others who share your sorrow. When your father died, the animals and the fields helped me. Grieving is natural, and we need God's natural world to heal us."

She looked around and for the first time she fully understood why this was called Clover Meadow. Jack was in a bed of wild clover, and all around him the bees and butterflies were fluttering on the tall grasses and wild flowers. She wanted to talk to Jack about it. She wanted Jack here with her to talk her through this terrible thing. Jack had always been here. Whenever anything went wrong, Jack was always here . . . Jack should be here . . . and he was . . . only he wasn't.

The dogs ran off again to meet Danny and Shiner as they came bearing the door between them. She wondered where Peter was and then remembered that he had gone to the village to tell Kate, but why was Kate here on her own?

"Aunty Kate, where's Peter?" she asked in confusion.

"He's gone to the village for Fr Tim and Dr Robert and to tell Sarah and the Nolans. I met him at the cottage. I had called in to see Jack on my way home from a call, but I knew by the cottage that there was something wrong because he had not been home."

"Oh," Nora said dully, "so poor Jack had been here all night."

The boys laid the door on the ground by Jack and waited for Kate to tell them what to do.

"We'll wait for Fr Tim and Dr Robert. I think that Jack would like to take leave of his fields with a little ceremony," she told them, looking across the meadow. "They're coming."

Dr Robert put his arms around Kate and silently hugged her and then opened his arms to Nora, who sobbed as he rocked her back and forth and gently rubbed her head. Then Fr Tim said quietly, "Now we'll anoint this saint of a man to help him on his journey." He put the purple stole around his neck, knelt beside Jack and slipped the holy oils out of his pocket. As he anointed him he prayed:

Proficiscere, anima Christiana, de hoc mundo!
Saints of God, come to his aid!

Come to meet him angels of the Lord.
Go forth upon thy journey, O faithful Christian soul,
Go forth from this world; from your family, your friends,
    your home.
In the name of God the Father who created you and
    gave you life,
In the name of Jesus the Son of Mary who gave his life
    for you,
In the name of the Holy Spirit of God who was poured
    into your heart.
May your home this day be in paradise with the angels
    and saints
And with your own people who have gone before you on
    the great journey.
May you see the face of the living God.
May you have the fullness of life and peace for ever.
May Jesus the gentle shepherd number you among the
    faithful ones
And bring you to the waters of peace.
May you have eternal rest. Amen.

As Nora listened in a daze, she wondered if all of this was
really happening or was she dreaming, but the sight of Peter's
ashen face as he joined the circle around Jack drove home the
terrible reality. Then Peter and Shiner eased Jack on to the
door, and with the two of them at one end and Danny and Fr
Tim at the other, they carried him across the meadow. David's
father put an arm around Kate and herself and they followed
behind. Nobody spoke, but when they came to the stalls the
boys stopped for a few seconds, and Nora felt the pain in her

gut swell up and choke her as she thought of Jack carrying his bucket of milk from the stalls every morning as she passed up to school. If he was not there, she always called into the stalls, "'Bye, Jack," and he'd call back, "'Bye, girlie," and sometimes added, though it was never necessary, "Say hello to Toby." Now Toby was running alongside their makeshift stretcher and every so often looked up at it questioningly. *Poor Toby*, she thought. When they reached the house they went straight up into the parlour where Martha and Sarah had the big black bed with the brass knobs set up. The table and all her books were stowed away, and now the parlour had changed into a wake room. They eased Jack on to the bed and Martha asked, "Who will lay him out?"

"I will," Kate said without hesitation.

"Do you think that's a good idea, Kate?" Fr Tim asked uncertainly.

"I'll help her," Sarah told him, "but first I'll run up to the cottage and bring down Jack's good good suit."

They all knew about Jack's good good suit. He had his good suit for Sunday mass and other events, but his good good suit, as he called it, was for Christmas and weddings and other big occasions. This was an occasion for his good good suit.

As they left the room, Danny said, "I'll do the cows with you, Shiner," and they went out to the yard. The doctor followed them, having told Kate that he would man the dispensary. Martha and Sarah went into the kitchen, and Fr Tim, Peter and Nora sat on the wide doorstep. They sat silently while Toby and Bran lay in front of them with alert ears, waiting for any unexpected movement.

"Wouldn't you wonder how much they know?" she said.

"Toby is never down here. The cottage is his place; he must be all mixed up."

"Like us," Peter said grimly.

"I hate death," she burst out angrily. "Why does it have to happen to Jack just now when we are all so happy?"

"There is no right time for death," Fr Tim said quietly.

"But if you are very old and can't do anything, it would be all right then," she protested.

"Maybe it's easier to go before that starts," Fr Tim told her.

"I wish I was like Toby, not knowing what is going on," she cried plaintively.

"Maybe he does," Peter said. "He had only Jack. Bran had all of us, but Toby was Jack's, and even though he liked us all, Jack was his master."

"It's like Dad all over again, isn't it?" she continued, trying to make sense of things in her head.

"But we're older," Peter said, "and whether that makes it harder or easier I don't know, but when Dad died we had Jack. He always seemed to make everything all right, didn't he?"

"When Jack was there, I always thought that nothing very bad could ever happen to us."

Peter and herself talked and cried for a long time. After a while she noticed that Fr Tim was saying nothing, and she was suddenly irritated by his silence.

"You're used to death," she accused him.

"One never gets used to it," he told her.

"But it's other people's deaths you deal with," she stormed. "No one like Dad or Jack ever died for you."

"My mother died when I was sixteen," he told her quietly.

"Oh, I didn't know," she gulped. "That was awful."

"Awful," he agreed gently. "I thought that we'd never get over it, but there was no other way only to keep staggering on, and eventually we got all right somehow."

"I suppose that's how it was for us after Dad, but only for Jack we would have been worse," Peter said.

"I suppose there is always someone to walk with us," Fr Tim told them, "or maybe sometimes a few people. You will have Kate and . . ."

"Kate will be gutted herself," Peter interrupted.

"That doesn't matter," Fr Tim said. "Sometimes people feeling bad together help each other."

The door behind them opened, and Kate said in a strained voice, "You can come in now. Jack is laid out."

Nora felt her legs go stiff; she didn't want to go in. It wouldn't be Jack in there any more. He would be changed into a corpse. She remembered when she saw Dad laid out. Her eyes were just level with the high white bed, and she could only see up Dad's nose. It was like a black tunnel. Jack had lifted her up and talked about Dad and then taken her out into the calf house. He had given her what Peter called "Jack's cure" and it had burned her throat but for a little while had melted the lump of ice in her belly. Now there was no Jack to make it easier.

She looked at Kate, who had a frozen look on her face. Kate was no longer Kate but a nurse who was somehow apart from them. Then Nana Agnes appeared from somewhere and held out her hand. "Come on, lovey," she said. "We'll go in together."

Nana Agnes was small and comforting with her soft grey hair caught in a knot on top of her head. Nora always found it strange that she was Mom and Uncle Mark's mother because they were so tall and Nana was so tiny. But for a small person Nana was somehow all-encompassing, and now it was she who took charge, and taking Nora and Peter by the hand as if they were small children, she led them to the side of Jack's bed.

"You know something," she whispered, "he looks a bit like he did when we were going to school together. He was a handsome little boy."

Nora had to smile through her tears at the concept of Jack being a handsome little boy, but Nana was right because, unexplainably, he had got younger in death, as if he had gone back down the road to his youth.

"'Tis true," Peter said. "He looks so young. How's that?"

"Sometimes happens," Nana told them, "and, of course, he had no long sickness and died easy."

"I suppose," Peter whispered, "if he was given a choice, this would be it."

"But he wasn't given a choice," Nora protested as the tears ran down her face. "Jack wouldn't have wanted to leave us . . . he wouldn't . . . he wouldn't . . ." and she shook with uncontrollable sobs and suddenly they were all crying.

After a while, when the sound of sobbing abated, Fr Tim suggested quietly, "Will we say the rosary?" They knelt around Jack's bed and all joined in the rosary. Nora buried her face in the starched lace bedspread, and the smell of lavender and mothballs drifted up her nose. She had never particularly liked the rosary, but now it was oddly soothing, and as the monotonous rhythm of the "Hail Mary, Holy Mary" wound around the bed, a strange stillness came into the room.

When they were finished, there was absolute silence, and into it came the sudden barking from outside. Toby was looking for Jack. With that Mom got to her feet and said firmly, "Down to the kitchen everyone and we'll have something to eat."

She already had the table set and went around filling bowls with warm porridge. *How can she expect us to eat that?* Nora thought. Sometimes it was hard to understand Mom. As if reading her thoughts, Mom pronounced, "Jack always said, when you're upset sit down and eat." They gathered around the table, and somehow, even though at first it tasted like sand, Nora forced the porridge down.

Nana Agnes had stayed in the parlour, and when Nora had finished she went back up to her. They sat quietly together in the silent room. Mom had the heavy cream drapes on the windows half drawn, and the four lighted candles around Jack cast soft shadows over the bed. It would be easy to believe that he was just sleeping. Gradually people began to filter in and shake her hand and kiss Nana; they sat around the room and chatted in low voices. They told stories about Jack, and as he lay there in the midst of them, his life's story was retold around him. Nora found it strangely comforting. Jack was still part of them.

Then Rosie came and they went down into the kitchen. Mom put soup in front of them, and Nora wondered how on earth Mom could get round to doing all this, but then she saw that Rosie's mother and Ellen Shine had taken over in the kitchen. People were sitting around eating sandwiches and drinking tea. Some of the men had black glasses of porter and little tumblers of whiskey, and Fr Burke's prissy housekeeper was sipping sherry.

The day wore on slowly. At times Nora thought that she was in a dream world and that all of this could not be happening, but then she looked at Jack in the high bed in his good good suit and it told the real story. Late in the evening all the talking and people began to stifle her, and she slipped out the back door and over to the calf house, where she sank into a pile of straw. Within minutes Bran and Toby found her, and she wrapped her arms around them and, in the semi-darkness, cried quietly. All their lives were changed. She was glad of the warmth and comfort of the dogs as they all curled up together in the straw.

When Nora awoke it was dark, but moonlight was pouring in the open door. As soon as she moved Bran started to lick her face. "Bran, what time is it?" she demanded in confusion as she straightened herself up and dusted the sops of straw from her skirt. Toby rubbed himself against her legs. When she came out, Peter and Shiner were sitting on the calves' trough in the corner of the yard.

"Hello, Sleeping Beauty," Peter said quietly out of the darkness.

"Why didn't you call me?" she demanded. "What time is it?"

"Kate said to let you sleep because there is a long night ahead and you would probably want to stay up."

"Of course," she agreed, stretching her stiff limbs.

She went over and sat with the two lads on the edge of the trough.

In the moonlight the tall trees cast dark shadows across the yard, and when the moon disappeared behind a cloud, the lights from the house sent yellow beams over the low hedge. The yard was a different place tonight.

"It's hard to believe that this is happening," she whispered.

"I feel as if I'm the cause of it," Shiner fretted.

"But why?" she asked in surprise.

"He was over with Danny and Shiner last night and went up the ladder to see the roof. Shiner says that he got some kind of a turn up there but was all right after and insisted on going home alone, even though they wanted to go with him," Peter told her.

"Jack hated being fussed over," she said.

"But last night was different," Shiner said desperately. "It was more serious than we thought."

"Stop it, Shiner," she said sharply. "When Dad died, I spent months blaming myself because I was so wrapped up in going to town to buy him a new pipe for his birthday that I never watched the road with him."

"But you were only a small girl then," Shiner protested.

"Makes no difference, maybe made it worse, because I could understand nothing then."

They sat silently, wrapped in their own thoughts while the two dogs settled themselves down on the yard beside them. The thought of Danny floated into her mind; if Shiner was feeling guilty, he must be more so.

"Where's Danny?" she asked.

"He went over to milk his cows," Shiner said. "I went with him this morning when we had ours done, and he came back to do ours this evening, but he insisted that I stay here, that I was needed here, though I'm not sure that I'm much use here either."

"Shiner," she told him, "it's a comfort to just have you here."

"Thanks, Nor," he said gratefully.

"I'd hate it if Danny was feeling guilty like you," she told him, "because Jack would hate that too."

They stayed for a long time while further down the yard

people went in and out to the wake, but gradually the stream of people thinned out, and eventually there was nobody there but themselves. *We should get up and go in,* she thought, but there was a reluctance in her to go back into the house. Out here, even though the pain was throbbing away inside her rib cage, there was comfort in just sitting here with Peter and Shiner, whom she knew were hurting in the same way. Eventually it was Shiner who made the move.

"As Jack used to say, 'This will never keep white stockings on the Missus'," he said, getting off the edge of the trough. "Come on, you two."

So they went back into the house where a pale-faced Kate was tidying up and Sarah Jones was washing ware.

"You had a little sleep," Kate said with a strained smile.

"I couldn't believe that I fell asleep," she confessed.

"You needed that," Sarah told her.

Nora took a tea towel from the rail over the Aga and started to dry the big stack of ware beside Sarah. She threw a tea towel to Peter, and the two of them dried the cups and saucers and Shiner stowed them away. *It could be a normal day,* she thought, but smiled when she thought that the two boys would never be doing this if it was an ordinary day. It would have amused Jack to see them now.

"What are you smiling at?" Peter asked in surprise.

"I was thinking that Jack would have been amused to see the two of you now," she told them.

"I'm not so sure that you got that right," Shiner told her. "Jack knew that we are domesticated at heart."

"Jack knew a lot of things," she told him, "but he didn't know that."

"Now that's better," Kate said, looking around the kitchen. "We're a bit straightened out anyway."

"Where's Mom?" she asked.

"She's gone for a bit of a lie down," Sarah told her, "and your mother is gone home for a while," she told Shiner.

"Who's above in the parlour?" Nora asked.

"Your grandmother and Uncle Mark and David," Kate told her.

"I'll go up to them," she said.

The night dragged on slowly, and they moved between the parlour and the kitchen, making tea and relighting the candles around Jack. They retold stories of the childhood that Jack had shared with them, and occasionally Nana Agnes shook holy water around the deathbed, and when crying threatened to take over from talking, she led them in the rosary. Finally the grey streaks of dawn filtered into the room, and Nora went out to the front garden. She needed fresh air and reprieve from the presence of death. Over the grove a golden glow was rising and the birds were beginning to twitter. As she watched, the gold turned crimson and the treetops fired red. Slowly the birds' twitter swelled into a crescendo. She remembered Jack's east-facing bedroom windows and how he kept them open to hear the dawn chorus. He loved to watch the sunrise. She wondered where was he now, and was he watching the sunrise?

Late that evening, the house, the garden and the yard filled up with people, and Fr Tim gave out the rosary. Afterwards, everybody filed out of the parlour, the coffin was brought in, and only herself, Peter, Mom, Kate and Nana Agnes remained. It was goodbye time. Memories of Dad were flooding back, and she was eight again and he was being taken away. A stony-faced

Mom stepped forward and put her hand on Jack's. There was absolute silence in the parlour. Nora felt as if something was going to break inside in her. Then Nana Agnes bent forward to kiss Jack on the forehead, and Kate laid her head on his chest and sobbed. Blinded by tears, Peter stumbled forward and grasped Jack's hand, and then there was no one left only herself and she could not move. She felt Nana Agnes arms around her gently edging her forward, and she was seeing Jack's face shimmering though a sea of tears.

"I'll never forget you, Jack," she sobbed, and then she was standing beside Peter looking out the window and remembering the night that Dad was going into the coffin and it was Jack who had been there beside her.

When she turned around the bed was empty, and Shiner, Peter, Uncle Mark and David were carrying the coffin out the door. Kate, Mom, Nana Agnes and herself walked behind it out through the garden and into the yard where the hearse was parked. She knew that people were standing along the way, but blinded by tears she could not see them. Then the coffin was eased into the hearse. Slowly it moved out of the yard, and they followed it up the long boreen. Jack was making his last journey from Mossgrove.

Chapter Twelve

THE MORNING OF Jack's funeral, Kate woke before dawn with a throbbing headache. While she lay in the darkness as David, deep in sleep, breathed evenly beside her, her feet were stiff and she felt like a block of black ice. Since she had seen Jack lying in the field, she had been enfolded in a wave of desolation. She had tried to function normally, but her legs and hands had become wooden and her mind had lost its coordination.

In the grey of the early morning her pain was unbearable, and because she did not want to wake David, she slipped quietly out of bed and went downstairs. She lay on the couch in the warm kitchen and let a wave of unrestrained sobbing wash over her. It was a relief to go with the tide of grief. When it abated she was drained but calmer. The yellow rays of dawn were filtering into the kitchen, and when she opened the back door the garden was full of golden light. As she walked down the path, the light encompassed her, and all around white butterflies rose from the flowers and filled the garden with their delicate fluttering. Jack and herself had shared great days in this place, planning and digging. Now she felt his spirit close to her.

She ran her fingers along the fronds of a tall moist fern and remembered him carefully planting it after digging it off one of the ditches in Mossgrove. He knew that she loved ferns, and one of her fondest memories of childhood was of playing hide-and-seek with Ned under the huge ferns in the glen behind the house. "It's good to have a little bit of the homeplace in your new garden," Jack had told her as he lovingly planted the fern into a shady corner under a young chestnut that he had already transplanted from his own acre. Now as she looked around, she realised that most of her flowers and shrubs had been nurtured from seeds and slips by Jack. He had green fingers and loved to grow from seed, and many of the young trees around her garden he had brought on from tiny seedlings with constant care. "Your garden should surround you with friends," he often told her as he brought in yet another little slip from Sarah or Agnes's garden. Now, as she looked around her, she felt the comfort of all the loving that Jack had given her through this little place. He would always be part of her garden.

She sat on the seat under the beech tree. The early morning sun slanted through the surrounding trees, turning their dew-laden leaves into sparkling halos, and a lone blackbird covered himself in silver spray as he hightailed across the grass. Kate felt that she had never before seen the real beauty of this place. Its tranquility soaked into her distressed mind and a calming peace enveloped her. A phrase that Nora had recalled yesterday came back to her: "Where there is sorrow, there is sacred ground." Because now, even though she was in deep pain, she also sensed she was in a sacred place. *When someone you love dies*, she wondered, *do you go a little bit of the journey with them?* Were Jack and herself now in a new place? Though parted in the physical sense, was there in these early days after death a new spiritual union? Here in her garden, where Jack and herself had worked together with earth and stone creating something beautiful, would there always be part of them here together? She felt his intangible presence all around, enfolding her in a delicate cobweb of kindness which she knew might not last but at least gave her peace for now.

Later in the church, as she knelt between a grim-faced Peter and a silently weeping Nora, her sense of peace prevailed. From where had this blessing come? She had no idea, but was just grateful to Jack that he had come to her rescue and was helping her through this black time. Was he telling her that now she would have to take his place and be the one to help the young ones cope? Was she now to be the comforter of the family? She doubted that she was up to it. As her mind wandered around in questioning circles, she suddenly became aware that while everyone else was now sitting she was still kneeling. Nora was squeezing her fingers, trying to bring her back to reality, and Peter was frowning at her. As she sat down between them, she heard Fr Tim talking about Jack.

"Maybe sometimes we could be accused of waiting until someone dies before we acknowledge how great they are, but in the case of Jack Tobin, I think that we all realised that he was one of the stalwarts of this parish. A hard-working, honest, kind man, who loved this place and all of us. To Jack we were all as good as we could be, and yet he never perceived us to be saints; but he was very tolerant of our weaknesses because he had the biggest, most generous heart in the parish. Everyone in trouble went to Jack, and he helped in the soundest, simplest, most straightforward way he could. Jack saw solutions where some of us saw dead ends, and his approach was all about application to detail and hard work. As he used to say himself, he knew the seed and breed of the whole place, and what he thought you should not know he kept to himself. Jack was an honourable man. He loved and shared the life of the Phelans through four generations and buried five owners of Mossgrove in his lifetime. He was the backbone of their life, and today they mourn him as a grandfather and father figure and loyal, loving friend. And yet his going, though sudden and unexpected, was just as he would have wished it, out in the quietness of his beloved fields where he was totally at home with God and creation. As a man lives, so shall he die, and Jack died exactly as he had lived."

As she walked down the church after the coffin, Kate raised her eyes and looked at the sea of surrounding faces, and many looked back with tear-filled eyes. How many of these people had Jack helped in his lifetime? Often when she came to his cottage late at night, there was a neighbour with him deep in conversation. Now they were all here to pay their last respects to this kindly man who had helped them though hard patches of their lives. She was glad to see that Danny was under the coffin with Peter, Shiner and David. It would mean so much to Danny and probably come as a surprise to many people unaware of Jack's recent effort to help him salvage Molly Barry's homeplace. Jack had been the peacemaker who had seen them through the feuding years with the Conways, and now before he left he had planted the seeds of future peace between Peter and Danny. For Peter to have Danny shouldering Jack's coffin was an amazingly generous gesture brought about, she felt sure, by some indefinable urge that Peter himself might not be able to explain. Jack was the source of that inspiration. *Is it possible,* she wondered, *that Jack gone from us is going to be as influential as Jack with us?* Now he had all the answers, and so far he was making his presence felt even in the formation of his funeral!

But when they arrived in the graveyard and she watched Jack's coffin being lowered into the deep, narrow grave, her newfound peace abandoned her. There was no easy passage through this physical separation, and an overwhelming sense of loss swamped her as Nora and Peter wrapped their arms around her and the three of them clung together. Martha stood blank-faced and remote beside them, while Shiner and Danny wept quietly side by side. Finally the grave was covered, and on the piled earth his old schoolfriends, Agnes and Sarah, laid little bunches of wild flowers. The flowers brought a sense of completion to the burial, and then the neighbours and friends lined up to sympathise. Kate had sometimes questioned the value of this exercise, but when old friends of Jack's or her own appeared in front of her, she found it comforting. Then the crowds ebbed away and only the family and close friends were left.

"Isn't it great that Dada's grave is just beside Jack's?" Nora whispered, her teeth chattering with the cold.

"I always thought that too," Kate told her, "but now it means far more with Jack here beside them all."

"There is only Jack and his mother in that grave," Peter said, trying to steady his voice and get a grip on himself with normal conversation. "Where's Jack's father buried?"

"He is with his own people," Sarah cut in. "That happened

when a husband or wife died young and there was a possibility that the one left might marry again."

"We'd better all get out of this cold or there'll be a few more of us joining the crowd here already," Martha told them impatiently, heading for the gate. They trooped after her in pairs and little groups, with the older people stopping along the way to pray at other graves.

Back at the house, Ellen Shine had the fire lighting in the parlour, and rounds of tea and chat began again. *The prospect of yet another cup of tea is too much for me*, Kate thought, and just then Martha shepherded a few of them out into the back kitchen where she had a row of steaming bowls of soup lined up.

"Thank God," Kate breathed as the warm creamy soup slid down her throat. "I'm burnt up from tea."

"Mom, how did you get round to it?" Nora said gratefully.

"Ellen had it ready, and she slipped it out here before the masses would descend on her," Martha told them.

"I'm so cold," Nora shivered.

"Graveyards are cold places," Kate told her gently, "and death chills you from inside out as well."

"Will we ever get over this?" Nora asked her piteously. "I can't imagine Mossgrove without Jack."

"We'll have to, Norry," Peter broke in determinedly. "If Jack taught us anything, it was that you had to keep going. Jack never gave up. I remember the day after Dad's funeral when we were all in a desperate state, he said to me, 'Come on, Peter lad, down to the river and we'll do a bit of fencing, because there is healing in doing.' And he was right, because we were better to be out in the fields than huddled up in here."

"All I remember of those days was the blur of pain and

feeling that my world had come unstuck," Nora said quietly, "and Jack was the only solid rock in the middle of the terror. Now there is no rock." As she started to cry, Kate put her arms around her and ran her fingers soothingly through her long, soft hair.

"It's not going to be easy," Kate said, "but Jack would have kept the flag flying, as he used to say. In many ways I suppose we have much to be grateful for because he gave us so much of himself, and maybe now we should be able to go it alone."

"I don't want to go it alone," Nora sobbed.

Her crying set them all off, and Martha, coming into the back kitchen, looked at them in disapproval.

"Will you for God's sake pull yourselves together and look after the people out there with Ellen and Sarah?" She marched back into the kitchen with a full teapot.

"I suppose she's right," Kate sighed. "We'd better help."

"She's not," Peter raged, heading for the back door. "She's all about law and order. I don't give a damn about that kind of thing."

"Let him off," Kate advised when Shiner made an attempt to follow him. "He needs time by himself. Some of us need to grieve alone and more of us need people. We all learn the best way for us."

"Well, I have learnt nothing," Nora said quietly.

"Come on, Norry," Shiner said gently, holding out his hand to her, "and we'll walk down along the fields. It will clear your head to get out."

"I can't go down to Clover Meadow where it all happened," she protested.

"No, no," he assured her. "We'll go up along the glen."

"All right," she agreed doubtfully, trailing him out the door.

When they were gone, only a white-faced Danny and Kate remained.

"I'm glad that you were under Jack's coffin," she told him quietly.

"I couldn't believe it when Peter asked me," he said tremulously. "It meant the world to me, as if I was being invited in from the cold. I feel kind of responsible for Jack's death, because when he got that turn over in my place, I should have insisted on coming over with him."

"I feel guilty too, Danny," she confessed, "because I knew that Jack had a dodgy heart, as he called it. I should have insisted on his looking after it. But he did not want to go down that road, and I felt that it was his right to do it his way."

"I can understand how you feel," Danny told her.

"The strange thing about death, Danny," she continued, "it's full of guilt. So over the next few weeks when you feel bad about Jack, just remember that it is part of the aftermath of death. But you have probably discovered that yourself."

"I thought that it was only me on account of how my father died. His death haunts me at times," he confessed.

"As time goes on the guilt will fade, and your perspective on the whole thing will balance out," she assured him. "Jack knew and understood how the whole thing happened."

"Did he tell you?" he asked in surprise.

"No, Danny," she assured him. "Jack would never betray a confidence."

"I have always felt since the night my grandmother died that you knew more about us than we do ourselves," he said ruefully.

"Well, I suppose if you are with families in childbirth and

death, you come very close to their inner core," she told him, "but the strange thing is that your grandmother made me feel that she knew more about the Phelans than we did ourselves. But remember one thing, Danny, that it was Jack's dearest wish that you would restore your grandmother's homeplace, because he felt that he owed that to my grandfather."

"Thanks, Kate," he said gratefully. "I might need that thought to keep me going, that and money."

"Sometimes, Danny, solutions come from the most unexpected corners," she encouraged him, though privately she wondered where on earth the money could come from to restore Furze Hill and to pay off Rory, "but for now why don't you follow Nora and Shiner up the glen?"

All afternoon she moved between neighbours and old friends, discussing Jack and his sudden death until eventually she felt that she had talked herself to a standstill. She saw Mark and Nora cuddled up close together in the window seat of the parlour, and she slipped gratefully in beside them.

"How do you keep going, Aunty Kate?" Nora wanted to know.

"Auto pilot," Kate assured her, "but now I need the sustenance of you two."

"Are you bleeding inside?" Nora asked.

"That's as good a way as any to describe it," Kate told her.

"But how can you behave so normally then?" Nora demanded.

"Maybe because it helps her cope," Mark interjected thoughtfully, his long sensitive face full of concern.

He was such a contrast to everyone else in Kilmeen, with his long hair and blonde beard and clothes that always looked, as

Peter had once put it, as if he was wearing the kitchen curtains. But all the disarray covered an artistic mind that turned out pictures of startling originality. Now Rodney Jackson marketed them all over America. Until Rodney became involved they had more or less considered Mark locally as a bit of an oddity. But nothing converts the public mind like the ability to earn large amounts of money, and now Mark was viewed with awe in Kilmeen. But either way it had never bothered Mark, who had little interest in the human and viewed the natural world as a wonder for his canvas. That he was Martha's brother was a puzzle that Kate had never been able to solve, because Martha was the most practical person you could imagine and Mark did not have a practical bone in his body. But Jack had an explanation.

"He's a throwback," he told Kate. When she had repeated questioningly, "a throwback?" he continued, "Every few generations a family can turn up 'a throwback' who somehow embodies the bloodline of someone long gone. The chances are that back along that family line there was a talent that might not necessarily have been developed, and then down the line it breaks out in a descendent and everyone is amazed. But sometimes the explanation is not lost in the mists of time, as is the case of Danny Conway, who embodies all the bloodline of his grandmother."

She smiled at the memory of Jack's words, and Nora demanded in surprise, "Aunty Kate, what are you smiling at?"

Kate gave them a detailed explanation. When she was finished, Mark chuckled in amusement, "So that explains me; I'm a throwback!"

"And you're a lovely throwback, Uncle Mark," Nora assured him, "and because there is a family connection between you

181

and Rodney Jackson, it probably makes him very proud of his bloodline too."

"Well, he believed in it anyway, that's for sure," Mark said.

"Did you hear from him lately?" Kate asked, curious to know if Mark knew anything more than she did.

"He was supposed to come for Easter as you know, but now he'll be coming in a few weeks' time, probably the end of the month," Mark told her. "He has some big plan up his sleeve that he is quite excited about."

"Like what?" Nora demanded.

"Well, for a hotel in Kilmeen," Mark told them.

"Where?" Nora persisted.

"I think it's the school, because he wants to take all those paintings down, and I'm to prepare new ones for the hotel," Mark told them.

"And where is the school supposed to disappear to?" Nora demanded.

"I've no idea," Mark told her.

"But, Uncle Mark, whose idea was it that we needed a hotel?" Nora wanted to know.

"Your mother's, I think," Mark said mildly.

"My God," Nora gasped. "Peter was right."

"Why?" Kate asked.

"Well, he said that it was Mom's idea. That while she had no notion of marrying Rodney Jackson, she would still use him."

"Dear, dear, but Peter has no false illusions about his mother," Mark said quietly, and then added thoughtfully, "but then I suppose he inherited that trait from her."

"Surely Rodney Jackson would not throw Uncle David out of his school?" Nora protested in dismay.

"I doubt it," Mark said.

"But you're not sure," Nora persisted.

"Well, no, I suppose I'm not," Mark admitted.

"Let's change the subject," Kate intervened. "Today is enough to handle without burdening ourselves with the future."

"Aunty Kate, you sound just like Jack," Nora said sadly.

Kate waited until all the neighbours were gone home and then walked up to Jack's cottage. Toby was waiting at the gate and went ecstatic with delight to see her. She gathered him into her arms and hugged him.

"Darling Toby," she asked him, burying her face in his bristly neck, "what are we going to do with you at all at all? We can't take you away from here after all your years, and anyway you'd find your way back, so you'll have to stay, but we can't leave you here alone."

The sight of the little dog looking at her with such absolute devotion brought a lump to her throat, and suddenly her tears were running down his coat.

"We all depended on Jack," she told Toby as he furiously licked her face and then jumped out of her arms and ran to the door ahead of her. She dreaded opening the door into the silent cold cottage, but to her surprise the fire was lighting. She almost expected to see Jack sitting beside it.

God bless you, Sarah, she thought. *You knew that I'd call.*

She sat by the fire for a long time, thinking of all the times that Jack and herself had shared these evening hours, and gradually a quiet peace came to her. Toby slept contentedly at her feet. Then she became aware of a subtle difference in the sounds of the cottage. The clock over her head was not ticking, and she wondered if Sarah had stopped it, or did it need winding? She got up to wind it and put her hand down into the base of the old clock to find the key. Her fingers touched a roll of paper, and she brought it out with the key. She was holding a little bundle of letters tied with a faded blue ribbon. It was the last thing that she would have expected to find in Jack's clock, and she slipped them back hurriedly, feeling guilty for having taken them out in the first place.

She walked around the cottage. The place without Jack filled her with pain, but still the sense of his past presence comforted her in another way. She opened the door of his bedroom and the smell of his pipe reached out to her. His brand of tobacco gave the room a sweet aromatic whiff. She went over to the window and looked out over his little haggard. All locked up for the night. Sarah had been at work here as well. How Jack loved this room, and when the lads had taken down the dividing wall last year, he was so pleased with his extra eastern-facing window to catch the morning sun. He loved the sky in the early morning and always said that it set the tone for his day. She drifted into his little parlour. He was so proud of this cosy corner where he lit the fire at Christmas. This was his treasure store for all his mother's beautiful cloths. When she opened the tall press beside the fireplace, a lavender scent floated out to her. All the cloths were neatly folded with little bags of his garden lavender hanging off the edges of the shelves. *How well he looked after them*, she thought as she gently slipped her hand along the top of the folded rows. Her hand touched a small flat box, and she drew it out and opened it. It contained more of the same letters tied up with the same blue ribbon, and this time she recognised the handwriting. She put the box back carefully and left the cottage, closing the door quietly behind her.

CHAPTER THIRTEEN

DANNY STOOD INSIDE the gate of Furze Hill and viewed with satisfaction what had been achieved in just a few weeks. Bill Brady had worked wonders! The house was free, standing proud and clear of the strangling growth that had smothered it for years. It now had a tight coat of close-cropped ivy that Bill had trimmed to well below the eaves and around the edges of windows and front door. When Bill had removed the sheeting from the windows, they were both pleasantly surprised to find that the high timber sashes had stood the test of time. But the dark closed shutters on the inside prevented any glimpse of the interior.

As Danny looked up the short driveway, he tried to imagine what the house would look like with all the shutters folded back and the windows and front door thrown open. He longed to see the house breathe again. The front garden and lawn were already taking shape. Gone was the wilderness of years, and now the sun shone down on grass that was turning from brown to green, and newly pruned shrubs and trees stifled for so long were already breaking into new growth. For weeks Bill had cut back and cleared, and every evening Shiner and himself had come and drawn away heaps of greenery. Bill had sorted out what was worth keeping from what was better discarded, and as Danny watched he was thankful that Bill had not allowed Fr Tim to let the Kilmeens loose in the garden. They would have cleared faster, but all the valuable old shrubs and trees of his grandmother's time might have been swept away and gone for ever in a tide of enthusiasm. But Bill's selective pruning was paying dividends, and the garden was recovering fast. The two weeping willows at each side of the driveway fluttered in the breeze and veiled the house from full view of the gate. As the design of the old place unfolded, Bill had nodded his head in appreciation

"Whoever laid this out knew a thing or two about gardening," he told Danny, but Danny felt that Bill himself was bringing out the best of the place. The day that he uncovered an old vegetable garden to the rear, his delight was infectious. Danny could imagine his mother's joy in having her own vegetable plot after years of struggling with his father to maintain a little growing area behind the yard. Invariably the bonhams had rooted it up or the calves broke into it, and sometimes he thought that his father had left the gate open on purpose. Now there could be no such happenings because this area was totally cut off from the farmyard, and he loved the way you had to walk through the arch to get to the yard. It was as if they were two different worlds. Bill was right that the whole place had been originally very well laid out. The now-exposed high stone wall extended from each side of the entrance pillars and surrounded the entire garden and house, back and front. It was easy to see now how his crazy grandfather and father had managed to lock this enclosed world away.

He opened the gate that now swung easily on well-oiled hinges; it had taken Bill hours of grinding and oiling for these simple, elegant gates to work smoothly between the tall stone pillars. Out on the road, he walked along beside the high wall just for the satisfaction of coming back to the gate and looking in at the amazing transformation inside. Jack's words came back to him: "I remember looking in across the garden at a blue door." He had decided then that one day there would be a blue door. But before this could happen, they had first to get in through that door. Occasionally Bill would inquire, "Any news of the key," but as he had now begun work on the barn he felt no pressing need to get the key. To Danny, however, the key had become an obsession that he thought about daily, and a consuming need to get into the house possessed him.

Last night he had a strange dream of the day that his grandmother died. He was a young boy, sitting frightened with the rest of them by the fire. His eyes were glued to the bedroom door behind which Nana Molly was dying. With Nana Molly gone, there would be no one to protect them from his father, who was now pacing around the kitchen in a controlled rage. So he had two things to fear: death and no one between him and his father's temper. In the dream the door opened and Kate Phelan came into the kitchen. In that few seconds that he could see beyond her, Fr Brady was leaning over Nana. Then the dream faded, but when he woke in the morning it came back to him, and since then it kept drifting into his mind.

"You could grow bananas in here it's so sheltered," Bill

188

declared as he came through the arch. "Time for grub, Danny boy." He brought his two flasks and sandwiches to the doorstep where they had their lunch every day. As he poured out the tea, Bill surprised him by asking, "Have you thought any more about the lost key?"

"I have thought about nothing else lately," Danny told him.

"Thought so," Bill smiled. "Your eyes have a longing look when you view those shuttered up windows and locked door."

"Bill," he began slowly, "if you were dying and had something very valuable, to whom would you give it for safe keeping?"

"Now that would depend," Bill began thoughtfully, "on who was around at the time. If I could trust one of my own, I suppose I'd give it to them, but if I couldn't I'd have to settle for whoever was available. Who else was there that night apart from yourselves?" Bill asked.

"Kate Phelan and Fr Tim," he told him.

"And you've asked them?"

"Well, Kate doesn't have it and, sure, Fr Tim knows that I'm looking for it," Danny told him.

"Tim has a head like a bloody sieve," his father declared; "always had."

"But surely he'd never forget something like that?" Danny said in dismay.

"Not making light of your predicament, Danny, but he's forgotten bigger things in his day," Bill told him. "Might be no harm to take him on a little jaunt down memory lane."

Later that evening Danny called on Kate to discuss his predicament, but he was taken aback at how white-faced and tired Kate looked when she opened the door. Jack's death had really taken its toll on her. He felt uneasy to be bringing his problem to her, but she smiled warmly in welcome and was obviously glad to see him, which was reassuring.

"Danny, it's so good to see you," she told him as she led him back the hallway into the kitchen. "You came at a great time because I'm all on my own and just taking a tea tray out into the garden, so you bring the teapot now and I'll get an extra cup."

As he followed her along the garden path, he looked around with interest. Kate pointed out her mother's old roses and the ferns that Jack had dug out of the glen in Mossgrove. In the profusion of growth, he was enclosed in shady woodland with something of interest around every curve of the long winding path. At the very bottom of the garden under the huge beech tree, Kate set the tray on a table and pulled up two chairs.

"I love your garden," he told her appreciatively, "and it must be great to have so much of Mossgrove here."

"That was Jack's idea," she told him, her eyes filling up with tears. "Imagine, I still can't talk about him without crying. But this garden is doing more to help me come to terms with his death than anything else. When I feel real bad, I come out here and get down on my knees and work away for hours, sometimes until it gets dark. David teases me that I will take root out here myself." She smiled tremulously through her tears. "But it's the only thing that helps, that and the likes of you calling."

He was touched by her words and felt a swell of sympathy for Kate, who was obviously going through a terrible time. As she poured the tea, he looked up into the branches of the giant tree.

"Jack used to tell me, pray for the person who planted this tree because they left me a great blessing, and Jack himself left this garden full of his blessings." She pointed out all the slips and plants that Jack had brought from Mossgrove and from the gardens of Agnes and Sarah.

"We'll be able to exchange now as well," he told her, and immediately her face lit up with interest.

"Tell me all about Furze Hill. Bill Brady tells me that it's coming on at a great rate," she said.

"Thanks to Bill," he told her and then filled her in on the details of the transformation.

"It's a bit of a miracle, isn't it, Danny?" she said when he finished.

"Sometimes I am afraid that something will happen to disrupt everything. I have no title and no money, and I feel like a fellow swimming across a lake who can see the shore, but there is always the possibility that he might drown."

"I don't think that Jack will let you drown," she told him with conviction.

"Well, so far I'm floating anyway, thanks mainly to Bill. I don't know how I will ever be able to repay that man for what he is doing for me. He has worked like a Trojan, and apart from the two friends who helped with the roof, he's been all on his own. When I asked him how we were going to pay the two roof men, he told me that they owed him one and were glad to help out. He works all day every day and never seems to get fed up with it."

"Fr Tim says that he is finding the whole thing a huge challenge and that he is a new man since he started on Furze Hill. As you know, he is staying with Fr Tim, and between the two of us, they are not an ideal partnership in that house, because Fr Tim is all over the place and Bill is as tidy as tuppence in a rag. But for Bill it's still better than being at home where he is not very welcome in the new set-up. I wouldn't worry unduly about the money thing, because do you know something Danny? The Bradys are amazing in that money does not figure big in their lives. Fr Tim is just hopeless about money, and Fr Burke despairs of him at times, and I must say that for once I can see what he is complaining about."

"Talking about Fr Tim," Danny began, "he is one of the reasons that I'm here." He went on to fill Kate in with the details of what Bill had told him and his own ideas about the night his grandmother died.

"Could it be possible that she gave Fr Tim the key that night?" he asked hopefully.

"Quite possible," she answered slowly, "because he was with her for a long time. I kept my distance because I'm always very conscious that when people are dying they might want to say things to the priest. So I stood away over by the window and then, I think, went down into the kitchen."

"That's right; I remember it," he agreed eagerly.

"But how could you remember, Danny?" she asked in surprise. "You were only a young fellow."

"I have never forgotten that night and I dreamt of it again last night," he told her, a little embarrassed, because he thought that relating dreams was a bit idiotic.

"How strange," she said thoughtfully, "but apart from that, as Bill says, the whole thing makes sense that she would have given something valuable to Fr Tim or to me, though probably not to me because I am a Phelan."

"But how come he didn't remember it," Danny asked, "that it didn't come back to him when he heard we wanted to get into the house?"

"I wonder, Danny, did he know what he had?" she asked.

"How do you mean?" he demanded, feeling that Kate was trying to justify Fr Brady's forgetfulness.

"I'm not sure," Kate said slowly, "but I have this vague memory of Fr Tim saying something about a packet, but because he was new in the parish at the time he probably did not know me well enough to discuss things with me. And to be honest, Danny, I forgot all about it as well until you brought it up just now."

"But if he got something, what would he have done with it?" Danny persisted.

"Probably put it in the parish safe and forgot all about it," Kate decided.

"Will you ask him about it, Kate, and find out if he did get anything?" Danny asked. "I might be on the wrong track, but I want to explore all possibilities. Apart from anything else, Jack was very anxious that the key would be found, and he was adamant that Nana Molly would have left it in safe keeping, and I can't think of any other safe keeping available to her that night."

The following morning just as he finished feeding the calves, Fr Brady's car shot in the gate, and as he strode across the yard he drew a small packet out of his pocket. Danny felt his heart jump with excitement. Could he possibly have the key?

"Danny, I have no idea what is in this packet. Your grandmother gave it to me on the night that she died, and I put it in the parish safe and it went completely out of my head until Kate rattled my memory," he said apologetically.

"It can only be the key," Danny breathed as he took the little parcel wrapped in stained brown paper and tied with knotted

193

cord. Faded writing scrawled across the packet, but he did not take time to read it as he slipped off the frayed cord and tore away the layers of crumpled paper to reveal a flat cardboard box. Gingerly he lifted the cover, and underneath were layers of old yellow tissue paper. He turned it back to reveal a large rusty key. He felt a wave of relief wash over him. His grandmother had minded this key for years in the hope that one day it would be used again, and when her wish had not been realised in her lifetime, she had wrapped it up carefully, hoping that one day someone, maybe even himself, would come looking for it. He was so glad that he had taken Jack's advice and waited for the key to turn up, because this big solid key was a link back to his Barry ancestors. It was almost as if they were handing on to him the right to come back into the homeplace. When he turned over the brown paper, the shaky writing read "Molly Barry . . . 10 March 1952." She had written it the day before she died.

"It's hard to believe that I have the key of Furze Hill in my hand," he said to Fr Brady in wonder.

"I feel so bad that I didn't remember and connect the two things sooner," Fr Brady told him regretfully.

"Never mind," he assured him. "All that matters is that we have it now."

"I think that it's Dad and yourself who should go in there together for the first time," Fr Brady told him, "so I'll head off back to the village. I'll call later."

With his heart thumping in anticipation, Danny eased the key into the lock, but when he tried to turn it, it refused to budge. Disappointment shot through him, and he looked at Bill in alarm.

"It isn't working," he said in dismay.

"Take it easy now, boyeen," Bill told him gently. "There's bound to be a fair share of rust in there. I'll get my oil can and we'll get it moving." He disappeared out to his red van. He was back in seconds bearing an oil can with a long spout that he tilted into the large key hole, and when he withdrew it he poured the thick blue oil over the lugs of the key. Then he reinserted the key into the door and stood back.

"Now, Danny, try again, but move it around a bit inside to loosen things up in there," he instructed. Danny moved the key back and forth a few times and then tried to ease it anticlockwise. It did shift a little but soon stuck again, and though he pushed hard there was no give.

"Don't force it, don't force it," Bill warned, "or the damn thing could split. We'll try the oil again and give it a chance to soak in."

When he had repeated the oiling, Danny tried again. The key went a little bit further this time, and then they repeated the same procedure and the key moved another fraction. After a few more oiling sessions, the key slowly ground the whole way round and the lock was open.

Danny had dreamt of this moment for so long that he was finding it hard to believe that it had finally arrived.

"Go on, Danny," Bill encouraged him. Danny gingerly pushed the door, but this door had not moved for many years. Bill poured oil over the hinges, and as the two of them pushed together, slowly the creaking door eased open. They were looking in. After the bright light outside, it took Danny's eyes a few seconds to adjust to the semi-darkness. Inside was a grey scene. Veils of cobwebs hung from the ceiling and draped the walls and staircase, but despite the mantle of age, there was a sense of spaciousness and height. Danny felt as if he was looking into another world. In there time had stood still. He was rooted to the floor, but Bill strode in and took the stairs two at a time. When he drew the groaning shutters of the tall window on the top landing back, light flooded down the stairs. The whole place was shrouded in crusted dust, but that did not disguise the simple elegance of the hall.

"This is some house," Bill announced from the top of the stairs.

Danny swallowed hard, rendered speechless by the immensity of the occasion. In here was a world that years ago his grandmother had locked away, and now he was coming back into it. Bill was running his hand lovingly along the curved rail of the staircase.

"Wait until this is polished up," he declared in awe, "and look at the width of this stairs. Makes you feel good just to walk down them." He scraped the floor with the heel of his boot and announced with satisfaction, "Just as I thought, fine old flagstones, and look at those grand doors! Wouldn't they do your heart good?"

In his enthusiasm Bill had forgotten Danny and was striding around surveying the place with gusto.

"Now, let me figure out the house plan before we look around. This door at the foot of the stairs, I'd say, leads into the dining room, and the one straight across probably into the drawing room, and back at the end of the hall the kitchen door is probably behind the stairs, and the morning room door straight across from it."

Bill was so carried away that it took him a few minutes to notice that Danny was standing motionless at the entrance.

"What's the matter, boyeen?" he asked in concern. When Danny remained silent, he came over and put an arm around his shoulders, inquiring worriedly, "What's happened to you?"

"I'm sort of dumbfounded," Danny whispered, "and maybe a bit frightened."

"Frightened of what?"

"Well, I wanted so much to get into this house, but now that I'm here, I feel that somehow I might be moving into something that's too much for me."

"Danny, don't lose your nerve now and miss the wonder of the opening of this door," Bill insisted. "You won't get another chance to relive this great occasion."

With Bill's words something clicked in Danny's brain, and he swallowed hard in an attempt to shake the burden of the future off his shoulders. This was a momentous occasion and he shouldn't let his fear for the future erode it.

"You're right, Bill," he breathed. "I lost myself there for a few minutes."

"Well, it's a big step for you," Bill told him reassuringly, "but I wouldn't want it to pass without you savouring it to the full. You will always look back on this day, and it shouldn't be spoilt by worrying about other things. So come on and we'll do the grand tour." He opened the door into what he had already decided was the dining room and went straight over to fold back the creaking shutters of the two tall windows facing out over the garden. Light poured into the high-ceilinged room that was bare of furniture but for one long table. There was a large fireplace on the wall facing the windows. While Danny stood looking at the room in awe, Bill was down on his knees with his head under the table.

"Oak, just as I hoped," he announced with satisfaction, getting off his knees and heading towards the fireplace. He began scratching the dirty surface of the mantelpiece and then looked at Danny with excitement.

"Boys, oh boys! This is marble. What more could we ask for?"

"Bill, I can't get over it!" Danny gasped.

"It's just as I had hoped it would be," Bill declared. "When this was built they only used the best, and luckily nothing was ripped out of it, at least not in this room anyway. Come across the hall now and we'll see how the drawing room fared." He almost ran across the hall and eased open the door into a room which was a duplicate of the other. There was no furniture, just the another marble fireplace with a huge overmantel.

"That mirror could be affected by the damp," Bill said regretfully, looking up at the cobweb-covered mirror.

Despite Bill's reassuring word, Danny was still mesmerised by the sight of everything unfolding before him. But Bill had no such restraints. He had worked in fine old houses all his life, and when he came on a real, authentic one, it awoke the restorer in him, and so it was with a glowing face that he led Danny back to the kitchen where he almost danced with delight at the sight of a huge range and old dressers that were cloaked in dust.

"This is like exploring an Aladdin's cave," he declared as he almost dragged Danny across the corridor to another room with windows overlooking the back garden. Not satisfied with folding back the shutters, Bill tried to open the windows, but there was no movement.

"Dozed cords, but all those can be replaced," he declared with enthusiasm. "These windows really stood the test of time, and do you know something, Danny? This place is basically sound. I have seen houses like this in London, and they were built by people who spared nothing in the building, and it paid in the long run. Come on upstairs, lad," and he was running up the stairs ahead of Danny. Upstairs there were four large, airy bedrooms opening off a wide landing and a little boxroom at the back.

"This is a grand house," Bill asserted as he led Danny down the wide staircase. "We have layers of dust and cobwebs everywhere, but even though it's been locked up with years, it's as dry as pepper."

Danny had trailed around the house after Bill, content to let him do all the talking while he endeavoured to absorb the fact that he was actually walking around Nana Molly's homeplace, the home that she had dreamed and talked about for years. As he walked after Bill, he could hear her voice describing each room. She had brought him here many times with her recollections, and when he had stood at the open door, he had been frightened that it would not be as she had described. But as they had journeyed around the house, her stories had come alive. It was exactly as she had remembered. The only difference was that she had remembered it furnished. In her old age she had forgotten that most of the furniture had been sold off. But at least now he knew how it could look if he had money. But lack of money for the farm and house was one of the nightmares that kept him awake at night.

When Fr Brady came back later, he felt a surge of pride as he showed him around the house where Bill was already getting down to work trying to free up one of the dining room windows.

"I'm going to need new pulley cord for all these," he told

them as they joined him after their tour of the house. "Well, what do you think of it, Tim?"

"Wonderful, but it's going to take some money to bring it right." Danny did not miss the warning look that his father shot at him.

"It's all right, Bill," he assured him. "I know that I'm in a deep financial hole between this and the farm, not to mention the title."

"I thought that I could help you about the title, but it did not work out," Fr Brady told him regretfully.

"How?" Danny asked in surprise.

"You remember the letter you gave me from Rory, saying that he would sign off for five hundred pounds? Well, I thought that if I took it into old Mr Hobbs in Ross that he could get Rory to sign off by assuring him that the money was coming, and that then he could transfer the title. Then he could give you the deeds, and you could get a loan and send the money to Rory."

"Sometimes, Tim, I think that you came down in the last shower," his father told him. "Sure, no self-respecting solicitor would go along with that, and old Hobbs is as set in legal concrete as they come."

"Well, I partly guessed 'twas a long shot," Fr Tim smiled, "but it was worth a try."

"Thanks for trying anyway, Father," Danny said appreciatively.

Later that evening, when he had the cows milked, he came back and walked around again. He wondered if he would ever get used to the excitement of just walking around and looking at this house. It was absolutely filthy, but he could see beyond the years of neglect, and this time round he was more relaxed and took in the details. All the high ceilings were edged with intricate cornice moulding, and panelled shutters framed the tall windows. When he came into one of the front bedrooms, he noticed a picture in the corner, partly obliterated with cobwebs. He reached up and rubbed the glass, but it was pitted with grime. His curiosity was aroused, so he went over to the poke and came back armed with a damp cloth. After a lot of rubbing, the face of a young girl smiled out at him. The picture was faded, and at first he thought it was Kitty but knew that was impossible. Then he realised that it was a very young photograph of his grandmother. She was quite beautiful.

He lifted down the picture to have a better look, and from behind it something fell to the ground. Resting the picture against the wall, he bent down to pick up what he thought was a small packet and saw that it was a small, hard-cover book. He carried it down to the front door and sat on the step to examine it. When he opened it, he was surprised to discover that it was not a book but a handwritten journal of sorts. The writing was quite faded but still legible, and he felt a flutter of excitement when he recognised his grandmother's writing. It was much better formed than the writing on the key box but still the same writing. On the first page was written "Molly Barry 1885".

He made a quick calculation and worked out that it was written while she was still living here and before she married his grandfather. But the entries were mostly jottings, or so it seemed at first. "This place is so dull, it is full of old people. Mama and Father are so old and Mary in the kitchen is ancient." Then there were pages of short entries about the goings-on in the house. But then, in underlined writing, as if to emphasis its importance, an entry read, "Someone young has come at last to Furze Hill, a lovely lovely girl called Emily, and we have become great friends. At night we sit in the kitchen and talk as she does her needlework." A few pages further on: "Emily has a secret. Last night I was looking out the window and saw her come up from the river and across the garden very late. This morning I coaxed her secret out of her. She goes down to the river to meet Edward Phelan. It's so exciting!" Then a few pages on another entry: "Emily says that Edward will bring his friend Rory to meet me. Delighted, delighted. Can't imagine anything more exciting than creeping out late at night when everyone is asleep to meet a stranger. What will he be like?"

Then the next entry was dated a few months later: "Emily has left. Edward and herself had a blazing row and she is gone to England. It's terrible here without her. Only for Rory I'd die and still nobody knows that I go out at night to meet him. Mama and Father would not approve of him. Father would call him a scoundrel." Then a lot of entries about Rory.

Danny, in view of what had happened afterwards, felt uneasy reading of her loving enthusiasm for his grandfather. But this was a young girl full of love and excitement. Then an entry: "Edward Phelan is getting married, but I'd say he still loves Emily." Later in the book the name Emily appeared again. "Emily is back married to Mike Tobin a merchant seaman and they are living at Mossgrove gate and now Edward is married in the house below. Today I am going to visit her."

The light was fading, but before he closed the journal he went to the back page and the last entry was "Tomorrow night I'm going out to meet Rory and I'm not coming back."

Dusk had gathered in around the house behind him, filling it with shadows. Tomorrow in better light he would read the rest of her journal and then give it to Kate Phelan.

CHAPTER FOURTEEN

K ATE SAT AT the kitchen table feeling miserable. Since
Jack's death she had not been able to lift herself out of
a black hole of loneliness. Despite all David's loving
efforts, she felt that a light had gone out of her life that might
never again come back. Now David looked up with concern
from the copybook he was correcting before going out to
school.

"Not having a great morning, my darling?" he asked
sympathetically, and her heart ached to see him so worried. She
could pretend that she was fine, but David knew her too well to
be fooled. He was already worried about the school, and she
hated herself for adding to his troubles now above any other
time of the year, with the exams pending.

She forced a brave smile and told him, "Well, I'll have to get
going today, because as you know Rodney Jackson is coming
this evening. Fr Tim and himself will be here for dinner, and I
asked Nora to come along because she needs a break from all

the studying. She is driving herself very hard, but she seems to be handling Jack's death better than me."

"It could be that she has it sidelined by burying herself in study, or it could be the resilience of the young," he told her. "They go down further and they come up faster."

"Well, I seem to be very slow surfacing," she said bleakly.

"Don't be too hard on yourself, Katie," he told her gently. "It's early days yet, and Jack was a big part of your life for a long time."

"Are you worried about what Rodney will tell us this evening?" She wanted to get the conversation away from Jack as she could feel the familiar lump in her throat, and she did not want to send David out to school with the memory of a weepy face.

"Well, at least we'll find out where we stand. At the moment, I don't know whether I'm coming or going, or even if I will have a school in the autumn."

"All thanks to wonderful Martha," she said bitterly.

"I suppose at the moment we are not even sure of that," he said reasonably, "so this evening should at least clear up a lot of confusion. Now I'd better get a move on or my pupils will be wondering what is happening."

He came around the table and, kneeling by her chair, put his arms around her and drew her face close to him to kiss her lingeringly.

"Kate, my darling, this black patch too will pass and the sun will shine for you again, and I love you more than I ever thought possible, and whatever happens with Rodney we will be all right," he told her comfortingly.

When he was gone, she sat for a long time, wondering why the hell she could not pull herself together. Then she heard the post thump through the letterbox and went to bring it back to the table. There were a few letters and one big envelope which she opened. When she saw the headed notepaper of Mr Hobbs, she felt a cold chill spread over her. It was a stiff legal letter and a copy of Jack's will. She recoiled with a shiver from the finality of this legal document. The uncompromising language of the will hammered home again the awful reality that Jack was now no longer part of her world. His voice was silenced into this unreal legal formula of words. She put her face in her hands and sobbed in desolation. Then slowly she picked up the will.

She had to read it a few times before she could take it in. Jack had left his cottage to her. The image of the cottage that was wrapped up in her love for him floated in front of her. She had spent much of her childhood there, and up to the night he died it was her first port of call in a crisis. Without Jack it was a shell, and yet she owed it to him to keep it as he would have wanted and make a home for Toby. She felt powerless, as if she would never again be capable of making a decision. What would she do with the cottage? She wished that she could live in it, but the practicalities of her job and David's made that impossible. But it was such a part of her that she wanted someone to live there who would appreciate, love and treasure the memory of Jack.

She was still sitting at the table gazing into space when Fr Tim rushed in, but he stopped short at the sight of her.

"Kate, are you all right?" he asked anxiously. "You look terrible." Without answering she handed him the will.

"Oh God, Kate, how come 'twas posted to you?" he wanted to know.

"I wouldn't go into old Hobbs," she told him listlessly. "I didn't want to see it. There is something so cold and final about a bloody will."

"And David was gone to school when it came?" he said, and when she nodded he sat across the table from her and asked, "Do you want me to read it?" When she again nodded silently, he picked it up and read it and then told her gently, "Kate, in time you will see this as Jack's final blessing, but just let it be for the time being." He folded it up and put it back into the envelope and slipped it between the books on a shelf beside him.

"Tim, what's wrong with me? I can't seem to get myself going," she asked plaintively.

"Grief can emotionally cripple people," he told her gently, "but you recovered after Ned and you will again."

"But I think that with Jack I buried them all again. He was the back wall of my world, and with him gone I feel that I have no past, and having no children I feel that I have no future either. I feel like an island."

"Grief is an island, Kate," he told her, "and you are isolated there with all your hurt."

"But why has not having children become such a big issue for me now?" she asked him desperately.

"Because in grief, Kate, all our vulnerabilities surface," he told her gently. "You have this dream of a little boy called Jack Ned, and maybe you see in him a way of perpetuating the two people who meant so much to you."

"It doesn't make sense, does it?" she asked sadly.

"But it's understandable," he told her gently, "and grief and reason are not fellow travellers." Changing his tone, he continued firmly, "But now we have a job to do. I came to help you prepare for the Yank."

"David sent you," she accused him, surprised that Fr Tim, who was a bit of a disaster around the house, was being enlisted to help.

"Well, what if he did? Any cook would be glad of a slave like me at her disposal. So, Madam, issue your instructions."

She looked across the table at this warm-hearted, forgetful, disorganised, lovable friend, and she forced a smile on her face.

"I'm glad you're here, and now we'll prepare a feast for the Yank that will hopefully give him indigestion if he brings bad news."

She was relieved to find herself actually enjoying the cooking and working with Fr Tim, who was not much of a help but good company. When they had everything in readiness and they sat down to have a cup of tea, he made her smile by telling her that his father kept the garden shed locked so that he could not get in and upset the tools.

"Was your father always methodical?" Kate asked.

"Always. I suppose if you were foreman on a building site in London, it came with the job. Then after my mother died and he was left with all of us, he had to keep law and order, so he ran the house and the bar like clockwork. He loves doing things well and restoring old buildings. Of course, he is in his glory in Furze Hill, and he treats young Danny as if he was one of us. If I was a bit more like him, he would find it easier living with me, but unfortunately I'm my mother's son."

"Fr Tim, how would your father feel about living in Jack's cottage?" Kate heard herself saying, but when a look of delighted astonishment filled Tim's face, she knew that it was the ideal solution.

"My God, he'd be in heaven," he declared.

"That settles it then," she decided. "Jack had great time for your father, and Toby will have a good home."

Shortly afterwards, Fr Tim had to go to the school for lunchtime football practice, and she began to lay the table in the front room, bringing out wedding presents that were seldom used.

Later David and Nora came home from school, and as soon as they were in the door Nora announced, "This house has the smell of visitors!" She made a beeline for the front room to inspect the dinner table. Kate could see the relief on David's face that she was looking better, and as he laid his bundle of books on the hall table she put her arms around him.

"Thanks for sending Fr Tim, and I've a good feeling about this evening," she assured him, leaving the news about the cottage until later.

"Come in here, Uncle David," Nora was calling. Kate followed him into the front room where Nora was surveying the table that Kate had covered with her best linen tablecloth, inherited from Nellie. She had used the best of everything, including the dinner service that she had got from David's father, the cutlery that she had got as a wedding present from Jack and the cut glass that she had got from Ned and Martha.

"This table looks fit for a king," Nora declared.

"Hopefully the king won't cut the head off us after the dinner by whipping the school from under us," David said wryly.

"If he does he won't get out of here alive, and my mother will have some explaining to do," Nora threatened.

It surprised Kate to hear Nora breathe criticism about her mother, and she decided that Nora was beginning to assert herself. Martha might not be queen bee much longer! Now Nora was looking up at the old picture of Edward Phelan above the mantelpiece.

"Doesn't great-grandfather look impressive? He kind of blends in with this posh table. Almost as if he is presiding over it. Aunty Kate, I think that we should all dress up," she decided. "Maybe we should rise to the occasion. The dress I wore at the dance is still upstairs."

"Well, if you dress up we must all dress up," Kate told her, "but is it a bit like dressing up for a public execution."

"Well, there is nothing like doing things in style, and maybe we might intimidate Rodney Jackson with our grandeur." Kate smiled at Nora's spirit.

"What do you think, David?" she asked as he stood quietly listening to them.

"Won't do any harm, I suppose," he said mildly.

"Ah, Uncle David," Nora protested, "we need to do a bit better than that."

"All decided then," Kate declared. "Upstairs for the transformation because he'll be here soon, but first I must check the kitchen in case I'll be serving burnt offerings."

When Fr Tim rushed in the door, he stopped short at the sight of them.

"My God," he declared, "you look like the royal family."

"Waiting to be beheaded," Nora told him as she kept watch by the window for Rodney Jackson's arrival. Kate was glad that she had asked her to be here, because she had introduced an upbeat note into the whole evening.

"What time exactly is he supposed to be here?" David asked pensively, and Kate knew that he was finding the waiting difficult.

"Oh my God, he's here," Nora cried and forgetting her resolution to be discreet dragged back the net curtain. "And look at that car! It's taking up half the street."

"Norry, for heaven's sake close the curtain," Kate protested as she headed for the door.

Rodney Jackson filled the hallway with his exuberant six foot four. His brown eyes shone with pleasure, and he was obviously more than pleased to see them.

"Kate, you look great," he enthused, and even though she knew that it was not really true, it still made her feel better. Then he was hugging Nora and shaking hands with Fr Tim and David. Kate could see that David's smile of welcome was a bit strained. She wondered how poor David was going to get through the whole evening and force himself to eat a dinner while wondering what the future of his school was. But she had reckoned without Rodney Jackson's forthright attitude.

"Now folks, I must apologise for all the delays in my coming, but I wanted to make sure that everything was sorted out before I left the States. Kate, can we adjourn to your wonderful kitchen and sit down around your fine kitchen table, because it's the nearest thing to a boardroom table available to us."

"A boardroom table indeed!" Nora declared indignantly as Rodney led them all back into the kitchen. He seated himself at one end of Jack's table and directed David to the other end and placed Nora and Kate at one side and Fr Tim at the other. Then he opened his briefcase and stacked a pile of documents in front of him. Kate felt her stomach heaving and hoped that she was not going to get sick. There was something very formal about all of this, and it scared her a little. It was almost like the reading of a will.

"I have big plans for Kilmeen," he began. Kate felt like saying, *Bet you have*, but he was continuing, "and I hope that you will all be pleased with them." Kate thought, *Doubt it*, but Rodney was only getting into his stride.

"The last time I was here," he told them, as his eyes travelled from face to face, "I walked around the school and saw that it was bursting at the seams and lacking facilities."

Kate saw that chairing meetings was a matter of course to him, and she felt a sense of resentment at his high-handed approach. *So now he's going to tell us that he is doing us a good turn by throwing us out*, she thought.

"Well," he continued slowly, "I worked out an alternative arrangement."

There was a sharp intake of breath around the table, and Kate's silent commentary was wiped out, but Rodney continued calmly.

"I want someplace with lots of space for playing fields, both for the girls as well as the boys, and development for the future. When I went back home, I made contact with your Department of Education regarding permission and grants, and the bottom line is that the plans got the go-ahead from the department. Now if you are wondering why I did not come clean sooner, the fact of the matter is that I did not want to raise false hopes, but now I think that we are ready to move forward."

The completion of his announcement was met by a stunned silence.

Nora was the first to recover. "Have you got plans for a

211

theatre in the school?" she wanted to know, and while the rest of them looked at her in horror, Rodney smiled in amusement.

"That's what I like about you, Nora," he told her. "You never lose sight of your dream. But, yes, when you get your degree and come back to Kilmeen to teach, we'll make that provision for you. You see," he said, turning to the rest of them, "that is why the right site, with plenty of space to develop, is so important."

Kate could hardly believe what she was hearing, and when she looked across at David there was such a look of delight on his face that she got up and hugged Rodney.

"Your news is such a relief," she told him. "We were so worried about the school when we heard of your plans for a hotel."

"Guess I should have kept my mouth shut on that one, but I wanted to trickle it out slowly and get you all used to the idea of change," he admitted.

"I'm afraid that I jumped to the wrong conclusions," David admitted, "and thought that I would finish up with no school, but what you have in mind is just beyond all expectations. It's any headmaster's dream come true."

"Well, you're the best, David," Rodney assured him, "and I know the best when I see it. But have a look at the plans. I got a top educational expert to do the design, but they are still open to suggestion. After all, you're the one who will be running the show."

The plans were handed around the table, but Kate found that she could not make head nor tail of the big sheet of paper covered with drawings. The rest of them, however, seemed to have no such problem, but she noticed that Fr Tim, having examined them carefully, looked across at Rodney with a puzzled expression on his face and said, "This layout is pretty extensive. Where exactly is this school going to be?"

"Well, that is where I thought I would be guided by local knowledge," Rodney told him. "Is there any suitable place available around the village?"

They all looked a bit perplexed, and Kate thought that it would be terrible if a suitable site could not be found. Fr Tim dismissed this possibility.

"There is bound to be a suitable place," he declared. "Sure, aren't we surrounded by farmland?"

They were all reassured by this, but Kate, knowing the farming people and their attachment to their land better than the rest of them, was not so sure. But she decided that she would not be the one to dampen their enthusiasm, and it was great to see David so happy. The entire discussion centred around the school, and after some time Kate decided that someone should show interest in his hotel.

"Are you looking forward to transforming the school into a splendid hotel?" she asked.

"Yes, I'm very excited about it," he declared. "It's a wonderful old building and as you know the original family home and has huge potential to be tastefully developed into a top class hotel. This is where your sister-in-law Martha is coming in. She has refused to marry me, so I must settle for a business partnership, and I think that it will work out very well. You know, Kate, property is very cheap in Ireland right now, but all of that is going to change. Tourism is about to take off here, and Kilmeen must be ready."

"You have always loved this place," she smiled.

"My roots are here. It was my mother's homeplace, and ever since I came back here to visit my aunts I've loved it too. I'm not ashamed to admit that my mother married big money in the States, but she had class and my father's people admired her greatly. The school for me is an opportunity to honour her memory. I can afford it, and I'll make money out of the hotel and other projects. I may be sentimental about my mother, but I'm a businessman. But family is very important to me too, and, Kate, I just want to say how sad I was to hear about Jack, because I know what he meant to you."

"Thanks, Rodney," she whispered and was relieved that no tears came.

Everything was happening so fast, and she wanted to go out into the quiet of the garden to take it all in, but she had people to feed and a dinner that was fast deteriorating in the oven, so she turned to Rodney.

"Will you call this meeting to a halt," she pleaded, "or the dinner will be burnt out of existence."

She shepherded them all into the front room where they had a dinner that was far past its best, but there was such an intense discussion about the school around the table that she doubted if the dinner was even tasted. It did her heart good to watch David glance down at the folded plans on the table beside him, almost as if to reassure himself that they were real, and to hear him discuss the layout of the playing fields with Fr Tim. She could see delight flowing out of him. Rodney and Nora were deep in conversation about her proposed theatre, and Kate thought that even if it never materialised it was the stimulus that she needed just now after Jack's death and to propel her through the exams.

When dinner was over, Rodney opted to take Nora back to Mossgrove, and David and Fr Tim decided to take the plans up to the school to check out classroom measurements. Kate determinedly refused all offers of help, and after David and Rodney had dragged Rodney's luggage up the stairs and the four of them had finally trooped out of the front door, she breathed a sigh of relief. She needed time to herself. As she cleared away the dinner table and stacked the ware in the sink, she reviewed the previous few hours. She sorted out her mind as she tidied up the table. When she finally folded up Nellie's tablecloth, she held the smooth linen against her face. This family heirloom had been on the table in Mossgrove for her First Holy Communion breakfast, and grandfather had been there that day as well. Now she smiled up at him.

"This tablecloth has been used for every big occasion since then," she told him, "and it's become precious through its intermingling in my life."

She carefully washed and dried Jack's cutlery and placed it back in its wooden box. She knew that Jack had put a lot of thought and care into the buying of her wedding present, and a bit like himself, it had quality and durability. When all was to her satisfaction, she went out into the garden.

She sat on the wooden seat that Jack had built into the old ditch beside the huge fern that he had brought in from Mossgrove. The evening sun slanted through the trees, softening the outline of the shrubs and filling the garden with long shadows. At this time of the evening, the shrubbery at the other side of the lawn was a mysterious corner. After a few minutes, a blackbird came out of there and began to explore the grass. She enjoyed watching him put his head sideways as if

215

listening for underground movement and, with a quick dart, come up with a tiny worm. Then he flew into the hedge where the hungry fledglings were waiting. Over her head a little grey bird was singing its heart out. Despite all Jack's efforts, she did not know his name. He had known them all, and when she got annoyed with herself because she could not remember, he used to say, "Kate girlie, you don't have to christen him to enjoy him." But the little bird was giving her such pleasure that she she felt she owed him that. She did not have that problem with the robin who now perched on a stone beside her, so close that if she reached out she could touch him. She loved his brave, cheeky approach to life.

Overhead the crows were flying home in perfect formation. In flight they were beautiful, but as they perched on the treetops at the bottom of the garden, they wrangled and screeched at each other and turned into cranky bedraggled old ladies. Now across the garden a thrush ventured out shyly from underneath the beech hedge, and she held her breath in case of frightening her. She was glad that the blackbird was gone, because sometimes he hunted the thrush away. In the late evening the birds, gathering in for the night, called the garden their own. They were all early retirers except the robin, who always seem to have a few last minute jobs to do. As if remembering one of them, he darted into the bluebells on the ditch beside her and then he was on the tree above her singing goodnight.

She breathed in deeply the heavenly smell of the bluebells that filled the air. She thought back over all that had happened since morning. It had been a good day. The pain of the morning had eased.

CHAPTER FIFTEEN

ANOTHER LETTER FROM Rory. As soon as he saw it, Danny knew that it meant more trouble. The letter was brief and to the point. Rory wanted his money and he wanted it now. Otherwise he would come home and make them sell Furze Hill. Danny knew that he could not force them to sell, but he could cause big trouble. He also realised that if Rory saw the house now his buying-out price would go up and there would be no getting rid of him. They had all thought that there was only a wreck of an old house buried under the rusty roof in the grove of trees. Now things were different. Rory had to stay in England! All morning Danny's mind went around in endless circles trying to find a solution. The letter put a time pressure on him. He knew that if Rory did not hear from him quickly, one morning he would walk in the gate, and then the real row would begin. When Bill and himself met for their midday break on the steps of the house, he showed him the letter.

Having read it Bill said grimly, "I've never even met this fellow, but I'm beginning to like him less and less."

"He's like the old fellow," Danny told him bleakly.

"You don't want that to start all over again," Bill said resolutely.

"To keep him in England is the answer," Danny said desperately.

"There must be a way," Bill declared. "There is always a way."

"Well, if there is then I can't see it," Danny told him.

"Well, it might take a bit of time," Bill comforted him.

"Time is one thing I don't have," Danny said.

"Well, boyeen, don't lose heart now, because so far you've soldiered it well," Bill praised.

They sat in silence and Danny was grateful for Bill's comforting presence. Nothing seemed as bleak when Bill was around. Bill had never previously mentioned his wife, but now he said, "You know, Danny, I seldom talk about Lucy because her going cut deep. But she was a great woman and I learned a lot from her. Not a tidy woman," he smiled, "a bit like her Tim in that way, but she had wonderful vision. It was her idea that we come back home and rear the children here. It was not an easy decision, because we were finally doing well over there after a few financial disasters. But Lucy always had a saying when I was facing a financial vacuum or a big decision. 'Fortune favours the brave,' she used to say. So this is your time to be brave, lad. We all think of the brave as the crowd who go out and fight, but more often than not they are the crowd who stay at home and survive."

After his chat with Bill, even though he was no nearer to a solution, he felt a bit easier, and he went to work on the stone

218

wall by the pillar. He loved working with stone and knew from previous experience that it would soothe his distraught thoughts. Sure enough, after a while his mind stopped racing and he became totally engrossed in marrying the stones together. Stones had a will of their own and would not stand together unless they were well matched, and wall building was an exercise in finding the right combination. He loved searching for the right one, and if he got the match wrong the stone let him know. They would not stay together. Getting all the stones to blend in a harmony of size and colour was completely absorbing.

He had not noticed that the hours had flown by and that it was cow time until Bill called across the yard where he was working, "What about the cows, Danny? They have no way of knowing that stone-walling is so fascinating."

"I think that I should have been a stonemason, Bill," he called back. "Stones are smarter than us. They only work with the right partner."

"I think that you are becoming a bit of a philosopher," Bill laughed.

"What is it about working with the earth and stone, Bill, that makes us feel good?" he asked as he walked across to admire Bill's digging out of the curved bed along by the drive.

"One of life's wonderful mysteries," Bill replied, leaning on his spade, "and it would be a tragedy if we lost touch with it."

"I'll see you in the morning, Bill," he said as he went out under the arch, "because you will probably be gone when I bring home the cows."

After the milking, he came back to the steps intending to reread Nana Molly's diary, but just as he was going in the front door, Shiner appeared through the archway.

"How's the slave?" Shiner asked cheerily. "You were started this morning before we begin across the river and you're still at it."

"I've a lot of catching up to do," Danny told him.

"Did you have any supper?" Shiner demanded.

"Well, no," he admitted, realising that he had forgotten all about it.

"Will you for the love of Mike come over to the poke and we'll hobble something together. You're like the handle of a bloody shovel," Shiner said as they walked across the yard into the small kitchen where, after the bright light outside, he blinked in the semi-darkness. Shiner already had the kettle on over the fire, and now he opened a paper bag and produced brown bread and a lump of cooked meat.

"You must be bloody starving," he asserted.

"Your mother is great," Danny told him appreciatively, "but Bill and myself always have a good spread in the middle of the day."

"But you know, Danny boy, that Bill has a proper dinner in the evening, whereas you're floating around on a wing and a prayer," Shiner proclaimed from what Danny knew was an extract from a sermon that he had got from his mother. Ellen Shine was into good eating, and Shiner's solid frame was evidence of it.

"Any news?" he asked to distract Shiner from his eating crusade.

"Oh boy, but there are big things about to happen in Kilmeen," Shiner declared excitedly.

"Like what?" Danny asked, scalding the teapot and shooting the rinsing out the door.

"If you ever get into that big house," Shiner told him, viewing the stream of water out the door, "you will have to improve your kitchen manners."

"That day is getting farther and farther away," Danny told him, thinking of the letter, "but let's have your news first."

"Well, we had the Yank for supper across the river the other night, and guess what? He is turning the school into a hotel for the Queen Bee to manage," Shiner told him with relish.

"Martha Phelan?"

"The one and only."

"And what about the school?" Danny asked.

"New school!" Shiner announced with glee. "The power of money works miracles."

"Who're you telling?" Danny said sourly.

"What's wrong with you this evening?" Shiner demanded.

"Bloody Rory," he told him, fishing the letter out of his pocket. Shiner scanned it quickly.

"He's some bastard," he declared, but Danny wanted to find out about the school.

"Tell me more about the plans of the Yank."

"Well, apparently he's looking for a site for this big scheme which will incorporate playing fields for both boys and girls, and if our Nora will have her way even a small theatre."

"By God, but that's going to be a huge layout," Danny declared. He wondered if Jack could be right when he said that worries were sometimes overcome by events. An idea was germinating at the back of his mind. He tried to control his rising excitement as he asked, "Where is all this going to be?"

"No site yet," Shiner told him, "but the Yank have the big guns on the lookout for him."

"That's Fr Tim, David and Kate?" Danny qualified, wanting to know exactly where things stood.

"Who else?" Shiner assured him. He felt his little glow of hope grow stronger, but he was almost afraid to articulate it in case that if he put it into words it would dissolve.

"What are you hatching?" Shiner demanded, frowning at him across the table. "You look like a fellow who has got a peep into heaven and is afraid that he might have the gate banged in his face."

"Exactly," Danny told him, amazed that Shiner had hit the nail so accurately on the head.

"Do you want to spit it out?" Shiner wanted to know.

"This idea that I have could solve this," he told Shiner, tapping Rory's letter on the table.

"How the hell?" Shiner asked in a perplexed voice.

"If the Yank bought my two fields outside the village," Danny told him slowly.

A look of amazement flooded Shiner's face, and for once he was speechless as Danny continued, "My problem is that I don't have the title to those fields to sell them. Fr Tim has already tried to crack that and failed because we had no cash to buy out Rory. But now if the Yank came up trumps, we might be able to get out of that corner."

"You're on a winner, Danny boy! You're out of the trap!" Shiner declared, throwing his cap in the air and thumping the table with his fist. "That's the ideal site. It's perfect! When you think about it, there is nowhere else better around the village."

"Do you think so?" Danny asked desperately.

"No doubt about it," Shiner told him delightedly, "and what you got to remember now, Danny, is to ask enough because you are holding all the aces. There is nowhere else as good as your two fields. So ask enough."

"What about the title?" Danny wondered.

"Fr Tim and Kate will sort that out with the Yank for you. It's all about knowing the right people," Shiner told him in an elated voice. "As well as the aces, Danny boy, you have the jokers as well. Now don't breathe a word about this sale to anyone, because when you are buying or selling land it's best to keep your mind to yourself. God, wouldn't Jack be thrilled with this?"

"He used to say that worries are sometimes overcome by events," Danny told him.

"He could be bloody right," Shiner declared.

The following morning when Fr Tim opened his front door, Danny was outside.

"Good God, Danny! What has you here so early?" Fr Tim asked in amazement. "Come in, come in." He led the way into the kitchen where the smell of fresh toast told Danny that he was preparing his breakfast. He put a second cup on the table and put on more toast, saying, "You must have something big on your mind to drag you away from your cows before milking."

"I've got an idea," Danny told him breathlessly, his chest tight with excitement. If this came off, he was out of the trap, as Shiner had said. He told Fr Tim slowly about his plan and watched with growing confidence as the priest's face lit up with enthusiasm.

"That's the answer to all our problems," Fr Tim declared.

"What about the title?" he asked worriedly.

"Kate and I will tackle Rodney Jackson on that one, and I can't see any difficulty. It's the perfect site, so it's to his advantage to acquire it. Only means paying earlier rather than later, and that should be no problem to him," Fr Tim said positively. "As soon as we have news, I'll be back to you. Does Dad know?"

"Not yet. It was late last night that Shiner told me about the school, and that put me thinking."

"That was good thinking," Fr Tim smiled and asked, "and you don't mind parting with the two fields?"

"Not with those two," he told him, "because they are not actually part of the main farm. More like an outside farm that's too small, and working them is a bit awkward. They are the two that my grandfather bought instead of paying back old man Phelan. They were the start of all the trouble."

"Well, maybe they'll put an end to it now," Fr Tim smiled.

All day he watched the gate waiting for Fr Tim's car to whirl in, but nothing happened. Bill assured him that it might take a few days to run down Rodney Jackson, but Danny knew that he was trying to ease his worry. Fr Tim was not one to hang around and would get it sorted out pretty fast. That evening after the cows he wanted to be close at hand, so he began to clean the front steps. A little later he was relieved when he heard a car stop at the gate, and then through the draping tendrils of the weeping willows he could see Fr Tim and Kate come along the drive. He held his breath, wondering if the news was good, and Kate, sensing his apprehension, called out to him, "Rodney will advance you the money to pay off Rory first."

He felt unrestrained joy sweep over him and high-jumped around in sheer abandonment and danced with uncontrolled exuberance up and down the steps.

"Light at the end of the tunnel," he shouted, and to Fr Tim's and Kate's amusement was off again, dancing up and down the steps shouting, "Isn't this great! Isn't this great!"

Finally he ran out of steam and collapsed on the steps gasping.

"Now I'll be able to get rid of Rory. Oh, the relief of that, and if there is anything extra I will buy a tractor. I need one badly to reclaim the farm."

"What about the house?" Kate asked.

"Kate, the last time that things went wrong here, my grandfather let the farm run down and then the house was sacrificed, so I don't want history to repeat itself," he told her. "But once I have the land signed over, I'll feel safe and then things will gradually sort themselves out."

"You deserve it, Danny, because you have swum against the tide long enough. Now the tide is turning."

"It began to turn the day you said that Jack would help me," he told her appreciatively, "and, Fr Tim, your father has turned this place around."

"It's beginning to look great," Kate said, looking down at the cleared garden and the delicate iron tracery of the entrance gate. "That's a beautiful gate."

"Bill spent hours of grinding and cleaning to get it swinging smoothly and closing properly. Now it fits perfectly," he said proudly.

"My father is in his element here," Fr Tim smiled, "bringing the place back to life."

"He is doing the same for me," Danny told him quietly.

They chatted for a long time and then toured the house. It was Kate's first time seeing it, and he was delighted with her reaction. Every time he walked around the house now he felt a glow of pride. Before leaving they told him that Rodney Jackson would be with him early in the morning to go to the bank and the solicitor.

That night he filled the old tin bath with water and had a good scrub-down in front of the fire. As he towel-dried his hair, he viewed himself in the cracked mirror behind the door. His hair was like the rusty roof of the barn, and he tried to comb it as flat as possible. He had inherited Nana Molly's mop, and now he saw images of her in the mirror. His father had always hated his Barry features. He opened a press by the fire and took out the jumper that Mary had given him for Christmas. It was dark green handwoven, and he had never worn it, feeling that it was a bit too good. But tomorrow he would need to look well.

Rodney Jackson swept into the yard in a car that caused Danny to gasp in amazement. It was like an enormous blue bird with sleek silver wings, and out of it came the long-legged, tanned American whom up to now Danny had only seen in the distance.

"I'm Rodney Jackson," he smiled, striding across the yard and showing a row of the most perfect white teeth that Danny had ever seen. "You must be Danny, and I'm so glad to meet you." Long smooth fingers grasped his hand and, looking around in delight, the American enthused, "What a place you've got here; this is the real Old World."

"Would you like to see inside?" Danny heard himself stammer, swept away by this wave of exuberance.

"Would I what?" Rodney asked, and he led him up the steps and around the house. *I'm a bit like a tour guide,* Danny thought as the enthralled American followed him around. When they reached the room with the picture of Nana Molly, he stood in front of it and for the first time was silent.

"So this is the famous Molly Barry," he said thoughtfully after a few minutes.

"You've heard of her?" Danny asked in surprise.

"My aunts often talked of her. They said that she was quite a beauty, and they were right." Turning to Danny he told him to his embarrassment, "I can see the family resemblance," and then he swept on, "so I'm glad to be doing business with one of the descendants of a woman of whom my aunts had such a high opinion. Now we had best get ourselves sorted out before we go to the bank and Mr Hobbs. How much are we talking about for those two fields?" He turned around and stood with Molly Barry looking over his shoulder.

Danny was stunned that things were moving so fast. He was glad that last night he had worked things out in his head and knew exactly what he wanted, but Rodney was not waiting for an answer, and looking him straight in the eye, told him, "I looked at those two fields this morning, and I was thinking that six hundred pounds would be a fair price, three hundred each."

"Eight hundred," Danny told him firmly, and when Rodney looked a bit taken back he added, "They are good fields and in a great location, and as well as that I need five hundred to buy out my brother Rory and three to buy a tractor."

"That's what I call a fair deal," Rodney declared to his amazement and put out his hand to shake Danny's warmly.

He could hardly believe that the deal about which he had done such deliberating was brought to such a fast conclusion, and without further ado Rodney Jackson announced, "Straight to the bank now and I'll transfer that money into your account."

Things were moving faster than Danny had ever thought possible. Rodney Jackson whipped the car around the yard and out the gate, and Danny arrived in Ross in less time than it would have taken him to walk to the village. Rodney strode into the bank where a surprised Mr Harvey found himself opening an account and depositing money for the young man who had come in months earlier in a torn jumper and smelling of farmyard. The blonde girl raised a quizzical eyebrow at Danny as he passed her cubicle and smiled.

"Will there be a return of the Vikings?" she asked, and he was glad that she seemed so pleased to see him.

Their next visit was to Mr Hobbs, whose firm had handled the family affairs since Nana Molly's time and who seemed well versed in all that needed to be done. He assured Rodney that he would get things sorted out as fast as possible. For the first time in his life, Danny wrote a cheque. It was a strange feeling to know that this piece of paper was the first step on his way to owning Furze Hill. He began to see that when you had money and the assurance of authority, people moved faster. He remembered Nana Molly's words about the arsehole of the world, but now he was discovering that the opposite was also true. Nana had come from the world that he was only now discovering. Mr Hobbs went to great pains to explain all the details of what was involved in the signing over, causing Danny to worry about the time span and the return of Rory.

"Will all this take long?" he asked.

"Not if you brother needs the money," Mr Hobbs told him. "He's the only one who can hold things up, because all the other have already signed."

"Oh, he needs the money," Danny assured him, but then

because he had an uneasy feeling that this old man did not understand what he was up against in Rory, he added, "but he will try to get the money and still keep his claim."

Mr Hobbs, who up to then had looked quite harmless, suddenly straightened up behind his cluttered desk and fixed piercing blue eyes on Danny and told him in acid tones, "Young man, I have handled your family business since your grandmother's time, so I know all that there is to be known about the two sides of that family. Rest assured that there will be no loophole. Is there anything else?"

"When the farm is being transferred over," he began tentatively, hoping that he was not going to draw further disapproval, "I'd like my mother's name to go on the deeds with mine."

Whereupon Mr Hobbs suddenly smiled benignly on him.

"Very well, but I will put in a rider that her claim reverts to you on her death. Things change, you know, and it is always better to have things in writing for long-term protection of rights. We don't want any loopholes. Is there anything else now?"

"There is," Danny told him, gathering confidence. "Would it be possible to have my name on the deeds as Daniel Barry Conway?"

"Anything is possible, young man. It will mean getting your name changed by deed poll, but that is no big problem. Then the Barry name will be on the way back to Furze Hill," a pleased Mr Hobbs told him. Looking keenly at Danny over his rimless spectacles, he added thoughtfully, "'Though the mills of God grind slowly, yet they grind exceeding small.'"

When he got home, Danny joined Bill sitting on the front steps to discuss the happenings of the morning.

"It's a great feeling, Bill," he confided with delight, "to be breaking free of the fetters of Rory."

"That was a nice thing to do to put your mother's name on the deeds," Bill told him.

"She worked like a slave here for years," Danny said, "and she had a terrible life. My father humiliated her in every way he could. Now I want to give her a sense of dignity and ownership."

"Does she know anything about the opening up of all this place?" Bill asked, looking around.

"Nothing, because I want it to be a big surprise for herself and the girls," he smiled.

"It's going to be some surprise," Bill asserted.

CHAPTER SIXTEEN

As SHE PASSED Jack's cottage on her way to school, Nora felt the raw pain reawaken. For her the cottage had died with Jack. Even though Sarah lit the fire every day and fed Toby and the fowl, it was now a dead place. She had not gone in there since the funeral, because the pain of even seeing it was almost unbearable. Kate went in every day. How could Kate bear to do that? She was very disappointed that Kate had not helped her more over the loss of Jack instead of becoming totally wrapped up in her own misery. She had pretended not to mind, but for the first time she began to think that Kate was self-centred. The invitation to Rodney Jackson's dinner had been the first time that Kate had reached out a helping hand, and, of course, the good news that night had made them all feel better. She was so delighted for Uncle David, who was much more understanding of how she was feeling than Kate.

Rosie was waiting out at the gate, which meant that she had news or wanted to know something and, as usual, went straight to the point.

"Nora Phelan, what were Fr Brady and your Uncle David doing waltzing around the Conway fields with sheets of paper hanging off them?" she demanded.

"No idea," Nora lied.

"That's a lie, Nora Phelan," Rosie declared.

"But you can't keep a secret," Nora protested.

"I can," Rosie boasted, "because I've a secret that I never told you."

"Like what?" Nora demanded.

Rosie looked at her steadily for a few seconds, determining whether to tell her or hold back, but her urge to share got the better of her and she burst out, "Peter and I meet in Jack's cottage at night."

"What!" Nora gasped in horror.

"Well, it's the ideal place," Rosie asserted.

"But Jack's cottage!" she protested angrily.

"You think that Jack's cottage is holy ground?" Rosie demanded.

"Well, no, but I think that Jack wouldn't like it," she protested, feeling that Peter had let her down.

"But how do you know?" Rosie demanded. "Peter loved Jack as well as you, and I think that meeting me in there is helping him. We don't get up to anything very much."

"That doesn't matter. I just do not like the idea of you two sneaking into Jack's cottage," Nora declared angrily.

"We're not sneaking," Rosie protested.

"I should have known that Peter was up to something," Nora

continued angrily. "He warned me after the dance not to be nosey, which meant that he had something up his sleeve. But I thought that you'd tell me if there was anything because we never have secrets."

"But Peter told me not to, and you know where he is concerned I'm not rational," Rosie said unhappily, "and as well as that I'm half worried that if Kitty comes back and shakes her red mane at him he'll bolt."

"In school she was always horrid to me," Nora declared, beginning to feel less annoyed.

"That's past history now," Rosie decided, "but Kitty is fairly tough competition for me."

"What makes you think that she fancies Peter?" she asked.

"The night of the dance she had eyes for no one else," Rosie declared, "only Rory upset the apple cart for her that night."

Nora felt that Kitty might well create another opportunity. The Kitty that she knew in school did not give up easily, and she was not a hundred per cent sure that you could depend on Peter to play fair. A bit like Mom, he went after what he wanted irrespective of the consequence. But at least he must be the cause of Rosie forgetting her singing ambitions for the time being, because she had settled down to study for her exam.

"Aren't you lucky that Danny fancies you alone?" Rosie broke into her thoughts.

"I'm not so sure of that," she answered, "and anyway, having anything to do with a Conway is too complicated for our family."

"Wouldn't it be great if that applied all round?"

"Well, Kitty is out of the running at the moment anyway," Nora told her.

"And I'm making hay while the sun shines," Rosie smiled. "When this bloody exam is over, I am going to bring back the Vikings and have another youth club dance, and we'll all celebrate a return to normal life with no damn studying hanging over our heads."

Nora was not very happy about Peter and Rosie in the cottage but decided to say no more about it. At least it was keeping Rosie in Kilmeen, and she knew that in the days ahead they would talk the whole thing to death anyway. That was the great thing about Rosie: you could discuss everything with her, and she was very honest and open. Maybe too much so at times! But now, as they walked along the road, she told her all about the new school and Rosie decided that it might not be such a bad thing to come back to Kilmeen after the exams and be part of all this exciting development.

"You could do music in college," Nora suggested.

"And come home and teach it to the natives. Are you trying to bring me into your arty-farty world?" Rosie teased, and then gave her a jolt by by adding, "But I don't have your fascination with a handsome uncle enticing me back."

"I do not," she protested in confusion, but knew that she could not bluff Rosie.

"For God's sake, Nora, we were in baby infants together!" Rosie asserted. "I know how you tick. The difference is that while I spit everything out you bury it inside."

"But, Rosie, in all fairness I couldn't tell anyone about that," she protested.

"I'm not just anyone, and anyway I've known for yonks. It's no big deal and you'll grow out of it because it's only puppy love. Not like me with Peter," Rosie assured her. "How is your

Aunty Kate? My mother is real worried about her, she looks so bad. Jack's death knocked her sideways."

"To be honest," Nora admitted, "I have felt that since he died that she has kind of withdrawn from me."

"That's because she can't cope," Rosie told her. "Do you call often?"

"Not really," Nora said.

"Well, this evening while I'm having a maths grind with the love of your life," Rosie teased, "you should call to Kate."

"All right," Nora agreed reluctantly.

When Nora opened the door into the kitchen that evening, Kate was sitting alone inside the window reading a book. She closed the book hurriedly and her face lit up in welcome.

"Nora, I'm so happy to see you," she cried in delight, coming across the kitchen to give her a hug. "Let's go out in the garden for a chat."

Nora felt slightly uneasy. She was not sure if it was the result of the conversation with Rosie this morning or the fact that she had resented Kate for not being more supportive. Kate, however, was obviously totally unaware of any undercurrent and led the way out into the garden. As they walked along the path, with the evidence of Jack's work all around her, everything else receded from her mind but the pain of his loss.

"He loved it here, didn't he?" she said quietly, tears filling her eyes. Kate put her arms around her and the two of them wept together.

"Aren't we two sad cases?" Kate smiled through her tears. "I know that you are going through a hard time, and I feel that I should be a bigger help to you, but to be honest I can only just handle myself at the moment."

Nora was tempted to say, "I'd noticed," but she remembered Rosie.

"It's not easy," she said, biting her lip, and then to change the subject, "but it's great news about the school anyway."

"And Danny," Kate added.

"Was he delighted?" Nora asked in a strained voice.

"Thrilled," Kate told her. "Have you seen Furze Hill since it was opened up?"

"How would I have seen it?" she demanded.

"Will we run back there now?" Kate offered, and Nora felt a rush of affection for her aunt.

"Oh, I'd love that," she declared, all her annoyance evaporating. "Shiner is for ever talking about it, and it would be great to see it for myself."

She was delighted that Kate had made the suggestion, because she was dying to see Furze Hill, and she could not go across the river from home because Mom would be mad. Sometimes Mom could be a bit of a pain.

They walked along beside a high stone wall and turned in an elegant gate that she had never even known was there, and the sight inside made her gasp in amazement. An ivy-clad house peeped out at them through the tendrils of two beautiful weeping willows.

"Mother of God! Where did all this come from?"

"It was buried for years," Kate told her as they walked past the weeping willows and the house came into full view.

"But it's magnificent," Nora breathed, taking in the limestone pillars and the stained glass fanlight above the door. "It was criminal to have a place like this locked up and buried. All that we could see from across the river for years was a thick grove of trees. I never knew that there was a house in there until Jack told me, but even when they began to slate it I had no idea that it was anything like this."

She was looking in wonder at the house. This was the place that Jack had wanted so much to have restored. It was easy to understand why!

"Pretty unbelievable, isn't it?" Kate agreed. "I think that Danny has never closed the windows since Bill got them to open, and any time I call the door is always open."

"I suppose he wants the house to breathe again after years of being stifled," Nora smiled.

"I wonder is Danny around or out the fields?" Just then Bill Brady came through the arch.

"Hello, girls," he called. "I thought that I heard a car but never knew that we were going to have two lovely lassies calling to see us." He called over his shoulder, "Danny boy, we have visitors." Nora liked Bill Brady; he was easygoing and always had time to listen. She was surprised one day when she had met him in Kate's to find herself telling him all about her plans for the future. He had been understanding and encouraging.

Danny came though the arch, and his thin, sensitive face filled with delighted amazement when he saw them. Nora felt slightly embarrassed that he made a beeline in her direction and ignored Kate.

"Nora, I can't believe you're here. Come in, come in, and I'll show you Furze Hill," he invited with pride in his voice. He led her up the steps and through the splendid door. She had not been prepared for the graciousness of the house. Despite all the cobwebs and dust, this was a far more splendid house than Mossgrove.

"I can only imagine what this will be like when it's done up," she told him in an awed voice as they walked up the wide staircase.

"That will have to wait, I'm afraid," he told her.

"But what about the field money?" she asked.

"Most of that will go to pay off Rory."

"But at least get it cleaned up," she insisted.

"Can't afford it."

"But, sure, the women around here would do that for nothing. Aren't they always doing it for each other for the stations?"

"We were never part of all that," he said grimly.

"Well, it's time you were," she decided firmly. "We'll ask Kate. She knows everyone who can do anything around here."

When they went into one bedroom which had an old picture hanging in the corner, Nora went over and stood in front it. At first she thought that she was looking at Kitty but then realised that this was a still more beautiful girl. It was a faded black and white photograph, but knowing Kitty she could visualise the colour of that wonderful hair.

"Uncle Mark would paint a super picture of her," she declared thoughtfully.

"Mark charges big prices," he told her ruefully.

"Uncle Mark would do it for nothing for a neighbour," she said.

"I suppose we were reared with a very low opinion of the neighbours," he confessed.

"Time to change."

When they came downstairs, Bill had gone back to work and Kate was sitting on the doorstep. Nora went straight to the point.

"Aunty Kate, wouldn't Ellen and Sarah and the other women clean up this house for Danny?"

"Well, I suppose they would," Kate answered in surprise. "I could get a few of the village women to help as well."

"That's settled then," Nora said decisively.

Kate surprised her by saying, "On Saturday evening I'm thinking of going into Ross to a old furniture place. Danny, would you like to come along?" When he looked dubious, she added quickly, "Just to have a look."

"Kate, I can't afford furniture," Danny told her firmly, and Nora felt that it was not the first time that they had had this conversation. "It will take most of the field money to pay off Rory."

"What about a bank loan now that you will have the deeds?" she suggested.

"No way," he told her forcefully. "I went down that road when I had no choice. It wasn't very fruitful, and I swore that I'd never put myself through that again."

"Now it would be different," she suggested.

"Different or not," he declared, "bank loans bring bad luck to this place."

"I can understand how you feel," she agreed sympathetically, "but it costs nothing to look at furniture. Nora, will you come too?"

It amused her that she was being thrown in as bait, but she could stay at Kate's on Friday night to avoid conflict with Mom, who was allergic to the Conways. It was agreed that they would pick up Danny and travel to Ross on Saturday evening.

On Saturday they set out for a place in Ross that Nora had never heard of but that Kate obviously knew well. She looked around, askance at what she considered to be a load of old rubbish, but Kate went determinedly into the shadowed depths of the long cavern of a room and started to look around with what Nora recognised as a well-practised eye.

"She's like a cattle jobber looking for a good animal at the fair," Danny grinned at Nora.

Kate called them to drag culled items out of her way, and when Nora was beginning to think that it was all a complete waste of time, Kate breathed, "Aha," and got Danny to lift a heavy chair and make a passage for her to something that she had spotted inside a bed and partly hidden behind a wardrobe. To Nora it looked beyond recovery, but Kate shouted, "Tom, where are you? We need help."

A man in a greasy brown shop coat appeared, whom Nora decided could not lift a chair, but he burrowed in, and after a lot of grunting and cursing and Kate's directing, he finally arrived at the spied object. Incredibly he got under it and piggybacked it carefully over the intervening articles, and Kate instructed him to carry it out into the light. It was a long narrow table, and even Nora's inexperienced eye could see its possibilities. Kate had Tom turn it upside down, and she pulled open the long drawer as she searched every inch of it for woodworm and finally demanded, "How much?"

Tom, who in the light of day looked far bigger and stronger, began to extol the virtues of the table, but Kate dismissed all his sales talk and demanded a price. When she finally extracted it from him, she haggled for so long that Nora began to feel sorry for the poor man. She whispered to Danny, "I'd come to his rescue, but Kate would throttle me afterwards."

"She surely would," he agreed. "Better to keep your head down and your mouth shut."

Anticipating a purchase, Kate had brought Bill's red van and they loaded up the table, but she made no comment as to where she intended to take it.

As Kate drove into Furze Hill, Nora wished that she could see Danny's face, but he was in the back of the van with the table. Without consultation, Kate directed them into the front hall and told them exactly where to put the table. Danny's face was inscrutable and he said nothing. The table was perfect. Even in its dusty state it still looked good.

"It blends in with the cobwebs," Nora smiled.

"That table was made for this house," Kate declared. Turning to a silent Danny, she told him, "It's a Phelan gift for Furze Hill. The first step. This house must be furnished slowly and the right pieces picked up carefully over the years. Mary can do the auction rooms along the quays in Dublin. They always have great stuff."

When Kate got going it was hard to put a stop to her gallop, and Nora looked at her in admiration. But Danny was not going to be swept along by her.

"Kate, I can't afford furniture, and the house will have to wait," he told her firmly.

"It costs nothing to be on the lookout," she informed him.

Danny walked with them to the car and handed Kate a small grubby book.

"What's that?" she asked curiously.

"Nana Molly's diary," he told her.

"Did she keep a diary?" Nora asked in surprise.

"Jack was the only one I ever heard mention the diaries," Kate told her. "He said that Molly kept one all her life but that when she died Rory burnt the most of them. This must be an earlier one that she had hidden away."

"God, Jack knew everything," Nora sighed.

"But why are you giving it to me?" Kate asked Danny.

"You'll know when you read it," he said evenly, walking back to the house.

"Let's go to Jack's cottage and read it," Nora said excitedly as they got into the car.

"I suppose we could," Kate said slowly.

As they drove along, Nora remembered that she had not been into Jack's since he died, and she did not like the prospect of going in now either.

"Kate," she began hesitantly, "I haven't been back to the cottage since, you know . . ."

"Well, maybe this is as good a time as any," Kate told her gently.

Toby went mad with delight when he saw them. Nora grabbed him up and hugged him, and then he jumped out of her arms and ran ahead of them in the path.

"He's welcoming us in," Kate smiled.

When they opened the door of the cottage, the fire was lighting and everything was just as Jack had left it. *If I closed my eyes*, Nora thought, *I could almost convince myself that he is gone out to close the hens.* She had to fight back the tears at the thought that he would never again be here. Toby settled himself by the fire, and when she sat in Jack's chair, he jumped on to her lap. Kate sat in the rocking chair and they were both silent, looking into the fire.

"He always said that he could think best looking into the fire," Kate said quietly.

242

"It's fierce hard without him," Nora said grimly, "and the cottage is like a dead place."

"How would you feel about someone else living here?" Kate asked tentatively.

"Like who?" Nora demanded in alarm, wondering what Kate was up to now.

"Bill Brady."

It would be hard to get used to someone else in Jack's cottage, but if there had to be somebody Bill Brady would be the best, and it would put an end to Rosie and Peter using it.

"Well, he'd be fine," she said in a relieved voice, "and he'd be very good to Toby."

"That was one of the reasons that I decided on him," Kate admitted

"Well, Jack would have considered that a good enough reason," Nora agreed.

As they sat in silence, she became aware that there was something different about the sounds of the cottage: the clock was not ticking.

"Jack never forgot to wind the clock."

"Jack kept letters in there," Kate said to her surprise.

"What a strange place to put them."

"Will we read this now?" Kate said, taking the little book out of her pocket and looking at it nervously. "Let's go over to the table and look at it together."

As they sat at the table with the book between them, Kate was reluctant to open it. She stroked it with her hand. Nora felt that she was almost afraid of the diary.

"Kate," she asked carefully, "what are you so nervous about?"

"I'm not sure," Kate admitted, "but old Molly Barry once hinted about dark secrets in our past."

"But what could they be?" Nora asked in alarm.

"We'll probably find that out now," Kate told her.

The writing was scrawling and faded but still legible, and the first few pages were full of a young girl's discontent at the inactivity of her life. Nora could identify with her. Molly Barry, she calculated from the date at the front, must have been the same age as she was now when she wrote this diary. She wanted to confirm that with Kate, but Kate was so completely engrossed that she was reluctant to interrupt. They both read silently, and she knew that Kate was reading ahead of her, but Kate waited wordlessly for her to catch up and then carefully turned the page. Then she heard Kate's sharp intake of breath. When she came on the name Emily she knew why. This was Jack's mother. When she read on and discovered the connection with old Edward Phelan, her own interest increased, and as she continued to read her interest turned to excitement. Then came the entry, "Emily is expecting a baby and only herself, myself and Edward know the truth." Nora's mouth went dry with the shock. Could it mean what she thought it meant? She felt Kate stiffen beside her. She was trembling with anticipation as Kate flicked forward through the pages looking for another mention of Emily and Edward, but there was no more reference to them.

Then they went back carefully over what they had already read. That last entry could only mean one thing. A tide of excitement spread over Nora, but could it really be true? What if she was wrong? She was almost afraid to break the silence and ask the question, but she just had to.

"Kate," she asked breathlessly, "was Jack one of us?"

A pale-faced Kate looked at her in disbelief.

"Doesn't it read that way?" she asked.

"If it is true," Nora wondered, "could he have known?"

"I've no idea," Kate answered slowly.

"It would be such a pity if it is the case that Jack died without knowing."

"It would," Kate agreed, "and now we might never be sure either."

They went back over the diary, but the diary had no more to tell.

With a thoughtful look on her face, Kate got slowly to her feet and went over to the clock and, to Nora's amazement, brought out a dusty bundle of letters yellowed with age. She put them on the table, and Nora looked at them in awe. They were ancient.

"In the name of God, Kate," she demanded, "where did these come from?"

"I found them in Jack's clock the night of the funeral," Kate told her, "and there are more in Emily's linen press." She went down into the parlour and came back with a little box.

"But whose are they?" Nora asked, feeling her mouth go dry with excitement.

"Edward Phelan's, your great-grandfather and my grandfather, and I'd say that they were to Emily. Maybe the answer is in these."

Kate took the letters out of the flat box. Nora looked at them and understood now why Kate had been nervous opening the diary. Kate undid the blue ribbon, and when the letters came loose she gave a gasp of dismay. Behind the old letters was a new clean envelope.

"Oh, my God," Kate said faintly, "this is Jack's writing."

On the plain white envelope was Kate's name in Jack's perfectly formed, strong writing. Nora thought that her heart would stop. She had a strange feeling that Jack had come into the kitchen and was here with them. With trembling fingers, Kate eased the letter out of the envelope and laid it flat on the table. Kate started to read aloud in a strained voice.

> The Cottage
> Mossgrove
> 7th May 1961

Dear Kate,

As you know, I have a dodgy heart, so any day I might embark on the great journey. There are certain things that I want you to know if that happens before the time is right to tell you this myself. You may or may not have read the other letters before you read this, but knowing you it will be this one first. These are the love letters between my mother and your grandfather. I discovered them when I knocked down the wall between the two bedrooms last year. They were in a small wall press that had been wallpapered over for years. They were put away carefully in a little box, so I imagine that my mother had intended that one day they would be found. These letters brought me the best news of my life. I am their son. It changed everything, and yet it changed nothing. I had loved the old man like a father, never realising that he was my father. But those letters explained something that had puzzled me for years.

When the old man died, he left me a small legacy in bonds with the specification that the money would never be invested in Mossgrove. We could have done with it there over the years, but my hands were tied. When I read these letters I understood. The legacy was my birthright. He felt that Mossgrove owed me that. I would never have looked at it that way because all of you were dearer to me than myself. I never told anybody about these letters, but I know Molly Barry knew who I was because she once passed a remark that I did not understand until I read these letters. I never cashed those bonds because I never understood why I got them and never felt entitled them until I found the letters last year.

But now a reason to use them has come up. It haunted the old man all his life that he was the one who introduced Molly Barry to Rory Conway and ruined her life. It was his dearest wish that she would get back into Furze Hill, and that was why he arranged the loan for Rory. When Rory betrayed his trust and bought those other two fields, all hell broke loose. Now that young Danny is restoring Furze Hill, I think that I owe it to my father and your grandfather to put his money into it. When we find the key, which I know we will, I am going to give the money to Danny. If I am gone to join the rest of them, you will be the one to do it. As you know, Kate, all my life I have believed that there was a time for everything. Now the time is here to bring peace to the living and to the dead.

Kate, please know that it was the greatest day of my life to discover that I was bone of your bone and blood of your blood. Please tell Nora and Peter. Danny will need to be told about the money.

God Bless.
Your Uncle Jack.

So it was true. Jack was one of them. They cried quietly for Jack, but as well as sadness there was peace and gratitude.

"It is so good to know that in his last months Jack had been fulfilling his father's and our grandfather's wish, and now he is giving us the privilege of finishing what he began," Kate said thoughtfully. "As he said, the love letters changed everything and changed nothing. But this letter is going to change everything for Danny and Furze Hill. Both Edward and Rory, in different ways, wronged Molly Barry. Now the two of them are correcting that wrong. The fields that old Rory bought in betrayal of Edward will be used to buy out young Rory. Furze Hill will go back to what Jack called the 'throwback' of the Barrys. Edward's money will restore the house. Jack was right: there is a time for everything, and the time has come."

They were both startled when the door whipped open suddenly. Sarah Jones breezed in with a welcoming smile on her face, but her expression changed when she saw the book and the letters on the table. She walked over slowly and looked down at the diary.

"This must be Molly Barry's diary," she said thoughtfully.

"You knew?" Kate asked, and Nora was not sure if she was referring to the diary or what they had just discovered. But Sarah did not appear to be listening.

"Jack thought that she might have written things down but that Rory could have burned everything," she said, slowly putting it back on the table, "and, of course, these are the love letters," she continued, gently touching the faded bundle on the table.

"You knew?" Kate repeated.

"I did," Sarah told her, drawing up a chair and joining them

248

at the table. Nora held her breath, wondering how much more Sarah could tell them.

"I knew for years. I knew before Jack. He found out last year when the boys knocked down the wall and the hidden press was revealed. I don't know if he would have told me, but that evening when I came in he was reading the letters. I decided then that he had a right to know what I knew. As you know, my mother was midwife here before me. She delivered Emily's baby. That night, in the pangs of childbirth, it was Edward's name she called out. Her husband was away at sea at the time. The following day Edward called, and my mother said that she knew by his face that it was his baby. She said that Emily and Edward were besotted with each other and were delighted with the baby. As you can imagine, my mother did not approve of the whole situation, but at the same time she told me that she never forgot the scene in the room that day."

"What a beautiful story," Nora breathed, looking around in wonder. "It fills this cottage with mystery and intrigue. It makes it a house of memories."

"Oh to be eighteen and full of romantic ideas," Sarah told her. "Another thing that you probably do not know was that Emily was a cousin of Molly Barry's. They had brought her to Furze Hill to keep Molly company."

"So Jack had connections with both houses," Kate said in amazement.

"He had indeed," Sarah said.

Later, after Sarah went home, Kate and Nora sat by the fire and read the love letters. The yellowed bundle from the clock were the letters written to Emily when she was in Furze Hill, and the ones that had come out of the little box were written later, after Jack was born. The earlier ones told of their meetings down by the river and of his life in Mossgrove. Some of them were in answer to letters that Emily had written to him.

"Wouldn't you just love to know whatever happened to the letters that Emily sent to Edward?" Nora said wistfully.

"The chances are that they were burned," Kate decided. "Women are more likely to keep love letters, and anyway Edward could not have kept them in Mossgrove."

"One day they might turn up," Nora said hopefully.

"Doubt it," Kate told her.

There was no trace of discord in the letters, only longing and love, and she wondered how come they had split up and gone their separate ways.

"I'd love to know what really happened," she said wistfully.

"It was all such a long time ago," Kate said, "that I suppose we are very lucky to have found out so much."

The later letters from the little box, written when Emily and Edward were both married and after Jack was born, were full of details about him.

"These letters are like a diary of Jack's early life," Nora said.

As they continued to read, shadows gathered in around the kitchen, but now she felt that the cottage was no longer a cold, empty place left behind by Jack. With the letters and Sarah's story, she felt that the spirit of Jack would for ever be alive in this place. Maybe Rosie and Peter had been right to come here.

Disturbing Toby, she went down into the small parlour, drew back the long lace curtains and looked across the river at Furze Hill. Kate joined her at the window and said thoughtfully, "Furze Hill is coming back to life, and with it the invisible links between the three houses."

CHAPTER SEVENTEEN

KATE WAS DEEPLY touched when Danny enlisted her help with the restoration of Furze Hill. The first time she had walked around the house, she had been intrigued by its possibilities. That the house had been part of Emily's life and that Jack wished to have his legacy spent there transformed the project into a journey of remembrance. The restoration would perpetuate his memory. As well as that, she would be spending her grandfather's money, someone of whom she had vague childhood memories. That he was Jack's father wove the entire undertaking into a deep connection with her own roots. These two men had given Danny and herself a key to transform Furze Hill.

She took Danny into an amazed Mr Harvey to transfer money from an old investment account into his name. Kate could see that the bank manager was wondering how on earth it could have happened that this young lad, who a few months earlier had come to him in desperation looking for a loan, had now in a short space of time acquired a substantial account. The whole village knew about the money from the two fields, but nobody would ever be told about this money, Kate instructed a surprised Mr Harvey. She wanted to impress on him that Danny's business and privacy were his personal responsibly. As they left the manager's office, a blonde girl came forward to greet Danny warmly, and Kate, remembering the night of the Vikings, smiled, thinking that it was not his bank balance that was impressing this pretty girl. She was glad to see Danny respond with such obvious pleasure. Danny, she decided, was beginning to blossom. But as they walked down the street he surprised her by saying, "Kate, I'm so glad that you are involved in fixing up the house, because without you I would not have the courage to take it on."

She realised then that he had been so long scrimping and scraping and being without that to him spending was a daunting experience, so there was no possibility of his losing the head and going wild. She decided that her role was one of reassurance and encouragement. To her the idea of going into antique shops, old furniture rooms and auctions with money to spend and an empty house to be furnished was heady stuff. As she confessed to a smiling David that night, "I'll be like a pig in muck."

"Kate, don't break the bank," he laughed. "Remember that Jack will be looking over your shoulder. After all, it's his money."

Now that the exams were over, David was free to concentrate on the new school. It was a relief to Nora and Rosie as well to have the exams behind them, and they were now on a mission to bring back the Vikings. The whole night was going to be bigger and better than anything Kilmeen had ever seen. It could prove to be an interesting night, Kate thought, with all the young ones, including Kitty, around. Remembering the pretty girl in the bank, she decided that Danny might have a distraction from his dedication to Nora.

Some nights when she came home from Furze Hill, the two girls were there with Fr Tim and David, who were trying to put a curb on some of Rosie's more extreme notions of entertainment. But most nights it was just Fr Tim and David, pouring over plans and new ideas for the school and playing fields. As far as Fr Tim was concerned, it was all about the playing fields, but for David the new school was a dream in the making.

Kate made out a list of all that was to be done in Furze Hill, and the first thing on the agenda was the big clean-up. Scattered around the parish were many hard-working women whom Kate knew would be glad of a bit of extra money, and she got in contact with them, but Ellen Shine was her first port of call. Ellen would be the ideal woman to put in charge of this undertaking. Ellen came very early one morning and walked slowly and silently around the house. Kate could sense her assessing every last detail, with the kitchen getting most attention. When she was finished her tour of inspection, she retraced her footsteps back to the kitchen. Standing in front of the big black range, she put her hands on her broad hips and pronounced, "We will start with this boy, because without boiling water we're going nowhere here."

Later that day she had Danny up on the roof with black chimney brushes, and Shiner, whom she had summoned from Mossgrove, was down below going from one fireplace to another. Buckets of old soot and generations of crows' nests made of twigs and horsehair rolled down the chimneys, and Shiner became a black ghost with red eyes. Finally the brushes ran smoothly up and down all the chimneys and the two lads cleaned away mounds of debris. Then she led them to the mountain of garden clearing that they had taken down to beside Yalla Hole and instructed them to cut it up into logs and firing. She sent a message to Mossgrove that Davey would not be over the following day, and Kate smiled, knowing that Martha would not question Ellen's decision. These two women understood each other.

Early next morning, Ellen tackled the huge grey range, and by evening it was transformed into a black shining monster with silver knobs. They all gathered in the kitchen as Ellen laid the first fire. The range belched smoke and turned the kitchen into a twilight zone where they all coughed and spluttered, but Ellen banged open and closed dampers with relentless ferocity and persistence until finally the fire glowed red and roared up the chimney.

"Your mother is one determined woman," an impressed Danny told Shiner in admiration.

"Who are you telling?" Shiner grinned.

But Ellen was not finished, and directed them around the house to lay fires in all the rooms. When there were no down draughts, Shiner declared, "I did a mighty job on those chimneys."

"Self-praise is no praise," his mother told him acidly.

Kate and Danny went into the garden and watched the smoke curl out the chimneys. Furze Hill was coming back to life.

The following day Ellen and her women began the big

clean. Kate had previously seen Ellen in action getting Mossgrove ready for the stations, but she had never seen anything like this. Ellen was a born cleaner; no cobweb or dust was safe in her presence, and she was able to inspire her helpers with her burning enthusiasm. Their combined aim was to rid Furze Hill of a common enemy called dirt. Every evening when she came back, Kate was impressed by their progress. Ellen herself took control of the kitchen and washed down the walls until sudsy water flowed around the floor and it resembled Yalla Hole. The table and dressers were cleaned and scrubbed until their original white wood emerged, and then Bill was summoned in to wax them. A few evenings later when Kate called, Ellen was on top of a ladder whitewashing the ceiling. Kate already had a colour scheme in mind for the kitchen and now without thinking she queried in dismay, "Whitewash, Ellen?"

"What's wrong with whitewash?" Ellen demanded, wielding a large dripping brush from the top of the ladder. Kate made a hasty retreat, feeling that she could well get a white shower. The following evening when she came back with Bill after Ellen had gone home, she was delighted with the transformation. The kitchen was immaculate. There was a smell of carbolic soap and Vim. The white walls gleamed with a tinge of blue that she knew Ellen had achieved with the blue bag that she used for washing her whites whiter than white. Against these walls, the waxed dressers gleamed golden brown, and the dark red quarry-tiled floor glowed.

"My God, Bill," she said in awe, "no germ would dare raise his cheeky head in here, and to think that I dared to question Ellen's wisdom."

"You were lucky that you didn't get a belt of a brush," he laughed.

"I almost did," she told him as she walked around in wonder, admiring the laden dressers where everything sparkled in the glow of the range, and then went into the long narrow pantry where the shelves were stacked with pots and pans that Ellen had scoured to perfection. She had been delighted to find most of the old pots and ware still in the kitchen. They had probably been unsuitable for the open fire in the poke, and of course the poke was so tiny that most of the things had to be left behind. It was ironic that in turning the house into a fortress old Rory Conway had guaranteed their survival. Now with this fine kitchen and the range back in action, they were coming into their own again.

What a dream of a place to work, she thought as she came back into the kitchen and looked around. She envied the woman who would work in this wonderful place. Then she smiled as she thought that it was probably the first time in her life that anyone had ever envied Brigid Conway.

As the cleaning continued around the house, faded wallpaper emerged, and Kate decided that this would be the colour guide to each room. She noticed that Danny and Bill had got the message loud and clear that their place was outside the front door. Inside it was Ellen who was in charge. Out in the yard, Bill's two friends had returned, and the farm buildings were being repaired and enlarged. The barn was now reroofed and the piggery was double the size. The hens had moved into luxury accommodation compared to their previous tumbled-down shack. The men had begun at one end of the yard and were working their way around it, and now next in line was the poke. One morning she found Danny viewing the poke thoughtfully, and she said impulsively, "Why don't we demolish it?"

"Would it be fierce extravagance, Kate?" he asked worriedly. "As a building there is nothing wrong with it."

"Maybe not as a building," she agreed, "but it's full of bad memories. I'm not saying that wiping that out will wipe them out, but I think that in some way it might help."

She knew what they had all suffered in there, but especially the girls, with whom she had kept in touch as she had been instrumental, with their grandmother, in getting Kitty out. Mary had at first gone to a convent in Dublin, where a cousin of Molly Barry's was reverend mother, and later Kitty joined her there. Now Mary was teaching and they had their own flat, but Kate still worried how they would survive the abuse they had suffered and had arranged with a friend of hers to keep in touch with them. But now she felt that wiping out the poke might be a good thing for all of them, including Brigid.

That evening when she came back the poke was razed to the ground. She knew by Danny's face that it gave him a sense of release that a reminder of all that they had endured was finally gone.

"The new stable for Rusty and Bessie is going there," he told her enthusiastically, pointing at the cleared site, "and we'll use the old stone of this place for the new calf house beside the cows."

"Where will you sleep tonight?" she asked, smiling at his delight.

"The barn," he told her, grinning at the prospect.

Gradually, Furze Hill began to emerge from beneath its

decades of dust, and shining windows let in the sunlight. Every evening when the women were gone home, Danny, Bill and herself did a tour of the house. Bill was delighted the evening the two fireplaces in the front rooms were revealed in all their simple elegance. He ran his hand lovingly over the white marble of the one in the dining room and grimaced in annoyance that the mirror on the other was, as he had expected, slightly tarnished.

"Let's look at it this way, Bill," she comforted him, "it gives it an aged look."

"This house does not need that," he told her indignantly.

When the cleaning was finished, she persuaded Danny to bring in a plumber and electrician and have the house wired and plumbed, and the little boxroom on the back landing became a bathroom. She knew that he was more than a little apprehensive about the amount of money they were spending, and on Saturday nights they sat down and added up their figures. It surprised her that he was so reluctant to spend, and she secretly worried that he might turn into a skinflint. But maybe it was understandable, she told herself, that he would have a tight grip on money having been without it for so long. They spent nights planning colour schemes, and he surprised her by how much he remembered of his grandmother's descriptions, which she kept in mind.

When the decorating began, the house became a hive of stepladders and white-overalled men. She had brought in Johnny the Post and his brothers, who decorated the houses of the parish for the stations. As this was such a big job, she had told Johnny to bring in his uncles, who painted in Ross, to help them. The window shutters turned from a dull brown to a gleaming ivory, and the oak floors that had absorbed years of dust and grime were polished to a golden hue. Bill was everywhere, seeing that things were done properly, and he moved between the building in the yard and the house. With the departure of Ellen, he was back with a free run of the house. His delight in the restoration of the staircase and the doors was infectious, and he gathered them all into the dining room to view the long table the evening that he had finally got it to his satisfaction.

The day the decorating was finished, Kate and Danny stood in the front hallway. It was transformed. As Bill had anticipated, the graceful staircase had come alive, and now the polished curved rail carried your eye upwards to the tall window that poured light down into the hall below. The pale grey flagstones complimented the rich oak doors and staircase. They went into the dining room where the white marble fireplace was reflected in the polished wood of the long table. The theme in here was blue, as dictated by the old wallpaper, and Kate had searched the shops in Ross to come as near as possible to the original. Now the embossed blue paper showed up the delicate cornice-work around the ceiling, and she had splurged out on a beautiful chandelier with a glint of blue. She knew on the day that Danny thought it was a step too far, but looking up now he smiled ruefully and admitted, "You were dead right!"

"Jack always said that you had to pay for quality," she told him.

They went into the drawing room, which was bare of furniture but for the black marble fireplace. In here she had replaced the soft rose wallpaper with one that was almost identical. Sunlight shone off the wooden floor. Upstairs the shining floors reflected the cream paintwork, and the sound of their footsteps echoed through the empty house.

"This house needs furniture," she told Danny, "but maybe you want to wait until your mother and the girls come home."

"They know nothing about all this," he told her.

"What!" she demanded.

"It's going to be a surprise," he announced.

"They'll die of shock," she declared.

"Well, Mary might have an inkling that something is going on, because she wanted to come down before they went to see my mother's sister in London. I put her off and she was a bit suspicious, but my aunt had sent them the tickets and put pressure on them to move once Kitty had her exam done and Mary had her school holidays. She had not seen Mom for years, and they were all so excited about it, that it kind of distracted them."

"So will we move on the furniture?" Kate wanted to know.

"But where will we get it?" Danny asked nervously, "and would it cost a fortune?"

"Not at all," she assured him. "You can be very lucky at auctions, and we'll watch out for a parish priest's auction because they always have quality stuff. Old furniture rooms are great too, and you can get fine pieces there. People are throwing out good stuff, and it's going much cheaper than the new ply and dye."

"But how come?" he asked in amazement.

"New money, new women, new taste," she announced.

"Furniture good enough for this house?" he queried.

"You'd better believe it," she told him, delighted at the prospect of old musty furniture rooms and auctions.

Kate enjoyed introducing Danny to a whole new world, and they spent enjoyable days at auctions where she watched him learn the procedure and develop an eye for a fine item. Soon he was no longer deceived by dust and grease. They got a splendid oak bed for his mother's room and two brass ones for the girls. Bill came on board if they brought home any piece that was damaged or ruined by paint or poor restoration. He polished the two brass bedheads until they shone, and the transformation that Bill could bring about was a constant source of wonder to Danny, but Kate assured him, "If you get the real thing, you can't go wrong."

Then one day the much-awaited parish priest's auction arrived when the PP of Ross died. She knew the house because she had visited it years ago with Nellie, to whom he was related. He had been a collector of pictures and nice furniture, and she knew that he would not have sold a thing over the years. She could picture the wonderful oak sideboard that would be perfect with the long table in the dining room of Furze Hill. The morning of the auction her mind was full of excited anticipation.

From across the breakfast table, David viewed her with amusement.

"Kate, you look as if you are going on a treasure hunt."

"Feels like it," she assured him blithely, and later as she left the house he called after her, "Have a good day, as Rodney Jackson is for ever wishing me."

"You can bet on it," she assured him.

"We could be lucky here," she told Danny as they went into the impressive parochial house. "If the damn dealers are not here we're flying." Amazingly they were not. How had this one escaped them? They usually came like wasps around a jam pot to priests' auctions. She could not believe her luck when the huge sideboard, which came up early, did not go as high as she had expected, and she almost lost her composure when a row of dining room chairs were knocked down to her at a good price. The chairs matched perfectly the dining room table in Furze Hill.

While she was inspecting an enormous oak bookcase, she saw Danny searching around for something. This was unusual. Finally he seemed to find it, a heavy gilt-framed picture stacked up with a row of other pictures. She saw him take a note of the number. It was a spectacular frame, but she wondered about the austere bishop behind the glass. Normally she did the bidding, but when the picture came up she told Danny to bid. He had to go a bit more than he had anticipated, and when he hesitated she egged him on, as she knew that the thin woman from Ross who was bidding against him would not keep going. Mrs Hobbs was a seasoned performer and never lost her head. Kate knew from experience that men were more likely to go stubborn at auctions and refuse to be outbid. Sure enough, Mrs Hobbs bowed out and Danny got his picture. It was his first independent purchase.

"Where are you going to put My Lord Bishop?" she asked.

"He's surplus to my requirements," he told her.

The bookcase that she had judged ideal for the drawing room was next up. She had seen a well-heeled, middle-aged couple examining it earlier, and sure enough when other bidders dropped out they stuck with her. She had to go more than she had planned to get it.

"That's the way it is at auctions," she told Danny afterwards, "and the secret is not to lose your nerve or your head."

When others left they stayed on late at the auction because she had decided that when the parish priest's bed and bedroom furniture came up she would go for it. It was a wonderful oak bed with two matching wardrobes and a dressing table that she knew in a few years time would be a collector's item. She was hoping that it might be too big for the houses of most people present, because on the instructions of the deceased it was going as one lot. *Wise man, Fr Kennedy,* she thought. *He wanted his wonderful pieces to stay together and go to a good home, not be split up and scattered around the country. A collector to the end!* Because she thought that Danny might put her off, she sent him out to the car for the flask and sandwiches just as the bidding began, and when he came back the bedroom set was his for a fraction of what it was worth. But she felt sure that Fr Kennedy would have been delighted that she had got it.

She looked forward to the arrival of the parish priest's furniture to Furze Hill with rising excitement, and the day it came Bill was in his element. As the delivery men unloaded, Kate directed them to the correct locations. She put Danny's picture under the stairs, and she was glad that he was out the fields as she led the men up to the front right-hand bedroom. The entire bedroom set looked magnificent, and Kate knew that she had struck oil. When she told Bill the price, he whistled in appreciation. Then they walked around the house admiring all the pieces, and she was thrilled at how they complimented the place.

"No touching up needed with these," Bill said with relish. "All in mint condition."

"Priests' furniture is always in great nick," she smiled.

"You're getting this place spot on," Bill told her

appreciatively as they stood in the hallway with the doors open into the different rooms. "What's the secret of being able to get it so right?"

"Anticipationary visualisation," she informed him loftily, and laughed heartily when he told her dismissively,"My mother put that outside the door once and it melted in the frost."

He had a wicked sense of humour, and working with him over the last few weeks had been such a pleasure. The better she got to know him, the more convinced she became that he was the ideal person to live in Jack's cottage. He was turning it back into a welcoming place. It was what Jack would have wanted.

"Do you think, Bill," she asked him now, "that Jack would have approved of how I am doing things here?"

"Without a shadow of a doubt," he assured her. "There was a touch of class about Jack, and he would only have settled for the best."

"Sometimes, you know," she worried, "I get the feeling that Danny thinks that I'm a bit of a big spender. But he has the money, so why can't he let it go?"

"You know, Kate, spending money is a new experience for our Danny," Bill said sympathetically. "You never knew what it was to be hungry, but I think that he got a flavour of it over the years."

"Is that it?" she wondered.

"I could be wrong," Bill said thoughtfully.

"Well, anyway," she said, brightening up, "let's have tea in Ellen's immaculate kitchen."

"We'd better not dirty it," Bill laughed as they walked back the corridor. "You know, I suggested putting in a big comfortable chair in the corner where you could read a book. She nearly had a fit, telling me that a kitchen was not for lounging around in but for cooking."

"Oh, I got that lecture too," Kate told him, "but we might slip it in later. Anyway, there is what used to be the morning room straight across from here. I think that will really be the living room, so I furnished that with mostly comfort in mind."

"Weren't they smart long go with their morning room for the breakfast and always facing east to catch the morning sun," Bill said, laying cups on the kitchen table.

"Easy for them," she declared, spooning tea into the big ware teapot, as Bill liked his tea strong. "They probably had retinues of servants to drag things back and forth."

"But 'twas good thinking all the same," Bill declared.

"Jack thought like that," Kate said thoughtfully.

"Still feeling the loss?" Bill said kindly.

"Yeah, but I think that he sent me a bit of a healer with the project of this house," she said quietly. "Bill, do you believe in the power of the dead?"

He watched her pour out the tea and waited for her to come back and sit at the table before answering.

"There was a time when I would have told you no," he told her slowly, "but over the years I know that Lucy helped me in many ways. When she was with us, she was the one who kept the show on the road. Calm and easygoing, she loved books and music and always had time to sit down and discuss everything. She was great with the lads, and when she died they were all fairly young and I was left high and dry. But I sensed over the years that at certain times she was around."

"I think that Jack is not far away either," she said quietly.

"Kate, you asking me to live in Jack's house was one of the nicest things that has happened to me since she died."

"You're making his not being there easier," she told him.

"He has lovely bits and pieces in that little cottage," he said.

"He taught me to appreciate so many things," she said, looking around the kitchen, "He would have loved this place."

"You are really enjoying the restoration here?" Bill asked.

"Loving it," she declared. "When I go into an auction or into an antique shop, I can feel my adrenalin rising."

"You'd love the antique business," Bill declared.

"Love it," she told him; "I have always been fascinated by old things."

"Maybe one day the two of us might open an antique shop," Bill said slowly. "You could do the buying, and I'd do the touching up and repairing."

"You mean it, Bill?" she asked in amazement.

"Well, we could think about it anyway," he told her.

Later, when Danny came in, they walked around the house. She could feel his mounting appreciation of how all the pieces fitted in so well. As they went up the stairs, she wondered how he would react to the appearance of his own room. When she opened the door, he gasped in amazement.

"My God, where did these come from? They're magnificent."

"Remember going out for the flask and sandwiches?" she asked mischievously. "Well, that's when I did it." She added hurriedly, "But they did not cost a fortune, you know."

Danny walked around the room, almost in awe of what he was seeing, and then went over to the window and stood silently looking out over the garden. Kate sat on the side of the bed and waited. She had known since she had told Danny about Jack's money that he had been wrestling with some dilemma but had not filled her in. She had wondered if she would ever be told. Now he turned around from the window and came across the room and sat beside her on the bed. To her surprise there were tears in his eyes.

"Kate," he began hesitantly, "I think that I owe you an explanation."

"An explanation about what?" she asked.

"About the fact that over the last few weeks I was so careful about the spending of the money."

"Well, I did think you were a trifle thrifty," she admitted wryly.

"I had a reason," he began. "I was not going to tell this to anybody outside the family, but you have been so brilliant to me that I owe you this. When first you told me about Jack's money, I was, as you know, dumbfounded. But the more I thought of it, the more certain I became that Jack was giving me more than money. He was giving me a chance to redeem myself and the family pride. Because of that, I have decided to give Mary and Kitty and the two in America the same as I gave Rory. It does not seem fair that he would get money for being greedy and that they would get nothing for being honourable. I don't want anyone to be wronged."

"But that will leave you with nothing," she protested.

"Six months ago I had nothing, and now I could be greedy. I own all this," he said with outstretched hand, "and I can work hard and reclaim the farm. I will enjoy the challenge. We were reared with no sense of self-respect because my father and grandfather stole it from us. Now I want to bring it back, and the starting point must be with the Barry sense of values. I think that Jack would have wanted it this way. He was an honourable man, and his was honourable money. I don't want to taint it with greed."

As he spoke Kate felt a lump in her throat, and she wrapped her arms around him.

"Danny, that is such a noble thing to do," she said tremulously. "Jack always said that you never knew anybody until you had money dealings with them. He would have been so proud of you."

"I hope so," he said. "He gave us the money, and it is up to me to give us the sense of honour."

"That's a strange twist of fate," she told him.

"How?"

"Well, my grandfather always felt guilty about being the cause of bringing the Conway name to this house, and now his money will buy it out."

"Old Mr Hobbs said something along those lines," Danny remembered, "about the mills of God."

"Do you know something, Danny," she smiled, "I'm glad that we got the house back to the way it should be before you decided to go all noble on me. If I had known, it might have cramped my style."

"Doubt it," he smiled.

"When are all these beneficiaries coming home?" she asked.

"As soon as they come back from visiting my aunt," he told her, "and the morning after they come home I am planning to have the stations here for the first time in decades. It will be a surprise welcome home for my mother."

"They are all in for some surprise," she declared.

They were so engrossed in their conversation that they had not heard Bill come up the stairs, and now he regarded them with amusement from the doorway.

"What are the two of you up to in the parish priest's bed?" he demanded.

"Rewriting history," Kate told him, "and preparing for the stations."

CHAPTER EIGHTEEN

THE DOOR WAS blue, a deep mystic blue creating a veiled invitation into the ivy-clad house. Then Bill decided to paint the gate the same colour, and when the old perennials in the curved border from the gate to the house began to bloom, they were interspersed with blue delphiniums, and the whole garden and house danced together.

"We are simply unveiling the plan of the original gardener," Bill told him. Danny had discovered who that was when he unearthed a small trunk of gardening books under the stairs, which had belonged to Rachel Barry, Molly's mother. Most of them had notes and sheets of drawings.

"I knew it," Bill declared triumphantly as they went though the books. "There was a well-planned garden here, made by a person who knew her gardening. These gardening books are by names that I have only heard on BBC gardening programmes. This woman took her gardening seriously, and now with these plans we can bring it back to exactly the way she had it."

Bill spent all his time in the garden bringing it back to its former glory, but Danny's days were spent out in the fields, because he knew that out there was the future of Furze Hill. A fine house with a non-viable farm would be a bubble waiting to burst. It had happened before. But now, because he had invested in a tractor that Peter had gone with him to buy, the work was easier. Slowly, with long hours of dedication, he would bring the farm around. It would take years, but this land was now his. He was free of the fetters of Rory, and the fact that all the others would get their share gave him a true sense of ownership. Jack had given him his freedom.

Then he received a letter from Mary saying that they were home and would be down as soon as they had recovered from their trip to London. He wrote back instructing her not to drive into the old yard when she came but to park out in the road and come to the gate of Nana Molly's old house. He wanted them to see it for the first time just as Jack had remembered it. Then he went to visit Fr Tim and asked about having the station mass in the house the morning after their homecoming. His mother had always regretted that she had never been allowed to have stations like the rest of her neighbours. She had a deep faith, and he knew that over the years it was at times all she had between her and total despair, so he knew that for her it would be a lovely homecoming welcome. It would also be a sign that they were no longer the outcasts their father had made them and that she could meet her neighbours as the woman of the house in the homeplace.

Now he was waiting in the garden behind the weeping willow from where he could see the front gate but could not be seen. He had heard the car pull up and wanted to have the thrill of watching their faces as they came in. As he expected, Kitty was first in, and with her glowing red hair and resemblance to the old photograph, it was as if Molly Barry was coming in the gate. But Nana Molly would never have been turned out in the little bit of nonsense that Kitty called a dress. In total contrast came Mary, in her dark, sedate suit, with short dark hair framing a quiet, reserved face that was now incredulous with delight. If he was expecting a surprised reaction he was getting it.

But he was not prepared for the surprise that awaited him. His mother was such a changed woman that at first he hardly recognised her. Gone was the skinny, frightened-faced woman with the clothes hanging off her and straight stringy hair pinned behind her ear with a steel clip. Now her hair was short and curled around a face that was smiling and relaxed, and she was dressed in a smart white suit that showed off her slim figure. Brigid Conway was a different person from the broken woman who had left a few months ago. He was so delighted at her transformation that he forgot his idea of watching her reaction and ran across the lawn. He hugged his mother and swung her around in delight, aware all of a sudden how much he had missed her gentle presence.

"Danny, what have you done?" she asked breathlessly, looking around in awe. "How did you do it? Did a miracle happen?"

"A miracle of money, I'd say," Kitty gasped. "In the name of God, Danny, how did you manage it? Where did you get the money? The place is absolutely staggering."

"I thought that you were up to something," a shocked Mary told him, her normally pale face flushed with excitement, "but not anything on this scale! How did all this happen?"

They gathered around him in stunned but delighted amazement, wanting all their questions answered together until he had to hold up his hands and promise, "I will tell you all when we have tea in the kitchen. But first, just walk around and see everything."

The girls ran to the front door and disappeared into the house, but his mother stood looking around in wonder.

"What a beautiful, beautiful garden," she whispered in an awed voice, and then walked slowly to the arch. He watched her stand there surveying the farmyard and then joined her. He stood beside her in silence.

"I'm glad you took away the poke," she told him quietly. "It is better gone."

They gathered in the kitchen, and he tried to fill them in on all that had happened. Questions poured out of the two girls. His mother sat quietly until the girls were finally satisfied and then she observed, looking at him thoughtfully, "Your grand-mother always said you were a throwback."

When he told them about the station mass in the morning, her face lit up.

"What a lovely welcome home, but what about the food?" she asked.

"I brought what I thought we might need," he told her, "but have a look, and we can get anything else we want in the village."

"Things have improved since we used to bring the big roast from Dublin to keep you fed for a week," Mary laughed.

"Thank God," his mother said, rising from the table. "And now we will get ourselves sorted out and see what we need."

He was glad that his mother was taking charge, and when he

took her to the window and showed her the kitchen garden outside, she smiled with satisfaction. Mary, looking over her shoulder, surprised him by quietly quoting, "Not to those who inflict the most but to those who can endure the most shall victory belong." His mother's eyes filled with tears, and Kitty lightened the moment by teasing Mary.

"Always the history teacher, big sister." Turning to Danny she laughed, "And now I'll bring in the big roast, because we still brought it, not knowing that you had become a man of means. But at least now you have a proper oven to cook it in."

The house hummed with the laughter of the girls, and the smell of cooking filled the kitchen. Bill, coming in the door, said to Danny, "This place is turning into a home." He sat at the kitchen table with Brigid and filled her in on the details of the garden and showed her the plans that he had found in Rachel Barry's gardening books. Danny could see that his mother was more excited about the garden than the house and knew that she was going to have hours of pleasure working out there. But for the girls it was all the house, and they had settled themselves into the two back bedrooms. Kitty jokingly told him, "I want to be able to look over at Peter Phelan," but he was not so sure that it was a joke. He had allocated the front bedroom at the other side of the house away from the yard to his mother. Kate, when he had told her that his mother's favourite colour was yellow, had fitted it out accordingly and with everything that she had deemed a comfortable bedroom should have, and he was very pleased with the result. When his mother opened the door into it, her face lit up.

"This is like walking into sunshine," she declared. "Look at that beautiful bed. I never thought in my wildest dreams that I would ever have a bedroom of my own like this," and then going to the window overlooking the garden she announced, "but the view is the best part of it."

"God, this room is lost on you, Mother," Kitty declared.

Later Kate called, and after a lot of kissing and crying, the women sat around the kitchen table. Danny knew that there were going to be hours of chat, so he went for the cows. Just as he was herding them out, Kate came across the yard to him.

"Danny, I brought you two of Emily's cloths for the stations tomorrow. They may even have been embroidered in this house, because you remember in the diary Molly made reference to Emily doing needlework in the kitchen. It would be nice to use the white lace-edged one on the altar because it would be a link between them all: Molly, Emily, Edward and Jack. The other one is a banqueting cloth which I'm sure was never used, but it would be ideal for that long table in the dining room. What Emily was doing embroidering a banquet cloth defies logic."

"Thanks, Kate, that's a lovely idea," he said appreciatively, loving her sense of occasion.

"You never told them about the diary," she said.

"No," he told her, "that's a decision for another day."

"Agnes and Ellen have arrived," she smiled. "Agnes is laden down with lace curtains that she has been sewing up for weeks, and Ellen has rounded up cutlery and ware from all the neighbours."

"But did they mind?" he asked in surprise.

"No, no," she assured him. "People always do that for the stations. Nellie's candlesticks used to go around to all the houses for the stations."

"Wasn't that great," he said. "We knew nothing about that kind of thing. It's so good having our first stations here."

"Well, with Agnes and Ellen you have two great women with you for the night before the stations, and Sarah will be on shortly."

It was one of the things that pleased him most about the whole restoration, the way the neighbours now felt free to come and go to Furze Hill. For so long he had had no sense of belonging in his homeplace. Even in school he had realised that they were not part of the sharing that went on between the neighbours, and as he had grown up it had become more evident. It was not the neighbours who isolated them but his father. Now Rory was gone and the neighbours were back. At least the most of them were back. He was hoping that Martha would come to the stations tomorrow.

When they went back into the house, it smelt of wax polish, and there was a clatter of activity coming from the kitchen. Kate and himself turned into the dining room and spread the flowing cloth over the table. Along the edge it was embroidered with tiny blue flowers that blended in perfectly with the delicate blues of the room. They both looked at it thoughtfully, and then he went over to the window and called Kate to join him. They looked out at the blue border.

"She must have done it for this table," he said in awe.

"This house is coming into its own," Kate declared.

They went across to the drawing room where the mass would be said and wondered about a suitable table for the altar.

"I know," Kate told him. "We will bring in our first purchase, the hall table, an ideal altar, and the white cloth will be the right size."

The following morning he was up with the sunrise to get the milking done early and be home from the creamery in time, but when he went into the yard, Shiner was bringing in the cows.

"Shiner, you're great to come," he told him.

"Well, we can't have you messing up your first stations with a yard full of cow's scutter," Shiner smiled, "and Peter is going to call for the milk on his way to the creamery, so all we have to do is clean up the place after these ladies."

"That's the job," Danny told him, "that will take the rush off us."

"You'll be on show today, Danny boy, you know," Shiner informed him. "There will be more than prayers on some of their minds when they come. A lot of the ould wans will be dying to see the house, but it will be this corner that the men will be looking at. So we're going to be ready for curiosity boxes and showing no weakness."

"I suppose you're right," he agreed, "but I never thought about it."

"You're still a bit wet behind the ears yet, Danny boy," Shiner assured him.

Later on, Danny stood on the doorstep and welcomed the neighbours as they trooped in. There was a big crowd, and he smiled remembering what Shiner had said. Then he felt a flutter of excitement when he saw Nora coming in looking like one of the border flowers. "How's the man of the house?" she teased.

"I suppose I am," he answered in surprise.

Kate and David joined her and they all moved into the hall, and Mark passed him in carrying a big parcel, and saying, "I'll put this under the stairs." Then the priests arrived, and Fr Tim winked conspiratorially at him behind Fr Burke's back.

He had been watching out for one face, but now that the priests were here, he decided that she was not going to come. He felt a stab of disappointment. But just as he was turning to go in the door, he saw Martha coming in the gate.

He had been mesmerised as he had watched her that night when she had cut the wires over Yalla Hole and laid the trap for his father. Not for a moment had she wavered, and it had taken him a while to figure out what she had in mind. He had been stunned at the simplicity of her plan and the calm unhurried way she had implemented it. At one point a rabbit or a bird had stirred in the ditch beyond him, and she had turned around and looked straight in his direction, and for one terrifying moment he had thought that she had seen him. But after a few minutes she had resumed loosening the stakes and cutting the wires. When all was to her satisfaction, she had crept quietly back across the river. He had remained where he was until the first streaks of dawn had started to creep across the sky.

It had been decision time for him then. He could let it all happen as she had planned or he could warn his father. But why should he warn him? Hours later, as he lay hidden in the trees across from Yalla Hole, he had heard the sound of the new tractor up the fields in Mossgrove. He had known at once that it was part of her strategy to bring his father running down the high field. From then on her whole plan had unfolded perfectly. He had felt as if he was watching a play where he already had the script. When it was over they were all free.

Now, in a straight black dress with her glossy hair coiled to the back of her head, Martha was a picture of understated elegance. As she approached the door, he went forward to welcome her.

"Well done, young Danny," she said, holding out her hand with an enigmatic smile on her face.

"Thank you, and welcome to Furze Hill," he replied.

He was glad that it was Fr Tim who was saying the mass and wondered how he had persuaded Fr Burke to take a back seat. From where he stood by the door, he looked around the room. His mother's face was full of peace, and with a start he saw that she now looked as young as Martha, who was standing a little apart from the rest of them. Then he noticed Kitty looking at Peter with an appraising look on her face, and he thought, *If she sets her sights in that direction, there will be trouble with Martha.* Then he saw Rosie watching Kitty and decided that there could be trouble from more directions than one. It looked as if the road to Mossgrove could be stormy!

After the long years of trouble between themselves and the farm across the river, it was good to see the altar candles glow in Nellie Phelan's brass candlesticks and to know that the lace-edged cloth was the work of Emily's hands. Emily, whose friendship had been the original link between the two houses. But the betrayal of that friendship had led to years of trouble and division, and now they had come the full circle, and it was her son Jack who had healed the wounds. He was glad, too, that Kate had decided to have the table that she had bought for the entrance hall used as the altar. It was as if this station altar was a darning back together of their many strands. Then Fr Brady broke into his meandering.

"This is a very special occasion. With this mass we are celebrating many things, but most of all we are celebrating a homecoming. Molly Barry left this house many years ago, and her dream was that one day she would come back. Well, today, due to the courage and determination of her grandson Danny, who never lost sight of her dream, it has happened. He fought against the odds and got there, but he was lucky, and he was also blessed with good neighbours. No man is an island, and I think that the restoration of this house has proved that. We all need each other in our struggle through life, and maybe the question that will be asked of us when we arrive at the end of our journey is 'How many did you help along the way?' If Jack Tobin, whom we buried recently, was asked that question, many of us here, including Danny, could give testimony for him. He reached the hand of friendship across the river and joined two families whom difficult times had separated. Today we pray for all who were part of that division. We pray for Rory and Matt Conway that they may have peace and that those of us left behind may have the grace of forgiveness. We remember especially Molly Barry Conway, and we pray that Danny, Mary, Kitty and their mother Brigid will have long years of peace and happiness in this house."

After the mass some of the men were shepherded by Brigid into the dining room, but many of them made their escape and headed for the yard on what Danny knew was a tour of inspection. He smiled to see that Shiner was part of the posse. He wished he could be with them! But he had to sit down beside Fr Burke, who looked at him sourly and proceeded to talk past him to David, on his left. Brigid was having difficulty in filling up her table, and Danny could understand why because nobody felt at ease with the overbearing Fr Burke. But then Martha sailed in and Danny had to smile, because it was mostly the men who breakfasted with the priests, which was exactly why she chose to do so. She soon turned the conversation to her visit to New York and told them vivid stories of her trip. He had never imagined that she could be so entertaining. There were many sides to Martha, but he hoped that he would never have to cross swords with her.

That evening when all the neighbours had gone home, his mother and the girls walked back with Agnes to see Mark's paintings. Alone in the house, he went in under the stairs and brought out Mark's parcel. He had given him the old picture, and now his heart was beating with excitement as he peeled off the wrapping. He whistled in appreciation when he saw the rich oil painting. It was stunning! The faded old picture was transformed into a living canvas, and a vibrant young girl with a halo of red hair looked out at him. He went back under the stairs and brought out the picture from the auction and carefully removed the glass and the bishop. With rising excitement, he fitted in the portrait and then rested the frame against the leg of the table and stood back. The deep frame and painting were a perfect combination, the gilt picking up the golden glow of Molly's hair. It filled him with delight. Taking her diary out of his pocket, he slipped it in behind her and then eased the bishop back into position. He hung the portrait over the hall table, and her beautiful face smiled down at him out of a blaze of red hair. She dominated the hall.

He smiled up at her and said, "Welcome home, Molly Barry."

SOME OTHER READING
from

BRANDON

Brandon is a leading publisher of new fiction and non-fiction for an international readership. For a catalogue of new and forthcoming books, please write to Brandon/Mount Eagle, Unit 3 Olympia Trading Estate, Coburg Road, Wood Green, London N22 6TZ, England; or Brandon/Mount Eagle, Cooleen, Dingle, Co. Kerry, Ireland. For a full listing of all our books in print, please go to

www.brandonbooks.com

WALTER MACKEN
Rain on the Wind

"A raw, savage story full of passion and drama set amongst the Galway fishing community." *Irish Independent*
0 86322 185 8; 320 pages; paperback

The Bogman
"In *The Bogman* Macken explores the deep recesses of the land and people." Alice Taylor, *Irish Examiner*
0 86322 184 X; 320 pages; paperback

Sunset on Window-Panes
"In his company, to use a fine phrase of Yeats, brightness falls from the air." *Newcastle Chronicle*
0 86322 254 4; 284 pages; paperback

City of the Tribes
"Does for Galway what the writings of Frank O'Connor did for Cork." *Irish Post*
0 86322 276 5; 256 pages; paperback

BRYAN MacMAHON
Hero Town

"*Hero Town* is the perfect retrospective: here the town is the hero, a character of epic and comic proportions. . . It may come to be recognized as MacMahon's masterpiece." Professor Bernard O'Donohue

"For the course of a calendar year, Peter Mulrooney, the musing pedagogue, saunters through the streets and the people, looking at things and leaving them so. They talk to him; he listens, and in his ears we hear the authentic voice of local Ireland, all its tics and phrases and catchcalls. Like Joyce, this wonderful, excellently structured book comes alive when you read it aloud." Frank Delaney, *Sunday Independent*

"*Hero Town* is a *Ulysses* for Listowel and it is more than a novel; it is a work of philosophy, the philosophy of a 'wild, old man', to quote Yeats."
Gabriel Fitzmaurice
ISBN 0 86322 342 7; Paperback

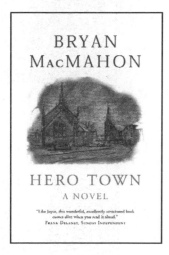

JOHN B. KEANE
The Bodhrán Makers

The first and best novel from one of Ireland's best-loved writers, a moving and telling portrayal of a rural community in the '50s, a poverty-stricken people who never lost their dignity.

"Furious, raging, passionate and very, very funny." *Boston Globe*

"This powerful and poignant novel provides John B. Keane with a passport to the highest levels of Irish literature." *Irish Press*

"Sly, funny, heart-rending. . . Keane writes lyrically; recommended."
Library Journal
ISBN 0 86322 300 1; Paperback

KATE McCAFFERTY
Testimony of an Irish Slave Girl

"McCafferty's haunting novel chronicles an overlooked chapter in the annals of human slavery . . . A meticulously researched piece of historical fiction that will keep readers both horrified and mesmerized." *Booklist*

"Thousands of Irish men, women and children were sold into slavery to work in the sugar-cane fields of Barbados in the 17th century . . . McCafferty has researched her theme well and, through Cot, shows us the terrible indignities and suffering endured." *Irish Independent*
ISBN 0 86322 314 1; Hardback
ISBN 0 86322 338 9; Paperback

EVELYN CONLON
Skin of Dreams

"A courageous, intensely imagined and tightly focused book that asks powerful questions of authority. . . this is the kind of Irish novel that is all too rare." Joseph O'Connor

"Conlon tells the extraordinary and unusual story of Maud's search for the truth, a journey that takes her not only to Ireland's past but to contemporary America and death row." *Sunday Independent*

"This astoundingly original novel stunningly portrays the close bond between twins that can be so easily severed. From drunken nights in Dublin to Death Row, Conlon traces the tale of two generations, through life and death, justice and execution, obsession and love. A beautiful novel, which will move you by its courage in delving into controversy and its imaginatively spun revelations." *Irish World*
ISBN 0 86322 306 0; Paperback

CHET RAYMO
Valentine

"[A] vivid and lively account of how Valentine's life may have unfolded... Raymo has produced an imaginative and enjoyable read, sprinkled with plenty of food for philosophical thought." *Sunday Tribune*

"His vivid tale conjures up a young doctor who falls for the blind daughter of a jailer in ancient Rome." *Mail on Sunday*

"This atmospheric, lyrical and sensual tale of epic proportions... Though Valentine's end is achingly poignant, there is a nice uplifting twist..."
Irish Independent
ISBN 0 86322 327 3; paperback

MARY ROSE CALLAGHAN
The Visitors' Book

"Callaghan takes the romantic visions some Americans have of Ireland and dismantles them with great comic effect . . . It is near impossible not to find some enjoyment in this book, due to the fully-formed character of Peggy who, with her contrasting vulnerability and searing sarcasm, commands and exerts an irresistible charm." *Sunday Tribune*

"I laughed aloud as I read *The Visitors' Book*. Although Irish, she reminds me of the best American comic writers. If you enjoy Alison Lurie or Carol Shields, you'll like this." Brendan Kennelly
ISBN 0 86322 280 3; Paperback